# WILD BOYS

# WILD BOYS

## GAY EROTIC FICTION

EDITED BY
RICHARD LABONTÉ

Published in the United States by Cleis Press Inc.,
2246 Sixth Street, Berkeley, California 94710.

Printed in the United States.
Cover design: Scott Idleman/Blink
Cover photograph: Redd Room Studios
Text design: Frank Wiedemann
First Edition.
10 9 8 7 6 5 4 3 2 1

Trade paper ISBN: 978-1-57344-824-6
E-book ISBN: 978-1-57344-838-3

*For my husband, Asa Liles:*
*Once a Wild Boy, never a tamed man*

# Contents

# INTRODUCTION: THE UN-WILD BOY, THAT'S ME

Wild was never my style.

I was the sort of twelve-year-old kid who was asked by adults to look after…their own twelve-year-old kids. When I played ice hockey on the hose-flooded rink behind the base's Post Exchange (I was a military brat), I apologized after board-checking a forward from the other team. I was the adolescent who convinced his peers that breaking into the bowling alley after hours was a bad idea (I set pins, so I had a key). When a schoolyard fight broke out, I inevitably played peacemaker (though I *did* enjoy hugging a brawler's tight-muscled body from behind).

And, a few years on, I always called back guys who gave me their phone number—even if that was the only connection we made. So polite.

An antonym for "wild"?

"Richard."

Well, I did stray from the straight and narrow on occasion…

precocious sex with young enlisted men when I delivered newspapers to their barracks rooms, trysts on the leather couch of my University Student Council President's office with a night cleaner, occasional forays into Griffith Park after I moved to Los Angeles in 1979, interludes of a threeway with two professional dancers (lovely legs!), some nude Radical Faerie cavorting through the 1980s, an et cetera here and there...but nothing particularly wild.

I was (am...) the un-Wild Boy.

Which is why assembling the stories for this anthology was such vicarious fun.

Wild young guys hooking up with more mature men; straight-arrow black college boys getting it on with a Southern redneck; a college kid bowing to the will of a wheelchair-bound older man; a wistful cop trying to recapture lost love with a street hustler; a young man thrashing a suit-and-tie businessman eager, after all, for a good spanking; two martial artists determined to best each other under the merciless gaze of their master...men taming youths, youths bringing men to their knees, young men living on the wild side getting their comeuppance—or the man of their dreams. Enjoy your read on the wild side.

Richard Labonté
Bowen Island, British Columbia

# CRUISING ON CARY STREET

J. M. Snyder

Monday, quarter after midnight, downtown Richmond. Neon lights glisten like wet paint off the cars parked along the cobbled streets of Shockhoe Slip. As off-duty police officer Willis Moore eases his 350Z Coupe down the narrow street, those same lights slide over his polished red hood and tinted windows like ephemeral flames, dancing over the car and disappearing behind him into the night. His side windows are down, his bass is pumping and dark sunglasses hide his eyes.

Here, he is anonymous, just another soul among those huddled in doorways or perched in the glow of streetlamps. The heavy hip-hop beat blaring from his speakers turns a few heads, but most aren't interested in his passing. They have their own lives to worry about and can spare no time for his. Will appreciates that mentality. Lately, he hasn't had much interest in his own life, either.

It's been a hellacious day for him. The first time back to work after a forced, month-long leave, and when five o'clock finally rolled around, Will was ready to call it quits. He didn't know what to expect but wasn't ready for the fake smiles, the inane small talk, the whispered conversations that stopped when he came into a room. Men he worked with for years now went out of their way to avoid him. When he tried to dive into a new case, he was told to take it easy, give himself time to get back into the swing of things.

Hell, he gave enough time already. He wants, *needs,* to move on.

Ahead, a stoplight flickers from amber to red. Will toys with the idea of not stopping—who'd notice? Who'd care? But the upstanding citizen in him hits the brakes at the last second, throwing him forward in his seat. Instinct causes his hand to stray to the volume knob on the radio; at the last minute, he catches himself before he can turn it down. Despite the nagging headache behind his eyes, he cranks the knob the other way. The car shudders beneath the increased beat.

Will glances out the driver's-side window. Two women stand on the curb, miniskirts hiked up to reveal tanned thighs, halter tops straining over ample breasts. One Asian, one Hispanic, neither Will's flavor of choice. They giggle and wave, but he turns back to the street and guns his engine, waiting for the light to change. *Sorry, girls.*

From the corner of his eye, he sees movement out the passenger-side window. He glances that way, sees a cluster of young men leaning against the side of an old movie theater and takes his foot off the gas as he does a double take.

Now *that's* more like what he has in mind.

There are five of them in all, the youngest probably not yet eighteen. They wear tight shorts and torn T-shirts that expose smooth, flat abdomens. Dyed hair spikes above dark eyeliner-rimmed, haunted eyes. Crotches bulge obscenely. Black leather ties form makeshift bracelets along pale arms. One kid wears a battered army jacket; another dribbles a scuffed basketball. Two have already paired off, rubbing against each other and snickering between stolen kisses as they move away from the others.

But the one Will notices, the one he lowers his shades to get a better look at, stands by himself at the front of the group. He has translucent skin that seems to glow in the lamplight, as if he hasn't seen the sun in years. His black hair shines almost blue in the night, the short bangs framing his face and ears in a pixie cut. He wears a silver mesh tank top cropped above his navel and a pair of black biker shorts pulled down low over bony hips. Will finds his gaze drawn to the flat planes of that bare stomach, the thin muscles taut and lean, the skin luminous against the shadows.

A car horn blares behind him—the light changed. Will hits the gas and shoots through the intersection, mind lingering on the scantily clad hustler and his friends. At the next block, without making a conscious decision about it, Will turns and circles back for a second look.

*Damn.*

*You shouldn't*, he tells himself, but his body doesn't listen. His blood rises at the sight of exposed white flesh, and when he closes his eyes, he can well imagine his own dark fingers splayed over that pale midriff like the shadows themselves.

*You didn't even see his face*, a voice inside him mutters.

Will doesn't care. He's been driving for hours, ever since he left the precinct, and for what?

*For this.*

Some part of him needs this, he knows. Why else would he be in the Slip, cruising the street? Music blaring, sunglasses on, an erection throbbing at his crotch? He needs release.

That damn voice in his mind won't let up. This is Tea all over again. Will turns the radio up in an attempt to drown it out, but it doesn't work. *You find another street rat like that, pick him up, take him home, clean him up, and what happens next? Where's Tea now?*

Dead.

Will grips the steering wheel tight and leans forward as he takes the next turn. He isn't thinking about Teabag anymore—that part of his life was over, done with, case closed. It's been a month already. Tonight is an escape, a way to move out of the past, a way to move on. And Will suspects a good, solid fuck is all he needs to do just that.

Back on Cary Street again, Will slows as he approaches the hustlers' block. This time he pulls over a bit, out of the flow of traffic, so he won't be rushed. The guys come into view and Will slows the car. A few of them elbow each other, nodding his way. Then the guy in the silver mesh turns and watches him come to a complete stop.

Will sits back in the driver's seat to wait. It doesn't take long. Within a few minutes, the guy breaks away from his friends and drifts to the passenger side of Will's car. As he approaches, Will turns the radio down to a mere whisper.

Leaning onto the open window, the guy flashes Will an easy grin. "Hey, dude," he drawls. His voice has a raw quality to it, as if he spent the previous evening screaming himself hoarse at a concert. "See something you like?"

This close, Will notices the guy's younger than he originally thought. Closer to Tea's age, maybe, barely a man…

An image of Teabag flashes in his mind, superimposing itself over the hustler's features. Freckles dot clear skin, the black hair turns a deep shade of russet, those green eyes deepen to a warm brown. The wide grin is replaced with a crooked one, thrown off by an eyetooth once broken in a club fight. Will hears Teabag's smoked-out voice when the hustler speaks. *"I know you want me, detective. And shit, I want you. So what's it to anyone else if we get our groove on, you know?"*

With a shake of his head, Will chases away that memory. Teabag disappears, leaving only the guy before him. Perhaps this isn't such a good idea after all. Putting the car into gear, Will starts, "Sorry, kid. You're not even legal—"

"I'm twenty-three," the hustler answers. "Don't go. I like black guys and you're kind of cute. It's been a slow night."

Will glances at the other hustlers, but they're calling out across the street to the girls on the opposite corner and aren't about to encroach on their friend's trick. The guy leans on Will's car. "I saw you looking."

When Will doesn't answer, the hustler straightens up and steps back, giving him a good eyeful. Large hands smooth down the mesh top over his belly, then dip into the waistband of his biker shorts to cup the cock hidden in his pants. As Will watches, a flick of those wrists has the shorts down and his dick out, both hands kneading his balls as the blind eye of his cockhead rises in Will's direction. A shuffled step brings him to the side of the car, and that long, thin dick dangles through the open window invitingly. Will clenches the steering wheel to keep from reaching out.

He watches strong hands stroke the length, teasing it erect. The guy moans as he fondles himself, hips humping against the side of the car as if he's fucking the vehicle itself. The way those fingers dance along the hardening shaft make Will's balls draw up with desire, and his own cock aches to be touched like that.

It's been way too long.

With a glance around to assure himself no one's watching, Will hits the release for the automatic lock. "Get in the car."

Instantly, the shorts come up again and the cock disappears.

The door opens and the hustler falls into the passenger seat, a knowing grin in place. He looks *much* too young for Will's taste, and twenty-three is a good ten years his junior, but in the dark, age doesn't matter. If the guy has a tight hole and knows how to fuck, that's all Will wants.

Releasing the clutch, Will pulls away from the curb and hits the button to raise the windows. Tinted glass rises around them, blocking out the street life. "You got a name?" Will asks as he pushes the car through the gears, heading for a high speed. "And buckle up."

"Yes, officer."

Will glances at the guy sharply. Did he know? Nothing in the guy's face gives it away, so Will writes it off as an innocent comment, a joke.

As the hustler cinches the seat belt into place, he asks, "You have a name you want me to use? Or just my own?"

*Teabag,* that voice in Will's head whispers, but he shakes it away. No. Tea is gone. Now that the car has hit a decent speed, Will cranks the radio back up again and shouts to be heard over the music. "Your own."

"Corey. I hate to bring this up, but do you want to hear my price list? Or do you have something specific in mind?"

Will hates this part. For a moment he considers pulling over, dumping the guy out on his ass on the street, letting him hike it back to his friends and bitch about the trick who dicked him over. But until Corey spoke to him, Will didn't realize how alone he feels. How much he wants this guy's touch, how much he *needs* it. Even if it costs him.

Without taking his eyes off the road, he hopes he sounds nonchalant when he asks, "You *do* bottom, right?"

A warm hand covers his on the gear shaft. Strong fingers fold into his palm, then guide his hand into Corey's lap. Will brushes over soft skin like velvet beneath his touch—the shorts are down again, tucked beneath Corey's balls. On their own, Will's fingers encircle that long shaft, a rod of iron in his palm, silk-sheathed, smooth and hard. His thumb traces the ridge of the flared tip, and beside him, Corey gasps. "Oh, yeah."

With one hand on the wheel, the other in Corey's lap, Will begins to look for a place to park.

Will finds a secluded spot in an empty lot behind an old, abandoned building that was once the Big Star grocery. In the far corner of the lot, two streetlamps have blown, giving the night free rein. When he turns into the lot, Will cuts off the radio so no one will notice them, then drives around behind the store, heading for that dark corner.

Each time he releases Corey long enough to shift gears, the hustler takes his hand back and places it firmly in his lap. Corey's dick juts hard from his crotch, the tip damp with precum, and only the Velcro cable tie he wears cinched around his balls like a makeshift cock ring holds back his orgasm. The pale erection has turned a ruddy color that rivals the plum-shaped tip, and whenever Will strums his fingers along the hard length, Corey whimpers.

Pulling into the last spot in the lot, Will yanks up the parking brake and cuts off the engine. He leaves the keys in the ignition and for a moment toys with them, their jangle loud in the abrupt silence. Suddenly he feels like a teenager again, alone with a guy for the first time, unsure of what to say or do next.

Corey takes charge. "You want to do this?" When Will nods, he instructs, "Then lie back. It's going to be pretty cramped, but I think we'll manage."

As Corey slips his shorts down his thin legs, Will obeys. The driver's seat pulls forward a few inches, then reclines. Will stretches back in the seat, hands smoothing down the long sleeves of his T-shirt, then straightening the material bunched beneath his seat belt, then down over his thighs to reposition his jeans. The denim bites into an erection that's been bothering him all night, and now he'll finally be taking care of it.

Or rather, Corey'll take care of it. Will hopes he'll be worth the price.

Beside him, Corey unbuckles his seat belt and climbs onto his knees in the passenger seat. His cock points at Will, whose hand drifts to grasp the hard shaft. He hears Corey gasp in delight and feels the car shake when those narrow hips buck into his palm. Using Corey's dick as leverage, Will pulls himself up into a sitting position and guides the hustler's dick to his mouth.

He misses.

The wet tip of Corey's cock brushes over his cheek and across his mouth before Will manages to close his lips around it. The musky scent of sex enflames his senses, and the dick fills his mouth, the bittersweet taste of cum like ambrosia. It's been *way* too long since he tasted another, but like an eager student, he relearns the fisted shape of a cockhead, the fold of skin at the end of the penis that bulges like a mushroom, the slit where the skin meets beneath the tip, the weeping pinprick in the center that quivers when he tongues over it.

Above him, Corey gasps, "Oh, yeah."

His words are mere breath between them. His hands play over the tight curls clinging to Will's scalp; his fingers tickle over the tops of Will's ears and down the back of his neck, guiding Will closer, driving his dick farther into Will's open mouth. Corey's breath draws in, a sharp hiss like a snake between them.

But when Will fingers the cable tie, ready to rip open the Velcro and drink down Corey's juices, the hustler pulls back. The tip of his cock slips from between Will's damp lips; he sticks his tongue out to chase after it, but Corey's stronger than he looks and holds Will back. "You're not paying for just this," Corey reminds him. "Lie down."

Again, Will does as he's told. Corey's fingers dance over Will's crotch, nimbly unbuckling his belt, unzipping his jeans, pulling the fly open to get inside. Will's shirt is rucked up, out of the way, exposing a flat stomach and chiseled muscles as dark as the night around them. Corey's hands look like searchlights flickering over the shadows of Will's flesh. The bright white briefs Will wears seem to glow in the darkness, but Corey pulls them down, tucks them beneath Will's chocolaty balls and runs both hands up the stiff length of Will's cock. "God *damn*," Corey sighs. He can't encircle the shaft at its base with just one hand. "You're fucking huge."

Will won't go that far—he's seen bigger guys in the shower room down at the precinct—but he likes the rasp of skin on skin in the close confines of his car, and he likes that Corey seems impressed. With difficulty he stifles a grin, instead concentrating on the shards of pleasure that spike through him each time Corey strokes his length. Through hooded eyes, he watches the pale hands fluttering over his dark flesh, white fingers plucking and rubbing over the reddish-black knob of his cockhead. He allows himself a slight moan and a whispered, "Yes."

Corey snickers. "You like that?"

Will doesn't have to answer—his lustful gasp tells the hustler what he needs to know.

Holding Will's dick with one hand, Corey runs his forefinger down the thick length from tip to base. The touch is ticklish, sending shivers of delight coursing through Will's body, and he writhes beneath the seasoned hands of the professional.

"Yes," Will says, the word escaping him to rise toward the roof of the car. Every time Corey runs his finger down the same path, it elicits another *yes* from Will, each louder than the last, until he clutches the seat beneath him and cries out into the night. "Yes, *yes*."

Just when Will thinks he'll explode, Corey's hands disappear. Forcing his breath to slow, Will sighs. "There's lube in the glove compartment."

In the passenger seat, Corey shucks off his sneakers, extracting a condom from the inside of his left shoe. With expert moves, he tears open the foil packet with his teeth then rolls the condom onto Will's cock without ceremony. Will fiddles with it, pinching room into the tip of the condom, as he hears the hustler rummage through the glove compartment. Too late, he wonders if his service pistol is in there. He turned it in last month with his badge, but can't seem to remember if the chief returned it yet or not. If it's there, and Corey finds it...

He hears a *click* as the glove compartment snaps shut, then Corey holds up a curvy bottle of Astroglide. "This it?"

Before Will can get a good look, Corey flicks open the pop-top and squirts a generous dollop of the thick gel onto the tip of Will's dick. Even through the condom, Will feels the cool liquid slowly drip down his shaft. "Don't use it all—"

But the telltale raspberry sound of the bottle emptying interrupts him. "Too late," Corey says, giving the bottle one good last squeeze before he pitches it behind his seat. Will ducks to avoid getting hit in the head with the bottle and feels the car move as Corey climbs onto him. "Guide me. I want your thick cock in my ass like now."

Will has never found such vulgar talk sexy. "You don't have to be so—"

"Now," Corey says again as he plops down to straddle Will's chest.

Will's hands are drawn to those pale buttocks—he cups them,

his fingers sliding into the cleft between the cheeks, massaging the firm muscle. One forefinger finds Corey's trembling hole, which puckers and flexes as he rims it. Above him, Corey fists his hands in Will's shirt and rocks back into his hands. "Fuck me already," he demands, jumping a little to rock the car. "You're paying for it, aren't you?"

Sitting up, Will covers Corey's foul mouth with his own, silencing him. The hustler sits back, surprised, and finds himself seated in the palms of Will's strong hands. Spreading those tender asscheeks wide, Will guides his dick to the hidden center of Corey's being. The wet tip of the condom slides over smooth skin, and Will uses his fingertips to angle it into place.

Corey makes a muffled noise, his lips pressed to Will's. When they part, allowing Will's hungry tongue entry, Will thrusts up into the hustler's tight ass.

*That* earns him a breathy gasp.

Will falls back to the seat, hips bucking to force as much of himself as he can into his lover for the evening. Corey follows him down, hands still clenched in Will's shirt, his mouth ardent, insistent, as it seeks Will's own. "Yes," he sighs into Will as they kiss, his words timed with each thrust, each fuck. "Please, god, yes, *god*, fuck, yes, *yes*."

They find a fast pace, a furious rhythm spurred on by Corey's half-whispered moans. The friction of Will's cock thrust between Corey's willing buttocks sets the night on fire around them. Will feels his blood blaze in his veins as he rocks toward release. Harder, faster, he forces his way into the body above his as he holds on tightly to Corey's hips. His fingers burn against the pale skin as if leaving scorch marks behind. Deeper, harder, *in*, as far as he can go, as far as Corey lets him. Will gives in to the ancient art of sex and lets the rest of his day, the rest of his *life*, fall away. Faster, yes, *yes*.

He needs this.

When his orgasm shudders through him, Will grabs the tie holding back Corey's release and pulls it free. Corey sits up, hips grinding above Will's, hand jerking as he comes in a white rush that slicks Will's lower belly. White cum streaks his black skin like spilt milk. One elbow hits the car horn behind him, and the 350Z blares into the night in time with Corey's strokes. The sound sets off in Will a second, more vicious orgasm, and he clamps his hands down on Corey's upper thighs to hold the hustler in place as he shoots his load inside him again.

For a long moment, they sit coupled together, Will panting as he lies in the driver's seat, Corey leaning back against the steering wheel. Neither seems able to speak nor has the energy to pull apart. Finally Corey runs a hand through his hair, and the short black bangs stand up from his temple from the lube on his fingers. He takes a deep breath, but his voice still shakes slightly when he speaks. "You know," he sighs, "I like you, so I'm gonna cut you a deal. Let's say a hundred fifty for the whole thing. That cool with you?"

Will reaches into his back pocket for his wallet, moving carefully to avoid dislodging Corey. At that price, he knows he could easily eat through his whole paycheck for this boy from the streets.

# SATYR

Jeff Mann

He stands in the rain, backpack over one shoulder, hopeful thumb cocked. Behind him, the woodlands of Draper Mountain are thick with August green. I never pick up hitch-hikers, but the afternoon's become a blinding deluge, and the boy looks waiflike and pathetic out here in the middle of nowhere, unkempt hair stuck to his brow. Besides, I've had my eye on him for months. I'd be a fool not to take advantage of such an opportunity.

Pulling my Jeep over onto the graveled roadside, I unlock the passenger-side door and beckon. The boy jogs over and climbs inside. He grins at me, drops his pack on the floor, shakes his shaggy hair like a wet dog and says, "Thanks, sir! I really appreciate it. It's raining cats and dogs out there. I'm drenched!" His voice is low and lilting, his accent country-thick.

I soak in his looks while he brushes thick brown bangs out of his eyes and wipes raindrops from his whiskered chin. I know his features well, despite the fact that we've never met. All summer, on my daily commute to Virginia Tech, I've admired him. Almost every time I've driven past that shabby apartment building on the wrong side of the tracks, he's been sitting on the stoop, beside a skinny, grizzle-jawed man I've assumed to be his father. Every time I passed I gawked; I couldn't help myself. The boy would smile at me; the father would glare. I wasn't staring at their obvious poverty; many folks in this little mountain town are poor, a constant reminder that I'm very lucky in such an economic downturn to have the job I do. No, I was ogling the boy's handsome face and lithe body.

Luckily for my voyeuristic lust, this summer's been hotter than any in memory, meaning that, every time I saw him, the object of my admiration was wearing nothing but shorts. Something about him made him look underage, not more than sixteen. Perhaps it was his short stature, around five foot six. Perhaps it was his oval baby face, the innocent brown eyes beneath thick eyebrows, the muss of wavy hair down to his shoulders. Some evenings he reminded me of a carefree child, bouncing a basketball or pedaling up and down the block on a bike far too small for him. Other times he looked perturbed, a sullen adolescent, sitting on the concrete stoop with glossy hair falling over his eyes, full lips set in a pout, his chin in his hands. The age difference both turned me on and made me squirm. I'm only thirty-eight, but my desire for a boy so young made me feel like a pervert.

Other things, mature details—and these were the elements that aroused me—made him look not like a boy but a miniature man. He wore a bushy chin-beard and thick sideburns, unshaven stubble perpetually shadowed his cheeks, vine-like tattoos wove around his wiry arms and shoulders, hair coated his lightly muscled chest and lean belly and his legs were so covered with brown fur they were practically shaggy. Two or three times, he was holding what had to be a beer can, leading me to believe that he was at least twenty-one. This conviction only fed my interest. Many was the time I'd drive straight home after such a sighting and jack off, imagining the little guy naked beneath me, legs spread, begging me to stuff his asshole full.

Now, amazingly, here he is, a few inches away, though fully clothed. He's wearing muddy sneakers, and, above dirty Madras shorts, a black muscle-shirt, so wet it's molded to his skin, showing off his torso's sweet shapeliness.

"I'm Timmy, sir. Timothy Keith Woodson. And I think I've seen you before. Don't you live around here?" He extends a hand.

Excellent, an excuse to touch him. We shake. For such a small guy, his grip's surprisingly firm.

"I'm Bryan Laurel. I moved here from Washington, D.C. this spring. And I've seen you too, sitting outside your apartment. On Jefferson Avenue, right?"

"Ah, yeah. The place's really hot this time of year, and my stepdad can't afford air-conditioning or cable, so we..." The boy trails off, clearly embarrassed.

"I understand. I think this is the first time I've ever seen you with your shirt on."

The comment's very deliberate. Being this close to the boy already has me half-hard. It's been a long time since I've made love to anyone, much less someone this hot. So I'm probing possibilities, making clear that I've noticed his previous states of undress. "Where you heading?" I ask, fingering the gearshift and clearing my throat. Lust this powerful always makes my palms sweat and my throat go dry.

"Sylvatus, sir, to visit kin. I grew up there. It's over the mountain a piece."

"You're walking to Sylvatus? That's a long way."

"Can't afford a vehicle. Next to no work around here. Only job I got's part-time at Sonic. And my stepdad won't drive me. He and I don't much get along."

Lightning flashes, and, immediately afterward, thunder crashes, shaking the vehicle. The rain thickens, pounding the Jeep's roof and hood. Beside us, the steep road's awash with muddy water.

"Sylvatus is a little out of my way, but I can drive you there. We should sit here for a while, though, till the storm slows up. Seems like it's right on top of us."

"Ain't in any hurry. Long as I get to Sylvatus by suppertime. I don't want to miss my aunt's pot roast."

"How old are you, Timmy?"

"I'm twenty-two, though, yeah, I know, I know, folks tell me I look younger. Always get carded when I buy beer. It's a pain in the butt."

"Well, speaking of beer, before this surprise storm set in, I was heading out to Claytor Lake for some fishing—I have a little motorboat there—which means there's a six-pack in the cooler behind your seat. Want a beer?"

"Hell, yes! I mean, yes, please. I'd sure appreciate it."

"You're sure you're twenty-one?"

"Yes, sir. I swear!"

"Your reward for good manners," I say, opening the cooler. "Been a while since I ran across a guy your age who's so polite. Lots of kids in D.C. are spoiled and rude. Here," I say, popping open a bottle and handing it to him. "This wheat beer's Starr Hill, from Crozet."

Timmy takes a pull and licks his lips. "It's great! Tastes a little like clove cigarettes I used to smoke in high school. Thanks, sir."

"The 'sir' isn't necessary. You can call me Bryan."

“I’m sorry, sir,” Timmy says, shaking his head, “but we country boys ain’t raised to call our elders by their first names.”

Elders. Ouch. So much for my attempt at reducing formal distance.

“Ah, okay.” I chuckle, stroking my beard. “I’m still not used to living around here. It’s pretty different from D.C.”

“City boy, huh? We hillfolk ain’t bad, once you get to know us.”

For a few moments we sit without speaking, sipping beer and listening to the rain. Thunder crashes again, even louder. “Shit, that was close!” Timmy says, looking startled. Heteros have it so easy. If I were straight, and Timmy were a girl, I could take this excuse to put a comforting arm around him. As it is, my guess is that most queers flee this rural region. The likelihood that my little friend here would share my erotic interests is pretty small.

“This brew’s real good,” Tim says, sipping. “Thanks again.” Then he continues, in a hesitant voice. “Sir, mind if I ask you something?”

Uh-oh. He sounds almost frightened. “Sure,” I say, taking a long swig.

“Are you gay?”

I choke on my beer. Doubling over, I hack and curse. “Fuck!”

“Sorry!” Timmy exclaims, slapping my back.

The coughing fit subsides. Face flushed, sides aching, I stare at him. He’s much smaller than I, so if he turns hostile, I can kick his ass with ease. “Uh, yes, I am. Why do you ask?”

“The rainbow flag on your bumper. My aunt drags me to church sometimes—I hate it, but she insists—and the preacher, he talks a lot about ‘the gay agenda,’ and how such ‘perverts’ are going to hell, and he’s warned us about ‘satanic queer codes,’ to use his expression. The rainbow flag was one he mentioned.”

I take a long breath, trying to regain my composure. I want to say, "This particular gay guy would love to suck you off right now" or "Is your butt as hairy as your chest and legs? Why don't you come home with me and I'll eat your ass for an hour?" but I've always been far too shy to make a pass if I'm not convinced that my interest is reciprocated, so instead I say, "And do you agree with your preacher?"

"Hell, no. I know better." Timmy grins, taking a swig of beer. "I'm gay too."

We have a second beer, waiting for the storm to move off. I tell Timmy a little about myself: how I moved here in May, six months after Ed, my partner of five years, left me; how I'd had enough of D.C., its traffic, its humidity, all the restaurants and bars that reminded me of Ed and how much he'd hurt me. Timmy tells me about his high school years, his successful attempts to hide his homosexuality with a series of girlfriends, his achievements in wrestling and track, his brief and very secretive affair with another runner, his mother's early death from lung cancer, his feuds with his stepfather, his desires to move to some queer-friendly city and the lack of cash that has hindered him in that and so many other hopes.

The rain tapers off; the sun comes out. When Timmy's stomach growls, I offer to treat him to lunch. He directs me up over the mountain and down into the tiny community of Draper. We sit on the front porch of the country store and snack on the rural Southern food he seems to favor: fried pork skins, pickled eggs, and baloney sandwiches. Then we're off down Route 100, along rain-swollen creeks. I drop him off in Sylvatus, in front of a rickety farmhouse overshadowed by a cigar tree. A couple of teenaged girls in bright colors are swaying in a porch swing. They cheer, seeing him climb from my Jeep.

"Them's my cousins. Thanks, sir," he says, smiling. "I really appreciate your kindness."

Again, I choke back what I really want to say: "May I see you again?" and "How about you come over for drinks and dinner sometime?" and "May I have your phone number?" and "Any chance a sweet little guy like you is a fan of smooth-pated, black-bearded muscle-bears like me?" Instead, I say, "No problem. It was great meeting you."

Timmy turns away, pauses, and turns back. "Where you live, Mr. Laurel? In town, right?"

"The brick house at the corner of Prospect and Madison. It's got green shutters and a big lawn. Set back in some trees."

"Got it. Well, maybe we'll meet again sometime." Timmy gives me another smile, tosses his hair out of his eyes, and heads for the farmhouse. I drive off, practically cross-eyed with lust, anxiety, curiosity, and hope, my frustrated dick tenting my jeans.

The following week, I'm enjoying an afternoon nap on the couch when the doorbell buzzes. I open the front door, still half-asleep. To my amazement, it's Timmy Woodson. He's smiling. He looks me up and down. His smile broadens. That's when I realize I've got nothing on but black nylon gym shorts.

I rub my eyes and yawn, scratching my belly's black thatch. The boy looks great. He's wearing cargo shorts that display his shaggy calves, short work boots that have seen better days, and a form-fitting white A-shirt that emphasizes the lines of his tasty torso and gives me a great view of brown chest hair curling over the top. His one flaw's the black bruise around his right eye.

"Howdy, Mr. Laurel," Timmy says. "I hope I'm not disturbing you. Did I wake you up?"

"Ah, no problem. Worked late last night. Fell asleep after lifting weights."

"You look like you work out, that's for sure."

My god, I think the boy's flirting. "Thanks," I say, flushing and looking sideways. "Yeah, I try to keep fit. How'd you get that black eye?"

Timmy fidgets. "Ah, got in a little street scuffle, that's all. Look, Mr. Laurel, I'm still only working part-time at Sonic, so I've been looking for odd jobs around town. I was wondering if you could do with a little yard work."

"Well, I usually mow the grass myself, but—"

"I could really use the money, sir. I'd do a great job, I promise. You have a lawn mower, right?"

"Sure, kid. Okay. Follow me."

It takes only a couple of minutes to bounce the mower from the basement and gas it up. Soon thereafter, I'm standing by the living room window, heart pounding and throat tight, watching the boy work and rubbing myself through my shorts. The slight swell of his chest beneath the ribbed white cotton, the effort knotting up his tattooed arms, the strain of his calves, the curve of his ass...I can't stop staring. The boy maddens and moves me. I can't believe he's here. I can't believe, after all I lost with Ed, I can still feel this hot mix of lust and tenderness. Long, lonely months of celibacy have only made my ardor sharper.

Timmy's a fast worker. As big as the lawn is, he's done in thirty minutes. I meet him at the door. His long hair's plastered to his brow; his A-shirt's soaked; his hairy armpits exude the rich odor of fresh sweat. Too late, I realize I should have put on a different pair of shorts. Gym trunks are none too effective at hiding a hard-on.

"You'll take a check, right?" I say, ushering him inside.

"Oh, sure, sir." He wipes sweat from his sideburns.

"How much?"

"Forty? Would that be all right?"

"Sure. Let's say fifty, actually. I have a good job, and you need the money. Want a beer?" Shy as I am, I'm also hospitable. Any excuse to keep him around longer.

"That'd be great! But, first, uh, do you mind if I take a shower? If it ain't too much trouble?"

Bold brute; damned tease. I lead him upstairs, show him the bathroom, and set him up with towel and washcloth. Downstairs, I sit on the couch, listening to the rush of water, fighting the urge to join him. I stroke myself, imagining him naked, then, with effort, pull my hand away so my erection will deflate by the time he's done.

The splashing stops. Silence, then a padding of bare feet down the stairs. Timmy appears in the door of the living room. He's wearing nothing but a towel wrapped around his lithe loins. Water beads his thick brown chest hair; bruises scatter his ribs, the result, I assume, of more brawling. "Sir, I've been thinking. Uh, since you were kind enough to buy me lunch and drive me to Sylvatus, today's yard work is on me. But, um, if you give me fifty dollars, uh, you can blow me."

I stand. My thighs betray me with an unseemly quiver. "I, uh, I've never paid for sex before."

"But you do want me, sir?" Moving closer, Timmy tosses wet hair out of his eyes. He looks at my crotch and the stiff evidence there. Beneath the towel, his own prick is clearly rising.

"Yes. God, yes. I do. Very, very much." I try to keep my voice from shaking; I fail.

"I'm not a whore, sir. I've never charged before. But I, I'm desperate. I need the money real, *real* bad, and I—"

Abruptly, he backs up and bows his head. "Oh, god!" he gasps. "I'm sorry, Mr. Laurel. I never should have—"

"How about fifty dollars if *you* blow *me*?" I blurt. "One hundred dollars if I get to eat your ass first."

Timmy drops the towel. He turns, bending over, presenting his bare butt. It's compact, perfectly curved, and covered with fine golden-brown hair. Gripping one cheek, he gives me a glimpse of his hole, barely visible in its grove of fur.

"Mr. Laurel, sir, it's a deal."

Bent over the end of the couch, Timmy moans with excitement. During those several years with Ed—well, before we stopped having sex—I perfected my rimming skills, and now my little yard-worker is about to receive the benefit of such practice. I knead and nip his fuzzy ass-mounds. Spreading his buttocks, I burrow my face between them, in the fragrant cleft-thicket I find there. I run my tongue up and down the crack, then around the tiny hole, then into it, jabbing and lapping, my face growing wet with my own spit. I emerge from desire's hot haze just long enough to realize that I'm growling and panting like a dog, then dive in again. It's been years since I've been so aroused.

Unlike many men I've pleasured in this manner, Timmy doesn't just lie there. His enthusiasm matches mine. He reaches back to spread his own buttocks wider. He bucks back against my face; he humps the couch; he accompanies my efforts with an appreciative chant. "Ohh. Yes, sir! Oh, yes. That's wonderful. Oh, man. Just great! Goddamn."

Now I give Timmy's ass a squeeze and a slap. He jumps, giggles and cocks his rear-end higher. I give him a few more open-palmed slaps. "Yeah! Mmm! Love it!" he groans, beginning to jack himself. I drag him to the floor, position us on our sides, and push my groin against his face. He wraps an arm around my waist, brushes my cockhead with his chin-beard, runs a stubbly cheek over the glans, tugs on my sack, then takes the head into his mouth. I grip his shaggy hair and pull him onto me. He chokes; my cock slams the back of his throat, once, twice, three times; he slobbers and sucks, head bobbing up and down. Within seconds, my thighs tense, my back arches, and, gasping, "Oh, shit, here I go!" I pound his mouth and cum.

Timmy giggles and swallows my load. He holds me in his mouth as I lie there, washed out, trembling, growing ever so slowly soft. I stroke his hair; he laps at my shrinking cock. He falls asleep like that, lips still retaining my flesh inside him. I drowse too, then drift off.

I wake to rapturous suction. I'm sprawled on my back on the carpet. Tim's stretched out on the floor between my spread legs, slurping frantically on my hard-yet-again dick. He releases me long enough to say, "Yum, whatta mouthful! Didn't think you got your money's worth the first time," before renewing his efforts. Before long, I've cum in his mouth again. Grinning, he rises; spits in his hand; grips his long, thin cock; straddles my waist and jacks off, spurting cream into my chest hair.

October's igniting the forest. Timmy gives me botany lessons as we drive the narrow road winding up the side of Big Walker Mountain. "That hot orange is sugar maples; the bright gold is tulip trees. And that there purple is aster. Pretty, ain't it?"

We've met every other week since August. I'm a little in love with my hillbilly hustler, and we both know it. He keeps charging me for sex, and his frequent bruises and black eyes indicate a worrisome addiction to street fights, and he hasn't let me ass-fuck him yet, which is, of course, what I dream of most, but otherwise he's the perfect companion. He's smart, despite the lack of a college education; he knows everything about the outdoors, able to identify plants, birds, animal tracks, even rocks. He's funny, and he's appreciative, thanking me for every little thing I do for him—buying him clothes, treating him to fast-food lunches, even making him a homemade pizza every now and then. Five times he's even spent the night, curled up in my arms. Those have been the happiest times of my life. I've only known him two months, but already I don't know what I'll do if he ever decides he's had enough of my cock and my cash.

The boy surely knows how to keep me hooked, that's for sure. Right now, his flannel shirt is unbuttoned, despite the chilly autumn air, giving me the luxurious sight of his furry chest. Every now and then, in between sips of beer, he squeezes his own denimed crotch, or plays with his tiny pink nipples, or strokes my knee as I drive.

"This here's the place," Timmy says, as we reach the crest of the mountain. I pull off onto the side road he indicates and park behind a moss-streaked boulder. "No one'll see us back here. Ain't no one comes up here anyway, 'cept deer-hunters next month. I can't wait to get your dick in my mouth."

With that, he swigs the last of his beer, shucks off his shirt, unzips my fly, hauls out my cock, kneels on the floor of the Jeep and starts sucking me off. I lie back, look out into the burning leaves, finger his stiff nipples and thrust gently into his mouth. We could be making love inside a bonfire, as bright as the autumn colors are.

As usual, it takes me only minutes to cum. In the months we've met, Timmy's become more and more adept at blow jobs. And, as usual, after he's swallowed my load, he keeps my cock in his mouth. He kneels there, happily sucking, for a long time. Finally, he rises. I hand him a fifty and another beer. We recline the seats a few notches, lie back and drink.

"That was wonderful," I say. "As always."

"Thanks, sir." Timmy blushes, as he does whenever I give him a compliment. "I love the taste of your jizz. When we get back to town, will you suck on my tits while I jack off? No charge for that."

"You bet, kid. So when are you going to let me fuck you? You know I really want to. Name your price."

"Naw, I ain't ready for that yet," he mumbles. "Maybe some day. I'm sorta saving that for..." He slurps his beer, wipes his mouth and stares out into the fiery leaves. Somewhere, a woodpecker's hammering.

"Look," he says, putting his half-drunk beer on the console, then scooting closer and resting his head on my shoulder, "I'm sorry to ask for money. I, uh, really, really like you, sir, and you've been super-generous. It's just that I need regular cash. I can't say why. I keep trying to find a full-time job, but..."

"You're not using, are you, Timmy? I know there's supposed to be a lot of drugs in your neighborhood. Just last week they busted another meth lab down the street from you."

"No!" Timmy sits up with a jolt. "I hate that stuff! I would never do that! How could you think that?"

"Relax, kid," I say, patting his shoulder. "You look tired. How about a nap? How about you put your head in my lap, curl up on the seat and sleep some? I'll just sit here and enjoy the quiet."

Without a word, he arranges himself. I stroke his hair; he sighs. "Can I sleep over tonight? Please? My stepdad's been a real shit lately, and I don't want to be around him."

"Sure, kid. Sure." My heart swells at the thought of another night together. "I'll make you a big meal of spaghetti and meatballs, okay? We'll have a nice bottle of Chianti."

No answer. The boy's already drifted off. I caress his bare chest, kiss his inked shoulder and watch him sleep.

* * *

"I didn't take them!"

Timmy grabs his backpack and heads for the door. He's poised to dash out into the cold night, the November rain, when I seize him by the arm.

"Hey, kid. I was just asking. Sit down and let's talk."

He's trembling beneath my grasp. I tug him back into the living room and push him down onto the couch. For just a second, the sweet memory swamps me, Timmy bent over this very piece of furniture, moaning with bliss as I work my tongue deeper up his asshole. But now, dammit, things have gone all to hell.

Timmy drops his backpack on the floor. He squirms; his eyes roam the room, avoiding mine.

"So what am I to think? You're always saying that you need cash. Now the watch my mother gave me has disappeared. So has my coin collection. So has my gold Phi Beta Kappa key. No one else has been in this house but you and me."

"Maybe someone broke in! Maybe somebody—"

"I have an alarm system, remember? Why, Timmy? Haven't I been good to you?"

Timmy leaps up. He grabs his backpack and pulls a knife from its side pocket. He flips the blade open and extends it toward me with a shaking hand.

"I'm leaving now! Don't you try to stop me!"

"What the fuck are you doing?" I say, taking a step toward him. "A knife? Seriously?"

It's over before I know it. One second I'm about to grab his shoulder; the next, there's sharp pain as he stabs my forearm; the next, I've punched him in the face; and the next, the boy's out cold on my living room floor.

Dazed, I pace about, then fetch peroxide and bandages. It takes a while to stanch the bleeding. I pick up the phone, dial nine, then one. I hang up. Knees wobbly with adrenaline, I hunker down beside my guest. He's still unconscious, his right eye already swelling. Gusts of rain spatter the window. I lift Timmy in my arms—he's heavier than he looks—and carry him upstairs.

I watch the clock. At least two hours, I'd decided. Greedy bastard. Charging me hundreds of dollars over the last three months. Then stealing from me. Let him suffer. Let him sweat and struggle and shout and whine.

Well, hard-heartedness has never been my strong suit, especially when it comes to handsome men or beautiful boys. I've tried to work through some online tasks, tried to read, tried to ignore the sounds upstairs—a thumping outrage waning rapidly into pitiful pleading—for only forty-five minutes before I relent. Rising, I finish my scotch, lope up the steps, and open the walk-in closet.

Timmy's naked, lying on his side in a mess of dress shoes and work boots. He stares up at me, brown eyes wide with futility and fright. Against the tight rope hog-tie, his limbs strain. Against the layers of bandanas and duct tape, he makes unintelligible sounds, no doubt pleas for mercy and release.

"Had enough, huh?" I say, nudging his butt with my boot. "I'm not done with you yet, bad boy."

I work loose the cord securing his ankles to his wrists but leave his hands and feet tied. I drag him out of the closet, sit on the bed's edge, pull him onto my lap, hold him down and swat his ass. Hard. Harder. He screams and struggles only briefly before his cock hardens against my jeans.

"You like this, huh?"

He nods wildly, grinding his crotch against me.

"I thought so." I chuckle, spanking him harder still. He

thrashes, humping my thigh. Within a minute, he stiffens, then, with a low groan, climaxes against my leg.

"Nice!" I say, wiping up the ejaculate and licking it from my hand. I lift him off me and roll him onto the bed, where he curls into a frightened ball, knees folded against his chest. "As badly as I want up your ass, I should rape you right now," I say, slipping a finger between his asscheeks and probing his butthole, "but I won't. If you tell me the truth. Why you stole from me. Okay?"

Timmy nods. He's shivering, so I strip off my clothes, climb into bed, pull the covers over us and wrap my body around his. I stroke his bruised face for a moment before peeling the tape off his lips, unknotting the bandana tied between his teeth and pulling out the spit-soaked ball of cloth stuffed in his mouth.

"Timmy, dammit. I was really starting to care for you. Why'd you ruin it?"

The boy sniffles. "I'm so, so sorry I cut you. Are you going to call the cops? Please don't."

"I might. But I'd rather strike a new deal."

"Whatta you mean? *Please* don't tell on me. I don't want to go to jail. My stepdad'll kill me."

"The new deal's this. I don't call the cops if you stop charging me for sex. And you give me your ass. And you never steal from me again, okay?"

"I was gonna give up my ass anyway. I was saving it for someone special, and, as sweet as you've treated me…that was gonna be your Christmas present."

I pat Timmy's hip and run a finger along his ass crack. "I'm someone special? So why'd you steal from someone special?"

"My stepdad!" Timmy gives a hoarse sob. "Fuck! Naw, I ain't gonna cry again. He's made me cry enough!"

"What are you talking about?"

"I owe you the truth. Why I needed the money. Here goes."

* * *

It's nearly midnight, the rain shifting to sleet. I pound the door hard. When Silas flips on the stoop-light and cracks the door, I size him up. He's shorter than I am, and skinny. Glad I lift weights. I'll break his jaw if he gets nasty.

"Are you Silas?"

"Yep. What you want? It's late."

"This won't take long. I'm a friend of Timmy's. He tells me that you beat him. That you charge him a high rent and make him sleep on the floor. That sometimes you even make him sleep in the alley when he can't pay what you ask."

"What the fuck? You can't prove any of that," Silas snarls. "And what business is this of yours? He's my stepson. I'll treat him any goddamn way I want."

"He also says that you're so addicted to a certain substance that you're in constant need of money, that you've stolen and you've forced him to steal. He's told me who your dealer is."

"That goddamn brat! That's all lies!" Silas throws the door open, fists clenched, and strides out onto the stoop. "Get the fuck outta here, or I'll—"

"I wouldn't do that," I say, flexing an arm and smiling. "I'm a lot bigger than you. You tweaked-out types tend to be scrawny."

He hesitates, takes in the size of my build, and backs up. "I got a gun inside."

"I'm sure you do. But I'm not here to bust you. The police don't need to be involved. I could report you for any number of crimes, but I figure the universe will give you what you deserve soon enough. I'm here to work out a gentleman's agreement."

"And what would that be?"

"Timmy stays with me. You leave us alone. We leave you alone. How's that sound?"

Silas chews his lip, then spits on the stoop, barely missing my right boot. "Why you want him around? You some kind of queer? God hates that kind."

"That's none of your business."

Silas's face twitches. He scratches his hair and rolls his eyes. "I'm tired of feeding that little shit anyway. You can have 'im. Is that it?"

"That's it."

"Tell him I said, 'Good riddance.'" Silas turns on his heel and slams the door behind him.

I find Timmy as I left him, snuggled beneath bedcovers behind a locked door. His mouth's taped, his hands bound behind him and his neck loosely chained to the bedpost. All necessary precautions. No way I was going to take the chance that he'd bolt before I got home.

Despite his restraints, he's fast asleep. I sit beside him, listening to him breathe. Then I undress, climb in beside him, wrap my arms around him, and kiss his stubble-rough cheek. He mumbles, sighs, and nestles back against me. We lie that way for a while before I remove the neck-chain and unpeel the mouth-tape.

"Still here, huh?"

"Yep." Timmy grins wearily. "You didn't need to tie me, man. I ain't going nowhere, I swear. So did it work?"

"I think so. Silas said you could stay here. Do you want to stay here?"

"Lord, yes."

"He'll leave us alone in return for our silence. You want me to go by in the morning and fetch your stuff?"

Timmy sniggers. "My *stuff*? All I own's some wore-out clothes and a few graphic novels. Hell, I ain't even got one of them fancy phones all the other guys my age are thumb-tapping on. So how long can I stay?"

"As long as you want. As long as you don't fuck up again. We'll see how things go. Maybe I'll adopt you. Adults adopting adults. It's the new craze. Think you can learn to cook and do laundry?" I run my fingers through Timmy's chest hair, then focus my attentions on a nipple.

"Whoa, that feels good. Keep that up. So I get to sleep with you every night in this big cozy bed? Rent boy graduates to houseboy, huh?"

"Yes. I think you just found a job, if you want it. No more sleeping on the floor or in the alley. No more stealing." I squeeze a fuzzy buttock and tug tufts of fine cleft-fur. "My salary's big enough for both of us. And maybe, if you'd like, you can start taking some classes at Tech. You'd make a fine forester or naturalist, country-wise as you are."

"Yeah, maybe so. Y'gonna untie me? My hands are going numb."

"In a little. First, I'm going to treat you to a lengthy rimming, and then a slow, deep finger-fucking. Then I'm going to screw you on your belly, your back and your side. After we've both cum, I'll untie you. That all right with you?"

"Christmas comes early, huh?" Timmy sighs and rubs his ass against me. "Yep, it's time you fucked me. I never told you about my real dad—he died when I was ten, and it's still hard to speak of him—but...he was so good to me, so protective, so loving. When I realized I was gay—I was fifteen—I swore only a guy who was as kind to me as my dad used to be would ever be...inside me the way you're wanting to be."

I stroke Timmy's asshole with my forefinger, then prod gently. "Damn, so you're a virgin here?" I sigh. "I want you so badly that way, little man."

"You got me. I'm ready to take your cock, sir. Just go slow, okay?"

"You bet, kid. I won't hurt you."

"Bryan, sir? Tomorrow, can we go for a walk along the New River Trail? If it ain't raining? I miss the woods. There's a great old white oak I want you to see. And the milkweed pods'll be splitting open. Their seeds are like little puffs of fog."

"Luring me into wild places, huh?" I caress a shaggy thigh. "My little satyr." Rolling him onto his belly, I nudge wide his legs. I rub my beard over his ass before spreading his cheeks and burying my face in the soft dark crack-moss growing there. "Lead on, little man," I whisper, tickling his clenched pink hole with the tip of my tongue. "Lead on. We'll enter that forest together."

# THE HITTER AND THE STALL

Michael Bracken

I clamped my hand around the man's wrist and squeezed until he whimpered and released my wallet, letting it drop back into my hip pocket. Without loosening my grip, I turned to face him. The subway riders crowded around us were oblivious to what was happening mere inches from them, and I spoke softly to keep it that way. "That's a terrible dip."

The slender young blond grimaced but also kept his voice low. "You're hurting me."

"You're lucky I don't break your wrist." I showed him his wallet. "Or keep this."

Astonishment overcame the blond's pain. "How did you do that?"

I flipped his wallet open and thumbed his driver's license out far enough that I could read his name and address. Then I thumbed it back into place, tucked his wallet into his shirt pocket and patted it lightly. "I have the gift, Sean."

The subway slid to a halt and the doors opened. I slipped out with the other exiting passengers before the amateur pickpocket realized I'd released my grip on his wrist. I tried to fade into the crowd but he followed me anyhow and caught me at the top of the stairs. He grabbed my jacket sleeve. "Teach me."

I examined Sean more carefully this time. At least twenty years my junior, he wasn't big enough for strong-arm work. Even so, there was a certain spark of intelligence in his pale blue eyes, something I'd not often seen in the young punks more interested in snatch-and-grab opportunities than in the subtle art of dipping. Sean wasn't bad on the eyes, either, and I suspected I could first teach him to be a stall, the same way an older hitter named Joey "Fingers" Johnson had taken me under his wing and taught me the trade when I was a young man. I asked, "What's in it for me?"

"What do you want?"

"We can discuss it over dinner." I'd been looping all afternoon, riding from one end of the subway line to the other, collecting hide along the way, and I was hungry. Even though I had a fat wad of cash tucked in a special pocket hidden inside my jacket that Sean never would have found even if he knew to look for it, I wasn't about to reveal its existence. "Are you hungry?"

Sean nodded.

"Good," I said. "You're paying." I handed him his wallet a second time, and this time I had stripped it of cash.

He stared at me. "How the hell did you do that to me again?"

I smiled. "There's a deli at the corner. They make a good pastrami on rye."

Without waiting to see if Sean would follow, I turned and headed up the block. He matched my stride and held the door open for me when we reached the deli. We ordered, found an empty booth in the back and sat with our sandwiches. The din of the busy deli prevented people around us from easily overhearing anything we might say.

"This is a terrible business to get into," I explained. I was working twice as hard as twenty years earlier just to maintain my lifestyle. "Fewer and fewer people are carrying significant amounts of cash."

"Cash is old-school," Sean said. "I'm after plastic—credit cards, debit cards, gift cards."

"You can turn those?"

"I know a guy."

"We all know a guy," I said. My leg brushed against his under the table. He didn't pull away. "Can you trust yours?"

Sean shrugged. "So far."

His cavalier attitude bothered me. It should have bothered me more but I was watching him eat—the way he wrapped his lips around the sandwich, the way he took the meat into his mouth, the way he wet his lips with the tip of his tongue between bites—and thoughts that had nothing to do with my profession distracted me. I shifted my leg, rubbing it against his in a way that could seem accidental, but he still didn't pull away. I said, "You need to have a lot of faith in a guy like that. He turns on you and then where will you be?"

"Having my room and board paid by the state."

"That's why I prefer to stick with cash," I said. "Less back-end risk."

Sean leaned forward, "But you have to dip more often than I do," he said, "which exposes you up front."

Above the table we were having a conversation that may have been about fences and risk, but under the table our legs were having a quieter conversation, one that made my cock hard.

We talked—above the table and below—for several more minutes, then finished our sandwiches and stood to go. I dropped some of Sean's money on the table before fanning the young blond. Fanning is the act of lightly touching a pocket to determine if it contains money or a wallet, but I wasn't checking Sean's pockets; I was determining the length, girth and firmness of his erection.

I was impressed and he didn't even know it.

Once we stood on the sidewalk outside the deli, Sean held out his hand and asked, "Do I get my change?"

I ignored both his question and his outstretched hand. I didn't like the idea of taking a stranger to my apartment, but if I wanted him I had no choice. "Follow me."

My apartment was a third-floor walk-up above a two-story used bookstore three blocks from the deli, and the entrance was a doorway sandwiched between the bookstore and a pawnshop. The building didn't inspire confidence, nor did the stairwell, but my living space occupied the entire top floor, with a large living room, eat-in kitchen, two bedrooms and large bath, all protected by a steel door with a serious deadbolt.

Once inside my apartment, Sean's eyes widened. My ex-boyfriend had decorated the place, and he'd had impeccable taste. He'd also had my bankroll to work with.

"You didn't get all this lifting wallets," Sean said, as I closed and bolted the door.

The young blond standing before me was correct, but I didn't admit it. Over the years I'd lifted many things: jewelry, bearer bonds and other easily fenced valuables, much of it when I was working with Fingers because it often required the work of both a stall and a hitter to walk off with purses, briefcases, courier pouches and other portable containers used to transport valuables. I had been working solo ever since Alzheimer's made Fingers worthless even as a stall, and teaming with my own stall I could again target high-end marks. My cock had grown flaccid during the walk from the deli, but the thought of once again taking down big scores firmed it right up.

I pushed Sean back against the steel door, covered his mouth with mine and shoved my tongue down his throat. I slipped one hand between us and had Sean's belt unfastened, his zipper open and his pants slithering down his thighs before he realized I had my fist wrapped around his cock. I could tell without looking that he'd manscaped his pubic hair into oblivion.

His cock quickly stiffened in my grasp and I pistoned my fist up and down the thick shaft. My weight pinned Sean to the door, and he could barely move his hips forward and back as I fist-fucked him. When he moaned in my mouth, I knew he was about to come and I quickly covered his cockhead with my hand. He came on my palm and when he finished ejaculating I wiped my hand on his shirt.

We shed clothes as I led Sean down the hall to the master bedroom where I kept a tube of lube and a box of condoms in the dresser drawer. By the time we reached the bedroom, we were both naked and I could appreciate his smooth, young skin; at the same time I realized that I had not manscaped in months, not since the night Leo realized exactly how I earned my living and declared that he would have no part of it.

Sean didn't seem to care that I'd not groomed. In fact, my mansweater seemed to turn him on in a way that it had never excited my ex. I grabbed the lube and condoms from the dresser, spun Sean around so that he was leaning over the end of the bed, and slathered his ass crack with lube. Then I pulled on a condom and pressed the head of my cock against his slick sphincter. I grabbed his hips and held tight as I pushed forward, easing my cockhead into him. Then I drove my shaft deep inside Sean, pulled back and did it again.

I fucked him hard and I fucked him fast, slamming into the

young blond again and again and again until I couldn't hold back any longer. I drove myself into him one last time and then filled the condom with wad after wad of hot ejaculate.

When I finally pulled away, Sean collapsed on the bed. I disposed of the used condom and joined him, holding him in my arms until he unexpectedly fell asleep. Then I eased away from him and, while he slept, went through all of his pockets and examined everything in his wallet.

When I finished, I shook him awake. "You have to leave."

"Why?"

"There's supposed to be honor among thieves," I said, "but I don't really know you and I don't trust you. Not yet. Maybe never."

Sean rubbed his eyes and crawled out of bed. He pulled on his clothes and I walked him to the door. He was about to step onto the landing when he stopped and patted his pockets. He turned back and held out his hand. "My wallet?"

I handed it to him and he shoved it in his pocket, not even realizing that I'd examined everything in it and that I knew far more about him than he knew about me. He asked, "When will I see you again?"

"Tomorrow morning, early." I told him what time and what subway station. "We'll work the morning rush. I want to watch you dip."

Sean was at the station awaiting my arrival the next morning. He'd already lifted two wallets and he showed me his paltry earnings: thirteen dollars and a stack of credit cards.

"Ditch the plastic," I ordered.

"Why?"

"We're going to spend the morning looping. We get caught with cash it'll be hard to prove where we got it," I explained.

"We get caught with plastic there'll be no doubt of its source."

Sean reluctantly discarded the credit cards into the nearest trashcan when we walked past. "What's looping?"

I glanced at my new apprentice. He didn't even know the lingo.

"We're going to ride to the end of the line, then to the other end and then return here," I explained. Some subway lines are only good for morning and evening rush hour during the week, other lines are best on weekends, still others are packed on holidays when out-of-towners visit the city. Over time I would need to teach Sean the differences.

Once aboard, I watched him work the subway train, noted how he picked his marks, and saw how often he failed to come away with anything. At the same time I was watching Sean I was also dipping, sometimes even lifting wallets from marks he'd been unable to hit. When we stopped for lunch I dissected his technique, from how he selected his marks to his actual handwork.

People near Sean's age are easy marks. Many of them wear earbuds, talk on cell phones, or are wrapped up in some other electronic device and pay no attention to their environment. Unfortunately, they were weaned on plastic and are the least likely to carry cash. The best marks are older people who came of age before the universal acceptance of credit and debit cards, who grew up paying cash and still often do, and who can tell a cashier their change before the cashier can get the answer from the register.

I explained all this to Sean over tuna salad on wheat. He ate a heavier meal despite my observation that it would weigh on his stomach and make him lethargic by midafternoon.

After lunch we returned to the subway and I taught him how to spot players and the jostling squad—fellow pickpockets and the police—and made him watch me work. He did, indeed, get tired midafternoon, but he also learned fast, and soon I had him working again. During the afternoon I fanned the crotches of a few attractive men, and I copped a good feel of Sean's crotch when we neared our last stop of the day, using a heavy touch so that he knew what was on my mind.

I took him back to my apartment, and we went directly to the master bedroom, where removing our clothes caused only a momentary delay. Sean dropped to his knees in front of me, cupped my heavy ball sac in one hand and held my stiff shaft with his other hand as he leaned forward and took the swollen mushroom cap between his lips. He painted my cockhead with his tongue and then slowly took my entire length into his mouth. As soon as I felt his warm breath against the dark tangle of my crotch hair, he pulled all the way back until his teeth caught on my glans.

He did it again and again, kneading my balls at the same time. Sean's oral skills were like his pickpocketing skills—they were effective but lacked finesse—and soon I wrapped my fingers in his short silky hair and held his head as I began pulling my hips back and pushing forward, meeting his descending face with each of my thrusts.

When it became obvious I was about to come, Sean squeezed my balls together and I slammed into his face one last time, spewing thick wads of hot ejaculate against the back of his throat. He held my rapidly deflating cock in his mouth until it stopped spasming, and then he pushed himself to his feet.

I wasn't completely satisfied and my cock rapidly regained its former stature. I grabbed the lube and condoms from my dresser drawer, spun Sean around and took him from behind, just as I had the previous day. This time, though, Sean's cock was hard when I entered him. As I pounded into his ass, he took his own cock in his fist and beat a staccato rhythm in opposition to the steady pounding he was receiving from behind.

He came first, spewing ejaculate across my carpet, and then I came, filling the condom and holding his ass tight against my crotch until I could easily pull away. I discarded the cum-filled condom and then we fell across the bed together.

We talked about the things Sean had learned that day, and we talked about the things he had yet to learn. He was eager, undisciplined and lacked the gift to be a truly great hitter. But he could develop into an excellent stall, a great lay and a partner in all things.

I looked into his pale blue eyes and smiled.

There's so much I can teach Sean, in the subway and in the bedroom, and I know we have a lifetime of adventures ahead of us.

# THE OUTLAW PAULIE CREED

Dale Chase

Paulie Creed is a wanted man and, as a lawman, I have a duty to pursue him. Problem is, I am a sheriff looking for more than justice. A newspaper account of his return to Arizona by way of holding up the Citizen's Bank in Benson brings on a recollection that gets my dick up to such extent I leave my deputy in charge of the office and go home, where I strip naked and indulge myself for some time.

Creed has to be twenty-two now, but I'd venture he still looks much the boy I knew four years back, the wild boy I fucked until I thought I'd expire, the wild boy who can kill a man so many ways.

I do not know if life turned him wild or he was born clawing, but his widowed Ma lost control early on. She managed to teach him reading and writing and get a few books into his head before he killed a man who fooled with her. He was fourteen, the golden child who took to guns and horses like he was born to the life.

An outlaw from then on, he made his name as a good shot, a ruthless killer and at times a most entertaining fellow. He rode with various low characters and did two years in a Colorado prison before he came to Globe, Arizona in 1884, back when I was Marshal there. I should have arrested him on sight but I was so taken with him laughing it up in the Silver Dollar Saloon that I held off. I'd been Marshal but a year and sought to keep the peace rather than tear it up, thus I studied him and his cohorts who played cards while I remained at the bar.

I had seen his picture on wanted notices, but none did him justice. It took light to make that golden hair shine, a riot of curls that set off his ruddy color and blue eyes. His fine features were smudged with dirt like some child resistant to washing and his laugh was infectious, all around him having a fine time by way of his antics.

I had known a good many men in a carnal manner, but here was one who drew me to him without any effort on his part. He could scarcely sit still which led me to believe him pent up, his young balls full of spunk. He'd be good for two or three rounds, maybe more, and though I was seven or eight years older, I knew I could give him just that. As I looked on, I reached down to arrange my privates as my dick was now stiff as a gun barrel.

It was brazen of him to come into a town as a wanted man and the law enforcement part of me believed I should quietly pull him from his game and cart him to jail. But the hard-dicked part said to wait awhile and enjoy the heft down below, and I had learned not to ignore that part.

I wondered, did he fuck his cohorts? They looked older, but then maybe he just looked younger as he had a timeless quality. Too bad he was destined to die young. It would be interesting to see one such as him an old man.

When he and his friends got serious with their cards, they

had been drinking for some time and soon came the expected argument. Drunks always found fault with losing and when one jumped up and sought his gun, I stepped in and knocked it from his hand.

"You there, Paulie Creed, you are a wanted man and I am taking you in. Your friend here can go on his way. You men clear out. Creed will not be leaving with you."

Creed grinned and gave no resistance as he stood. Scruffy as hell, he looked to have been on the trail a month, which I suppose he was. I took him by the arm and led him outside. He was not so drunk as to stumble, and he allowed himself to be put into a jail cell then begged for water to wash. The request amused me enough to comply.

"You got Paulie Creed?" asked my deputy, Carl Conlon, when he came in.

"Yep. Playing cards at the Silver Dollar like he'd never done a single wrong."

Carl looked through the window into the back, then came over to me. "I hear he's a cut up."

"I hear he's a killer."

"Well, yes, but he is said to be likable. That's how he keeps on the run, people helping him out."

"Go back out around town," I said. "Keep things quiet. I'll stay here tonight."

"Yes, sir. Good night."

Globe, being a small town, had just one deputy for me but we did fine between us, handling drunks mostly and claim disputes. The jail cells were in a room behind my office, the door between having a window that bore a shade that could be pulled down. I could thus look in on a prisoner, though there was little concern of escape as the walls were adobe and the one window was near the ceiling. Alone, I busied myself at my desk but found I could not settle and so I took a peek at Creed. To my surprise he was buck naked.

Though not tall, he was sturdy, a hard life adding muscle to his frame. He was browned all over, which surprised me as most men's under parts were stark white since they seldom shed their clothes. The sight of Creed sun-colored set me to wondering if he ran bare at times like some animal on the plain.

He had his kerchief in the basin and squeezed it out, then ran it over his body. His back was to me and I saw him run the kerchief onto his buttocks, then between them, and once he'd gotten this part clean, his finger stole back to get into the crack and play around. My mouth fell open at the sight and my dick rose up in approval.

He spread his legs and half squatted, then stuck a finger up his butthole and began to work himself, at which I let out a gasp that he must have heard as he looked back over his shoulder and grinned. He did not stop his prodding as he squirmed upon the digit and I saw his other hand engaged up front, which proved too much for me. I opened the door and went in. When I reached his cell, I saw him working his prick with a frantic pull while still poking his bottom. Then he looked at me, let out a laugh and began to spray come. I fixed on the sight, my breath all but gone, my crotch afire. When he'd pumped out all his juice, he pulled out of his backside and stood, holding his softening prick.

"Soon as I get clean," he said, "I want to get dirty."

Words failed me. I could not stop looking him up and down as he stood grinning and holding his dick. I scoured legs covered in fine golden hair, thighs thick from long hours in the saddle, a patch of gold between them and more of it running up his front to where it spread across his chest. It was fair enough so I could see his pink tit nubs and my gaze lingered there as I thought what it would be like with my tongue on one. As if to read my mind, Creed ran a hand up and began to pinch the thing.

When I looked upon his face I found his mouth open and his tongue out, wiggling as if to beckon me. His expression was dead serious now. He knew what he was doing to me and that I would have to unlock the cell, go in there and fuck him. As I sought the key, I wondered how many lawmen had succumbed to such promise.

I locked the door to the office and pulled down the shade though I did not expect Carl back this night. Didn't matter. If the Marshal was going to be fucking his prisoner, he'd best not be observed. I drew my gun, unlocked the cell door, put the key into my pocket and stepped in.

"Lemme see," Creed said soon as I was inside. "I figure the marshal is going to have a big dick." He continued to pull on himself and I saw his thing was starting to fill again. Such a blatant arousal further agitated me though I tried my best not to reveal my anxiousness. I then began to undo my pants, which I found near impossible with a gun in hand.

"Why don't you put that down," Creed said. "I am not about to run from a fuck."

He had a point. I set the gun on the floor, undid my pants and got out my prick. I was proud of my size and most men I did commented that it filled them and then some. Creed looked down and clicked his tongue as you do to get a horse moving. He then got onto the bunk and stuck his bottom up at me.

I shed my gun belt, pushed down my pants and drawers, got in behind him and drove my prick in to the hilt. I then began a fuck that could not be held back. Too worked up to last but a few strokes, I came such a gusher that my entire body reeled from the release, my heart pumping as much as my dick. Breath escaped me as I rode the tawny bottom and Creed made me welcome by way of squealing as he took my juice. When I was done I pulled back and sat on my haunches, trying to regain some air.

Creed flipped over to show me his stiff prick and he opened his mouth again, tongue beckoning. I got the idea and bent over to take his cock into my mouth, sucking with a fury until he spurted into my throat. When I pulled off after this, I fell back onto the bunk, leaning against the wall, bottom half still bared in a very unmarshal-like manner. Thoughts were fleeting as Creed crawled over and began to run his hand up under my shirt. He found a tit and began to tweak and rub. "Why don't you shed the rest," he suggested, and I was powerless not to do as asked. A minute later, I was fully naked, lying on the bunk while he played with my tits and I with his dick.

When he got his lips onto the nub, I got a hand onto his bottom and put a finger up him. He squirmed in welcome, so I added a second and began to work him. In response, he grabbed my soft prick and began to play around with it. Soon we were writhing on the bunk, him licking my chest, me wanting to get into his ass again. He then pulled off my tits and got down to my dick, pulling it into his mouth, which caused it to rise. I had to force him off else I'd come in his mouth and, pretty as it was, I preferred to spurt my stuff into his passage.

This time I put him onto his back, threw his legs up over my shoulders and drove into him with such force that the bunk gave way, some part of it falling down a couple of inches which I figured just short of total collapse, but I did not care. I would fuck on the floor if it failed. I would fuck until he was raw, as my juice was boiling and I needed to come so badly I ached.

It took longer this time, which did not matter as I wanted to stay inside him, taming the wild boy the only way possible. He made it plain he was eager to be had, rolling his eyes, thrashing his head from side to side, sticking that tongue out and moaning something awful. This drove me crazy yet in my frenzy I managed to consider that we, going at it, had traded places, me the wild one, him the prey. Never had I felt so unleashed. Never had any man brought me such molten urgency. I needed to possess him until I expired, if it came to that. I would fuck him the whole night and again in the morning. He would keep my dick stiff by way of that mouth or that body, and there was still much I wanted to do to him.

At last the rise beckoned and I began to thrust in earnest, pounding him as he fixed his eyes to mine. He grinned as he drilled me a most eager look, telling me by way of his eyes that he wanted me to fill him with spunk and keep on filling him. I then hit the peak and cried out, the come a long one, as if only Creed could fuel me so. I pounded his bottom until I'd emptied, then fell back and slipped out. I let his legs down but crawled on top of him. I put my mouth to his, even as I fought for breath, because I had to have that tongue and those wicked lips. He was most ardent and receptive and as we descended, we began to ascend for I could not leave off him.

I had no idea the hour and could not have told the day, such was my need of this creature. The fact that he encouraged me to partake of more and more drove me to an excess I could not have imagined. Soon we stank of sweat and come, yet I licked his every inch. And when I got my tongue onto his back, sliding down to taste his buttocks, he reached back and pulled them apart, inviting me to do the worst. "Lick me," he urged. "You know you want to. Stick your tongue in and taste your cream. I guarantee you'll never get enough." His pucker began to wink at me and he chuckled as he worked the muscle. I ran a finger up his crack and rubbed the place where my dick had gone.

"Go on, lick it. I can feel the want coming off you."

He was right. I had feasted on every part of him except the

place I most coveted and the more I looked, the more I realized it was my greatest desire. I was beyond myself now, a frenzied beast sliding into a wallow, eager for filth. My mouth was open, my tongue out like a hard prick ready to fuck. And that, I realized, was what it was about to do. I knew that once it touched that pink pucker, it would shove in just as my dick had and it would give him what we both wanted.

When I touched the tip of my tongue to his hole he let out a squeal. I could feel him with a hand up under himself, milking his prick for surely he had more spunk in him. Young men have a supply beyond belief, as I well knew, having enjoyed excess in my own youth.

I began to lick him like some dog going at his own bottom and the mere act of touching the filthy hole fired me. I hesitated but seconds before descending into a slopping that finally was not enough. Frantic to slake the awful thirst, I pushed into him and found a bitter taste yet I did not recoil. I accepted the foulness as fitting the depraved act, and I began to do with my tongue what I had with my prick.

As if to get deeper into his chute, I plastered my mouth to his buttocks, which I held wide. I then speared him deep as humanly possible. As I went at him, he cried out and I knew my eating his hole had driven him over. As he bucked and came, I held on, going at him until my jaw ached so much I had to quit.

Soon as I pulled out, he rolled over and sprang up to get his mouth onto mine and he sought my tongue with his, eager to taste his own filth. As he did this, he found my cock up again and he began to pull me as we continued the terrible yet wonderful kiss.

At last, I spurted what seemed the final drops of my lifeblood, which allowed Creed to ease his efforts and fall back. I in turn slumped onto the bunk. He purred like some big cat as he lay down across me. I was completely drained of all desire and much of my substance, feeling more like some dirty puddle than a satisfied man. We were in darkness now and I had no idea the hour, nor did I care. Sleep beckoned and she was every bit as alluring as Paulie Creed. As I shut my eyes, my last sight was Creed's beautiful smile.

"Marshal," somebody said. "Marshal, wake up."

I could barely rouse my eyelids, much less the rest of me. Feeling as wrung out as a Sunday morning drunk, I allowed enough light to find Carl Conlon standing over me. "What?" I demanded, not yet aware of my circumstance.

"Creed is gone," the deputy said.

This sent a jolt through me and I raised my head to look down upon my naked body. A host of swearwords came to mind, but I uttered none as embarrassment hit me like a flash flood. I sat up, reeling, and Carl handed me my under drawers. "Get out of here," I commanded. "I'll see you in a minute."

He seemed relieved to be dismissed. I could not begin to imagine his mix of horror and amusement at not only finding the prisoner gone but his boss laid out naked. I got into my clothes, finding as I did so that my gun and the cell key were gone. I did not strap on my gun belt but carried it out into the office where I got another gun from my desk, holstered it and put on the belt. Carl had his back to me, busying himself to spare me further distress. As I attempted to regain some measure of the dignity due my position, I realized I should get up a posse and go after Creed. I also knew Carl would expect to be a part; Carl, the only man who knew how I had been bested. Knowing men love to jaw and Carl one of the best, it would not be long until all of Globe knew Creed had escaped by way of my dick. All I could ask was for my deputy to hold back the worst.

"Carl," I said and he turned.

"Yes, Marshal?"

"I have been compromised in the worst way any lawman can possibly be and admit it my own fault. I let base instincts get the better of me but I am asking you now, as both deputy and friend, not to reveal it to anyone. Bad enough Creed escaped but if the how becomes known, I am ruined in law enforcement. Would you please not reveal the details? Tell them he got the drop on me and nothing more. Can you do that for me?"

Carl was a good man with a wife and two kiddies and I saw him consider the situation just a second before agreeing to do as I requested. "You are a good man, Carl. I will not forget this."

"Are we going after him?" he asked.

"You and I will ride out and look around, but I do not wish to find Paulie Creed. You understand."

"I surely do."

Now, as I lie in my room and pull my dick while replaying every minute of that night, I gain little relief beyond the momentary spew of come. Though it is a gusher that leaves me sweating and spent, Paulie Creed is back upon me the next minute, beckoning from Robber's Roost or some other outlaw camp, loot from the bank job spilled on a blanket. It is then I allow that the marshal who failed to pursue him four years ago has become the sheriff with new responsibility. Though suffering a stiff dick at the mere thought of the outlaw, I accept that I must go after him.

Spunk is all up my front and as I sit up and throw my legs over the bedside, I think how it's the best come I've known for a while, but then Paulie Creed does that to a man. I wonder how many other lawmen have failed as I did, not to mention how many outlaws have celebrated Creed's robbing with a good fuck.

When I return to my office, I tell my two deputies I'll be

getting up a posse to go after Paulie Creed. "He always favored Charleston and Globe. We'll try both, see what we can dig up. I'll go round up a couple more men as Creed is said to have two others with him."

Prestige had come with my election as sheriff of Cochise County. My reputation as marshal of Globe helped make me a good candidate, as Carl Conlon kept his word and never told of my embarrassment. I recommended him for the marshal's job when I left there, and he was duly appointed. Now I have two good men as deputies and for the posse I get two others I know to be good shots. Next morning we tie on our bedrolls, fill our saddlebags with ammunition and head to Charleston where Creed is known to have friends.

Riding hard toward our destination, I suffer a churning of the stomach at what I will face should I catch my prey. His golden curls and boyish face, all grins and mischief, might well be painted to my eyes but his body affects me lower and thus I suffer as we head to Charleston. When we get there, I go into the Rawhide Saloon as I know the owner, Chuck Fraser. It takes only minutes to learn Creed was through two days before, flush with money and cutting up like usual.

"Try Globe," Fraser suggests. "I hear he likes it over there."

As night is coming on, we make camp and I sleep fitfully until, in the cover of darkness, I get out my prick and have a pull while thinking on getting it into Paulie Creed.

Going to Globe the next day is not easy. Though a fine little town, it holds the low point of my law enforcement career, never mind only one man knows the truth. I too know it and riding in and having folks look at us brings back that morning when Carl Conlon found me naked. I make myself inquire around town but discover nobody has seen Creed. Finally I go over to the marshal's office where I find Carl talking to his deputy.

"Harlan," he says, springing to his feet, hand outstretched. "How the hell are you? Jim, this is Harlan Hurst. Used to have this job back before he became sheriff of the whole damned county."

I shake the deputy's hand and he then departs. "Have a seat," Carl says and I settle opposite him. He remains behind his desk.

"Place looks the same," I note.

"Pretty much. We've got more people leaving than coming in as the silver is playing out. Saloons keep us afloat."

"I have a posse with me," I tell him. "We are after Paulie Creed who robbed a bank in Benson and killed two men."

"I heard he was back," says Carl. "Did a stint in prison once, didn't he?"

I nod. "Didn't do him much good."

Carl studies me as we speak, the secret between us sitting there on the desk as naked as I'd been. Finally I make mention. "You kept your word on what happened and I am grateful," I say.

"You are a good man, Harlan," he replies. "I would not have wanted to damage your chances."

"Well, thank you again."

"How is it, though, going after Creed now?" Carl asks.

I have put this question to myself with every mile we've traveled but do not know the answer. Thinking on it as Carl waits leads me to enlightenment. "Good and bad, I suppose. I want to see justice done, but I know him to be a danger to me and I don't mean gunplay."

"A danger you do not wish to face?" Carl asks. "Or do you?"

As the man who has seen evidence of my depravity, he has a right to probe and so I answer with as much honesty as I can muster. "He is my devil," I say, "and you know how a man sometimes opens his arms to Satan. I both fear and crave him."

"Must be hell."

"The very pit. I would not go after him at all if my job did not demand it, because I am not sure I can do any better around him now than I did back then."

"You are strong, Harlan."

"Strong men can fall harder than the weak."

"But this time you know what you are up against."

"I hope that helps."

Here we turn from personal things to practical matters, but Carl has no good information as Creed has not been to Globe. "If he's flush, he's in some town throwing money around," he adds. "You just have to find which one."

"Any suggestions?"

"Charleston maybe, or Galeyville," he offers with a shrug.

I stand and offer my hand. "Many thanks, Carl."

"Most welcome," he replies.

We ride on to Galeyville, but Creed has not been there so we keep going. We scout one town after another for two days, covering much of the county before I learn Creed rode into San Simon with his friends the day before but left there alone as he got into an argument and shot both. As I attempt to maintain a solemn tone, my insides are frantic and my cock is rising. I take off my hat and wipe my brow, attempting to divert myself.

"What's the plan, Sheriff?" I am asked by one of my men.

"Let me think on it," I say. "Go get yourselves some supper, get your horses fed, and meet me here at six. We'll camp outside town and I'll let you know what is next."

I have to get away by myself as the idea of Creed on his own is too much to bear. I see to my horse, then go into a saloon and throw back a few whiskeys. This eases me somewhat but I still cannot regain my composure, so I go out back to the privy and pull my swollen dick to a come. Of course I do this while thinking on Creed running naked and me roping him and getting him down and fucking him.

Once relieved, I get a meal and as I eat I consider a plan. What I want is to trail him alone so my first concern is how to dismiss my posse without raising eyebrows. I am the sheriff, I remind myself. I run things, so they must do as I say. And five men are not needed to capture one, no matter how crafty. I can make my way quietly, I reason. I can slip up on him.

At six the men and I ride from town and set up camp. Around the fire I tell them to head back to Tombstone next morning. "I am going on alone," I say. "Better to slip up on him."

Nobody questions or objects though I do see a couple of skeptical looks exchanged. Early next morning I watch them ride away and I head east, as Creed is said to be going. When I find him, it is the stuff of dreams and I wonder if he planned it, knowing I'd likely come on my own. He lies sleeping on his bedroll beneath trees at a watering hole called Sandy Springs, a place I have stopped many a time while riding with a posse. It is late morning and his horse stands drinking from the spring. Creed is naked on his blanket, prick as stiff as a post. I tie my horse a few yards away, draw my gun and approach on foot.

"I knew you'd be along," he says without opening his eyes. "Caught sight of you early on. My old friend."

Here he begins to stroke his cock, which of course causes my entire self to seize like a noose is tightening around my neck. My prick cannot fill fast enough. "Get up," I command. "I am taking you in."

"How about you fuck me, then we talk about it."

He raises his legs to show me his butthole. "Come on, Marshal, you know you want it and I sure as hell welcome that cock of yours. Pick up where we left off. Nobody around to see."

"So you can run off again? No. Now get up."

"I will not get to my feet until I've had your dick. You can see I'm ready for you. Been lying here thinking on you chasing me down and getting at me, so you sort of owe me. Come on, Sheriff, get it out. I can see you are hard."

"You are the devil, Paulie."

"Then why not enjoy a trip to hell?" He works a finger down to his crack and pushes into himself. "I need me a dick the worst way," he adds.

I know from first sight I will do as he wants but the lawman still argues the matter, empty shell slaving for justice. Creed keeps grinning all the while I do battle, not saying anything more as he knows he's won. With my free hand I unbuckle my gun belt and let it drop. At this Creed eases his legs down, gets his hand back onto his prick, and starts to pull the thing.

I do not strip naked as I refuse to let myself indulge too far. I put down my gun, undo my pants and push them down enough to free my hard cock. Then I pick up the gun. "Get your legs back up," I say, motioning. "Around your ears."

He grins, wags his tongue at me and does as told, his butthole now there for the taking. "Fuck me, Sheriff," he begs. "Put your dick in and fuck me."

I kneel down, look into his blue eyes and see the boy he once was, sweet faced, eager, happy. Except there also lies a serpent, that tongue poking out. As he tantalizes, I grip my pistol tightly, then slide the barrel into him. This causes him to gasp and I figure this is the first time in maybe ever that someone has truly gotten the drop on him.

"You need to be done away with," I tell him. "You are a curse to mankind and worse to me." I prod the gun and see genuine fright come over him. "I figure the bullet will rip your innards to pieces but not kill you outright. You'll die slowly, which I see as fitting payment for the lives you have taken."

The tongue retreats, the flashing eyes widen with fear. A

shudder runs through him, but he does not speak.

"Maybe I will fuck you after I shoot you," I tell him. "Seal the deal."

We pass a good minute in this position. It is the first time I have felt any control in his presence. His expression remains stricken but at last breaks. He smiles. "Go ahead and shoot," he says. "What do I care? I am wanted in three states, I have no life but robbing and killing, and if you do not kill me I will go to prison, which I do not want. So I don't care if you end my life right now. And you are right, shooting me inside is fitting, a deadly fuck from the man who knows how."

I ram the pistol into him but he does not flinch and I see I've lost the upper hand. Doesn't matter I have the gun. A man willing to die gains all the power, and I can see he is serious. My thumb pulls back the hammer, and I make ready to shoot. Creed shows no fear now. He gazes at me almost peacefully, and I see he has truly come to terms with his end. One squeeze of the trigger and I am rid of him. Arizona is rid of him, dead men avenged. The urge to get off the shot rises up and fires me yet falls just short. My finger weakens on the trigger and I ease the hammer down, then withdraw the barrel from Creed's bottom. I look down to see it pop out of him and know my only recourse. I inch closer and shove my dick in where the pistol has been.

# SPARE THE ROD, SPOIL THE ADULT

**Landon Dixon**

"What the fuck you gawkin' at, old man?"

Danny stared defiantly at the distinguished-looking businessman sitting across from him on the subway. And he kept his hand on the bulge in his torn jeans, rubbing his cock.

Conrad shook his head and shook out his newspaper in disgust, chiding himself for not getting a company driver to take him home after he'd worked past midnight. He glanced up and down the car, but it was empty except for him and the nineteen-year-old. So he dipped his head back into the stock quotes, ignoring the punk.

Danny slumped farther down on the plastic bench, sprawling his skinny legs out wider, stroking the long, rigid outline of his cock and glaring at the man in the gray trench coat from under his blond bangs. And when he caught Conrad's eyes wandering up over the edge of the newspaper, he slid his other hand under his ripped T-shirt and pinched and pulled on a stiffened nipple.

His green eyes flashed a *What the fuck you gonna do about*

*it!* at the silver-haired gentleman on the opposite bench, as he openly felt himself up. And the older man watched.

Conrad's jowly face flushed red. He shifted in his seat as if he were about to get up to find refuge in another subway car where insolent young punks weren't committing public acts of indecency.

"You ain't goin' anywhere, geezer," Danny sneered, rubbing faster, harder, rolling his nipples. He fluttered his eyelashes and groaned for Conrad's benefit, pushing his pelvis higher, his huge erection almost splitting his jeans.

"Someone should teach you some manners, young man," Conrad snorted. "Your parents obviously didn't do a very good job of it."

"Maybe you can teach me some manners, old man?" Danny challenged, his body flooding with a tingling heat as he heavy-petted himself. "Or maybe you can just shut the fuck up and sit there and read your paper like a good old boy. Huh?"

Conrad rose to his feet. "Now listen here, if you don't behave yourself, I'm going to...call the conductor, the driver. Get you thrown off this train. Or arrested."

Danny laughed. He arched his lean body off the bench and pushed his jeans halfway down his thighs. His cock bounded into the open, head pink and swollen; a thick bush of blond pubes covered his heavy balls. "You ain't in charge here, old man," he taunted, lacing long fingers around his vein-ribboned shaft and pumping, grunting with pleasure. He fingernailed a clear pearl of precum off his gaping slit, stuck the finger in his mouth and sucked on it.

Conrad advanced on the jacking young man, his newspaper rolled and raised like he was going to swat him. But he stopped himself in time and tried to compose himself. "You're a filthy little punk, aren't you?" he growled, looking down his nose at

Danny, the words dripping with contempt. "Your parents must be very proud."

Danny stomped his rainbow-laced black boots down on the floor and sprang to his feet. And before Conrad could even react, he shot a hand between the flaps of Conrad's open trench coat and grabbed the man's cock. "Yeah, I'm a fuckin' filthy little punk," he spat into Conrad's shocked face, squeezing swollen cock through pin-striped pants. "And you're a fuckin' dirty old man."

Conrad's mouth opened and closed, but no words came, his erection surging in the vise of Danny's hot hand, his body flushing, like his face, with heat.

"Fuckin' hypocrite!" Danny jeered. "Complaining about me pullin' pud while you're pullin' boner. Maybe I should teach *you* some manners, old man. About carrying this thing around in your fancy pants when you're dishin' out the morality lectures."

He jerked up on Conrad's cock. Conrad jumped onto his toes in his Oxfords. Danny pumped the man's clothed cock with his left hand while he pumped his own bared cock with his right, both throbbing in his hands. The men were only inches apart, breathing hard into each other's face, until Danny roughly shoved Conrad back into a metal pole.

The businessman banged his head against the connecting overhead bar. Before he could recover, Danny spun him around, tore the trench coat off his shoulders and down his arms and smacked his pin-striped ass. "My god!" Conrad gasped.

Danny stepped on the tailored coat where it lay on the dirty floor, grasping Conrad's cock with his left hand again, smacking Conrad's ass with his right. "This how you discipline your well-behaved, well-mannered kids at home, old man?" he hissed.

"What—what do you think you're..." Conrad began to protest. But he never finished the thought, never commanded the angry young man to release him. Or tried to push him away. Because Danny's gripping hand on his pulsating member, pumping hard, felt so very good. And Danny's flattened hand on his flabby ass, smacking hard, felt even better.

Conrad flailed for the overhead railing and hung on, a solid, successful, middle-aged corporate executive getting spanked and jerked by a punk kid on the subway. And reveling in it.

"Now you're gettin' a taste of your own medicine, huh?" Danny rasped. "Like you deserve." The power in his hands, the pulsing of the older man's engorged cock and the trembling of his buttcheeks, filled him with a wicked eroticism that turned his own bobbing meat electric.

Every blow, every pump stoked the fire higher in the both of them. Conrad's hands slipped on the metal bar, his palms bathed in sweat, his body shuddering with the impact of Danny's blade of a hand smashing down on his stinging rump, the pulling pressure on his cock building to the boiling-over point.

"Oh, god, yes, spank me!" he gasped, just before his cock exploded in Danny's pistoning hand. He shook uncontrollably, dancing to the younger man's tune, hot, sticky semen spurting out of his cock and soiling his silken drawers.

Danny kept up the pressure on Conrad's clenched buttocks and ruptured cock, feeling the inferno of the man's orgasm, hands fanning the flames. His own cock went steel-hard and numb, bubbling precum, aching to be jacked.

"Okay, what's going on back there?" a voice crackled over the intercom. It was the driver, finally intervening after getting an eyeful of the strange scene—even by subway standards—through the train's CCTV system. Either he seldom paid attention to it—or he'd been transfixed...

Danny released Conrad, pushing the flustered, flushed man onto the hard plastic bench. He took in the stain on the front of Conrad's suit pants, panting, grinning, his big cock tenting his jeans again. "Guess you'll remember this lesson for a while, huh, old man?"

They met again on Train #18—financial district to the suburbs—two weeks later; same time, late at night, same car. It had taken Conrad that long to work up the courage, to come to grips with what had happened to him.

Only this time there were two other passengers in the car with them. Which didn't bother Danny one little bit. He rubbed his bulge through his denim skater shorts and toyed with his nipples through his Black Flag T-shirt. Conrad, in his gray trench coat—open again to show off another five-thousand-dollar charcoal suit—pretended to read his newspaper as he warily eyed his fellow travelers and the blond-haired punk blatantly playing with himself on the bench opposite.

They were a mother and her daughter, making the connection home from a visit to a relative in an outlying area. And while the girl was trying to enjoy the show, craning her head around her mother's blocking body to get a glimpse of Danny, the woman muttered, "Disgusting," under her breath and stared at Conrad, silently urging him to do something.

Conrad crossed his legs and coughed uncomfortably, his newspaper shaking, until Danny belligerently slid one hand down inside his shorts, the other hand up under his tee. And he felt obligated to act.

"Now, see here, young man," Conrad said, folding his paper over his lap. "You, uh, behave yourself...while there are other people on the train."

Danny pulled his hand out of his shorts and shot Conrad the middle finger, slick with precum at the tip. "Make me, old man."

The woman harrumphed.

Conrad rose to his feet, keeping the newspaper over his crotch. "That's it! You're getting off at the next stop." There was pleading in his gray eyes.

Danny glanced at the sign showing the next stop, then back at Conrad. "I'll fuckin' tell you where we get off," he stated. "And when. And how." He stuck his hand back into his shorts, regripped his cock and tugged.

They traveled along in strained silence for two more stops, the mother clasping her daughter tightly to her side and glaring at Conrad, who'd slumped back into his seat. He hid behind his paper, face burning red, erection engorged all the more by Danny's public putdown.

The sign flashed ARLINGTON STREET. Danny kicked up his boots and jumped to his feet. He grabbed Conrad by his two-hundred-dollar canary-yellow tie and jerked him to his feet. "We're gettin' off here, geezer."

They waited, Conrad swaying on the end of his leash, head down and shoulders slumped to loosen the pressure, Danny grinning contemptuously at the heavily breathing executive. He yanked Conrad's head close and kissed him hard on the mouth, then bit into the man's lower lip, drawing blood in a hot, salty spurt, like cum. The woman screamed and the girl giggled.

The train slid to a stop, and the skinny punk strolled off, dragging the brawny businessman after him. Up the steps and out of the subway, along the sidewalk of the cool, quiet, darkened street. When they arrived at the huge stone staircase that led up to Arlington High, Danny pulled Conrad up the steps, the older man stumbling to keep pace, wheezing, coat flapping in the breeze.

"Fuck, I hated this fuckin' place!" Danny spat, when he'd reached the top step. He glared down at Conrad. "Too many fuckin' tight-ass authority figures like you, old man."

Conrad looked up at Danny, waiting.

Danny dropped Conrad's wrinkled tie and ordered, "Take off your coat. Pull down your pants."

Conrad glanced at the street and surrounding buildings. "But—but someone might see us," he said in a strangled voice.

"Fuckin' do it!"

Conrad shucked his coat and let the wind take it, unbuckled his pants and let them drop to his patent leather shoes. He stood, knobby knees and pasty legs shaking, as Danny dug his dirty fingernails into the sides of the humbled man's striped shorts and yanked them down.

"Oh, god," Conrad whimpered, his hard cock bobbing up and sniffing the night air, vibrating in the breeze for all to see.

Danny laughed at the business emperor with no pants. He slapped Conrad's cock, and the man groaned. Then he sat on the top step and told Conrad to lie over his knees. The older man rushed to comply, and his bare ass was instantly jolted by the wooden ruler Danny had stashed in his shorts.

He smacked one flabby cheek, then the other, then both at once. The crack of hard, unbending ruler against hot, flaccid flesh echoed off the stone walls of the school and out into the street, the blows coming faster, harder. Danny shoved Conrad's head down and wielded the whistling ruler like a judgment, sweat shining on his forehead, his own hard-on throbbing under the man's squirming bulk.

*Whack.* "You dish it out," *whack*, "you better be able to fuckin' take it!" he screamed. *Whack!*

Conrad's body jumped with every stinging blow, face blazing as crimson as his beaten bum. He could barely breathe, his blood was boiling, his heart was beating in his ears. His straining cock pressed against Danny's leg, and he gulped, "I'm—I'm going to come!"

"Not fuckin' yet you aren't!" Danny shouted.

He stopped whaling Conrad's ass and pulled the man's cock up between his legs, bending the inflamed appendage back like he meant to break it off. Then he dropped his head down and lashed Conrad's purple cap with his tongue, licking up the tears of lust leaking from Conrad's slit.

The man groaned. Danny dropped his cock and picked up the ruler again, crashed it down on Conrad's battered cheeks. He flailed Conrad until white ridges began forming on his flaming skin, obscene outlines of the vicious ruler. Conrad was beyond feeling pain.

"On your feet, geezer!" Danny barked at last. "Time you got a taste of total obedience."

He shoved Conrad off his knees and the man tumbled down a couple of steps. Then Danny stood and pushed his shorts down to boot level, spreading his blond-dusted legs. His long, smooth cock stood out arrow-straight in the shadows. Conrad made for it, crawling back up the steps and grabbing on to Danny's mounded buttocks, engulfing the punk's mushroomed, pink hood in his mouth.

"Yeah! Suck my cock, old man!" Danny cried, digging dirty fingers into Conrad's silver hair as the man inhaled more and more of his engorged prick.

Danny stood between Conrad's legs, shaking, savoring the smooth lips and the velvet-sandpaper tongue sliding and gliding wetly along his boiling shaft, and the manicured fingernails biting into his trembling buttocks. The sensations filled his body and brain with wicked eroticism, sent him soaring with pleasure.

"Jerk yourself off!" he commanded. "All over my boots!"

Conrad grabbed on to his dick and fisted it as eagerly as he was blowing Danny. He clawed the fingers of his free hand between Danny's asscheeks and hung on to the groaning young man, fast-stroking himself with the other while sucking the punk's cock with his drooling mouth—right down to the thicket of blond pubes and back up to the bloated cap, over and over. Desperate to please.

"Fuck, yeah!" Danny howled, jolted by ecstasy. His cock exploded, spurting white-hot gouts of cum into Conrad's eager mouth as his own cock burst into a blazing orgasm, spraying semen over Danny's scuffed black boots.

Just like the punk had ordered.

Danny washed and changed in the garage, entering his parent's house dressed in a conservative white polo shirt and tan pair of chinos, a stack of textbooks under his arm.

His father glanced up from his newspaper. "I thought the library closed at eight-thirty!" he said sternly.

Danny smiled at the old man, brushing his soft blond hair to one side with his hand. "I had some tutoring to do afterward, Father," he said pleasantly.

His dad grunted, while his two sisters doing their homework at the dining room table giggled.

A steely look from the old man put their heads back in their books again, as Danny headed up the stairs to his bedroom.

"Are you aware that your son was brought home by the police again today?" Conrad's wife shrilled as soon as he stepped through the door and into his house.

His unemployed bum of a son was slumped on the living room sofa, an empty bottle knocked over on the coffee table next to him, while his sullen goth of a daughter, parked in front of the blaring television, yelled at her mother to shut the fuck up and have another drink herself, why didn't she?

Conrad hung up his trench coat and walked away from the chaos, down the hall and into the bathroom. Anxious to see his backside in the full-length mirror—see and feel the red stripes and white welts of cleansing discipline he'd received from the blond-haired punk.

# BOY FROM WILLOW CREEK

## Martin Delacroix

"Leopards never change their spots."

That's what my mother taught me as a kid. "Once a thief, always a thief," she said. "A cheater will always be a cheater."

I believed her then, and I *guess* I still do, but not entirely.

Let me tell you why.

A while back—about a year ago it was—I spent a summer in San Francisco, a true adventure for a guy like me who'd never traveled beyond Ohio's borders. My uncle Roy, my mom's brother, had died and left me a small inheritance. I was between jobs, and I thought: hey, I should go live someplace completely different, stay among people such as I had never known. I'd always been interested in the Bay Area: the Giants, the Golden Gate and, of course, the gay scene. So I thought San Francisco would be a good choice. I contacted a rental service and leased a furnished apartment for three months, a one-bedroom on Folsom. The rent was a bit high, but I found a cheap flight, and next thing I knew I was hailing a taxi outside SFO's baggage claim, juggling three suitcases and breathing the bay's salty air.

I met the kid a few weeks into my stay. Our first contact was through the Internet, via a website called *Lads for Dads*. After trading several messages, we spoke a time or two by phone, and I thought we'd be compatible. A high-school dropout with a knack for computers, he was twenty-one and still lived with his folks. His grammar was okay, he seemed amiable and he was eager to leave his hometown of Willow Creek—someplace up north—to visit me in San Francisco.

"I need to get out of here," he said.

"Sure," I told him, "come on down. We'll have a good time."

We met at Transbay Terminal. The weather was warm the night he arrived. I watched him move under ceiling lights in the bus, heading for the door. He was a small boy and his head barely reached the shoulders of some men he passed. Though I'd only seen his face picture, I knew it was him, right off. Even before he stepped onto the pavement, I recognized him because he moved with deliberation.

From our phone conversations, I knew there was nothing reticent about him.

I waved and he approached. We shook hands, standing on the sidewalk next to his bus, and he gave me a hundred-watt smile. He wore all black: T-shirt, jeans and sneakers. One leg of his pants was rolled to the knee, I don't know why. Three days of stubble sat on his face and his black hair was in tangles. He walked curiously: his shoulders rocked from side to side, as if he were moving through a crowd and dodging people, only there wasn't any crowd.

During conversation his gaze never stuck with me long. He'd look at me with his dark eyes. Then he'd glance at something in the distance. After a few seconds, he'd return his gaze to me. I found this somewhat weird, but everyone has his peculiarities, right?

Like many boys, the bulk of his weight was below the waist—in the ass and legs—but his shoulders were broad enough for a young man his height, and there was nothing feminine in his appearance or manner. He kept smiling while we walked down Mission Street, heading toward my apartment and speaking of things I can't recall now. He smoked a cigarette as we walked, all the way down to the filter. His voice was deep for a guy his age, a raspy baritone. He carried a backpack and his laptop computer—that was it.

Now, I'll admit I was sold on him, even before we reached my place. The boy was good looking in a rough-around-the-edges sort of way. And, my *god*, he was young. A tension dwelt within him. His fidgeting never seemed to stop, as if he were plugged into a wall socket. Walking next to him, there on the street, energized me like amphetamine.

I'd hidden my valuables—camera, wallet and so forth—because I feared he might be a thief. But as soon as I met him I sensed he wouldn't steal, and this turned out to be true. He lived with me three weeks—I had all sorts of cash and credit cards lying about—and nothing ever went missing.

We drank beer at my place that first night while we chatted. He was easy to talk with and his story was a bit sad. A week before, he said, his mom had broken some news to him: she told him he was an adopted child. She and her husband had found the kid through some agency up in Oregon, when he was a baby.

For a long time before then, the kid told me, he'd suspected his parents were hiding a truth from him, and now he knew what it was. When he told me this, I tried to imagine how the kid must've felt about the situation, but I couldn't. It's hard for me to put myself in someone else's shoes. Know what I mean?

He told me something else that first night: At age fifteen he'd taken a bus, alone, from Willow Creek to Portland, Oregon—a nine-hour trip—just to have sex with some guy he'd contacted over the Internet. At age *fifteen*. Crazy, huh?

Also, like I mentioned before, he had dropped out of high school before graduating. He said, "Why should I stay in school when I can make plenty of money doing programming and website design? I'm smarter than those other kids. Why sit around in classrooms learning stuff I'll never use in the real world? I already have several clients, and they pay pretty well."

That first night he arrived, right after we drank the beers, I looked into his dark eyes and knew I had to get him in bed. We sat on the sofa. I reached for the back of his neck and pulled him to me. We kissed a good long while, and I tasted the last cigarette he'd smoked. Sticking my tongue in his ear, I twirled it and the kid cooed while a shiver ran through him.

I reached for the hem of his T-shirt and told him to raise his arms. I peeled the shirt off him and, my god, you should've seen his body. He wasn't muscular or anything, but his chest was defined; he had a washboard belly. I placed his hands behind his neck and licked his dark armpits; they had a sour smell to them I found appealing. His nipples were tiny as raisins, and they hardened when I sucked them.

I reached between his legs and felt his boner. Its size and firmness made me salivate. I'd never touched a boy his age before, and my hands shook with excitement. I popped the button at his waist, ran down the zipper, parted the flaps. He wore black briefs beneath and I slipped my hand inside them. My fingers passed through his pubic hair. I grabbed his cock and squeezed it, making him groan. My heart pounded so hard I thought I might pass out. I asked myself, *Is this really happening*?

The kid took his sneakers and socks off, so I could get his

pants and briefs over his feet. His thighs were smooth, his calves dusted with dark hair. His cock was uncut, about six inches and thick as a flashlight handle. The foreskin was crinkly, caramel in color, as delicate as tissue paper. I retracted the foreskin, exposing his bullet-shaped glans. I smelled his dick cheese; it excited me and I couldn't help myself: I took his cock into my mouth and swallowed it whole, feeling the tip nudge the back of my throat.

The kid groaned again while I worked his cock with my tongue and lips; I slurped away like a child with a lollipop. He sifted his fingers through my hair while he bucked his hips. My own cock throbbed between my thighs. *This is great,* I thought, *truly unbelievable.* And then I wondered, *Will he let me fuck him*? *Probably not, but maybe…*

Holding his hand, I brought him to my bedroom. His cock bobbed before him. After lighting a candle, I killed the lights and turned down the covers. Then I got naked too.

The kid whistled. "Your cock's pretty big," he said.

I sat on the edge of the bed and motioned him to me. The candle cast our shadows on the wall: two silhouettes with raging boners. He sat beside me and looked at me with those dark eyes. My pulse raced while I stroked his temple with a thumb. "Tell me," I said, "what you'd like to do."

He dropped his gaze and licked his lips.

"What is it?" I said.

He looked at me again. "I want you to spank my ass—hard."

His request took me by surprise. I'd never done such a thing. But I thought, *Hell, why not?*

He positioned himself across my lap, face down, so his hips rested on my thighs. His hands and feet met the floor and his ass was right in my face. I patted his buttcheeks; they were firm and rounded, white as cream. A stripe of dark hair grew between them. His hole winked at me—a pink rosebud that flexed when I stroked it with a fingertip. The kid shoved his genitals back between his thighs, so I could touch them. I squeezed his cock, stroked his smooth sack and bulging nuts.

"Go on," he said, "make this hurt."

I gave him a couple of swats with an open hand, one on each cheek.

He moved his shoulders. "Not hard enough."

*Okay,* I thought. *Give him what he wants.*

I laid into him. The slaps sounded like pistols shots going off in the room, and I wondered if the neighbors could hear. The kid's head jerked as I went to work; his toes dug into my carpet. In just a few minutes his asscheeks looked like a pair of ripe tomatoes. I mean, they must've been on fire 'cause they were hot to the touch. I spanked his thighs, got them nice and red, too. The kid panted, sweat beaded on his skin and he kicked his legs while I continued delivering swats.

Now, I'm not a violent man; I don't like hurting people. But this was what the kid had requested, and I figured I should perform adequately. I kept on spanking till he was crimson from his waist to the backs of his knees, until he whimpered like a six-year-old. His cock remained hard during the entire spanking, so I guess he enjoyed himself.

I'll admit I found the whole thing exciting, especially the kid's submission to me, his acceptance of the discipline I'd administered. But again, I found his behavior curious. Was the spanking something he found arousing? Or was it atonement for some wrongdoing?

"It's enough," he finally cried.

He rose to his feet, rubbing his bottom. His face was flushed and tears glistened in his eyes. "Thank you," he said.

"You're welcome," I told him. "What now?"

He sniffled, still rubbing his ass. "Whatever you'd like; just say."

*Go on, ask.*

"Can I fuck you?"

He nodded.

And I thought, *Oh, yeah...*

We didn't rush into it. I took my time, holding him in my arms, stroking his hair while we tongue kissed. I patted his steaming bottom, pinched his nipples. He writhed like a snake and rubbed his skin against mine. His fingers gripped my cock; he thumbed my glans until I leaked precome.

At my suggestion, we did a bit of sixty-nine. The kid knew how to suck, that's for sure; he took all of me down his throat. His tongue caressed the contours of my cock. He used his stubble to scratch my ball sac, raising goose bumps on my arms and legs. When I asked if he was ready to fuck, he nodded. He said he preferred riding topside, which was fine with me.

I reached for the lube and greased myself, then his hole. My cock was stiff as PVC pipe. He straddled me and looked into my face while he lowered himself onto on my cock. I pierced his pucker and felt the heat of his gut. He clenched his jaw and looked at the ceiling. Candlelight reflected in a film of sweat on his forehead.

I worked on his nipples, pinching and twisting, drawing sighs from the kid. He commenced riding me while he used a fist to stroke his cock. His foreskin smacked like a man chewing gum. Scents of sweat, smegma and shit grew strong in the room. The bedsprings creaked and a breeze fluttered drapes at the window. I felt unworldly, like I dwelled on a distant planet, occupied solely by me and the kid. Already, his eyes had lost focus. His head rocked as I fucked him. My cock stretched his hole, again and again. Our shadows on the wall moved; we looked like two ancients performing some tribal rite.

The kid came first; he cried out and his chest heaved. His cock flung gobs of semen onto my chest; they glistened like opals. A buzzing sounded inside of my head. A tremor ran through my limbs and my lungs pumped. I grabbed the kid's asscheeks, squeezing his reddened flesh while my cock throbbed inside his gut. When I unloaded, my body jerked with each shot.

*Holy crap,* was all I could think.

Then the weirdest thing happened: the kid began to *cry*. He thrust his arms around my neck and buried his face in the crook between my jaw and chest. His body shook like a sapling in a gale. I didn't know what to think; I figured his orgasm had overwhelmed him, or something like that. My cock was still inside him. I put my arms around his shoulders and held him, not saying anything. After a while, he calmed down.

"Want to call it a night?" I asked.

He sniffled and nodded.

I blew out the candle and we climbed under the covers. He laid his head upon my chest, crossed one leg over mine and draped his arm over my stomach. His hair smelled like damp grass. I drew a breath and released it while I stared at the ceiling. I listened to traffic pass on the street below, wondering where all this was headed.

When I woke the next morning, he was there, naked and beautiful, and I could not believe my good fortune at having him with me. Already, you see, I'd fallen for the kid. He had stirred emotions deep inside me, ones I hadn't felt before. Everything about him—his lithe physique, deep voice and ready smile—enchanted me. You should understand something: I was in my early forties, and I'd never had a boyfriend. Right out of high school I'd married a woman; I thought I was supposed to. The marriage lasted eight loveless years. We didn't have any kids, thank god.

After my divorce, I finally worked up the courage to visit gay bars. Once in a while, I'd get lucky and pick up a guy. We'd have sex at his place or mine, but that was it. I never saw the same guy twice; I'm not sure why. Maybe I was afraid of emotional involvement. I spent most evenings alone, falling asleep in front of the TV, and I figured that's how things would continue.

But now, with the kid in the picture, I envisioned something more. I know it sounds crazy, but there in bed, that first morning, I told myself, *This is your chance. You could build a life with him.*

I bent my arm at the elbow and propped my head against my hand, staring at the kid while he slept. He lay on his back and his chest rose and fell. His dark hair was tangled, going this way and that. I studied the curves of his nose, mouth and eyebrows; they were so...delicate. Fingering his earlobe, I shook my head in amazement. I told myself, *Things are going to be great, aren't they?*

Well...

The boy liked his sleep. If he ever rose before noon, I don't recall it.

Now, I'm not saying he was lazy about everything. He worked at his computer business like there was no tomorrow: hour upon hour, tapping at the keyboard, taking online classes on programming, doing encryption and decryption for his clients' projects and so forth. They paid him via electronic bank transfers, once a month, how much I had no idea. But his work consumed much of his day. And he was a slob. His shit was strewn everywhere: clothes, packs of cigarettes, wads of paper, his computer and all its wiring and headset. The shelf over the bathroom sink was stacked with his stuff: toothbrush, hair gel, deodorant and hairbrush, all of it. Not an inch of space left for me!

Then there were his cigarettes. I don't smoke, never have. What's the point? You're only ruining your health. But the kid puffed like a chimney; at least a pack a day. At my place, I'd make him sit by the window and blow the smoke outside, but the stink still got in the apartment. His hair and clothes smelled of tobacco, and so did his breath when I kissed him. A time or two, I gave him some shit about the cigarettes, but he only shrugged and said, "I enjoy nicotine and don't want to give it up."

Another thing: I'm always horny in the morning. When I'd wake up, I'd want to feel him up and jerk off, maybe suck his cock. But he didn't like it when I touched him at that hour. He'd push my hand away. "Don't shoot a load on me," he'd tell me, or some such crap And I'd lie there thinking, *Hey, I'm giving this punk a place to stay in San Francisco—paying for the food, beer and all of it—and he's griping 'cause I want to jizz on his ass? What kind of bullshit is this?*

The kid could eat, too, tons of food for such a little guy. I nicknamed him "Dagwood" because he'd raid the fridge two or three times a day. He'd build these enormous sandwiches of ham, cheese, cucumber, onion and such—*huge* sandwiches. I hit the supermarket most every day, just to keep up with him. And did I mention the beer? I won't call the kid a drunk because he wasn't. I *never* saw him drunk. But he liked beer, and not the kind I drank, but some Czech brand. He'd always grab a six-pack at the store and place it in the cart. I paid for it every time, of course. I paid for stuff he drank whenever we went out, as well.

We went out often.

The World Cup matches occurred during this period, and the kid was a fiend for soccer. If Germany, Italy or France played in a match, we *had* to go see them on a large-screen TV, at some bar patronized by Europeans: weird people wearing soccer jerseys and speaking French or whatever.

I'm sure soccer's exciting if you played it as a kid. But I didn't, and I found the sport rather boring. Still, I sat there for hours at a time, watching this crap while the kid smoked cigarettes, drank beer and hollered at the screen along with the rest of the folks in the place. At the end I'd pick up the tab and shake my head, feeling a bit like a fool. Again, I asked myself where this was all headed. *We're so different, me and the kid. Is he the right guy for me*?

Somehow, despite his many flaws, I still liked him. He had a good sense of humor; we traded jokes and found many things to laugh about. He drew funny cartoons of himself and me doing stupid shit, like disco dancing or reading comic books to each other on the sofa. Every day, he'd let me bathe him in the tub. I'd scrub his back, his legs and feet, his armpits and ass crack and his genitals. Then I'd shampoo his hair. He'd groan when I massaged his scalp; it was all very sexy.

And despite our age difference and the newness of our friendship, our conversations clicked as if we were old buddies. I spoke of my life in Cincinnati and various jobs I'd worked. I talked about ball games and bowling and the horse track.

Mostly, though, he talked about his parents. "They're constantly criticizing me," he said. "My dad's a bully, too. He used to whip me with a belt when I was younger, 'til I got old enough to fight him."

It seemed the kid had been a loner most of his childhood and adolescence. His only friends were people he'd met over the Internet—his "cyber pals" he called them. These were kids he'd never actually met in person; he'd just talked with them in chat rooms, which I found rather odd. How can someone be your friend if you've never heard his voice or shaken hands with him?

Okay, okay…he was twenty-one and I was forty-one. I know kids today are not the same as when I was young. They dwell in a different world, don't they? They don't play pickup basketball games; they play something called World of Warcraft on the Internet, instead.

*It's a different time,* I'd tell myself; *accept him for who he is.*

Sex with the kid was the best I'd ever had: explosive, sweaty sessions that made me shout like a crazy man when I came. He was uninhibited; he liked it when I talked nasty to him. I'd call him my "fuck boy" and my "sweet little cocksucker" while I pinched his nipples and slapped his ass. I'd have him straddle my face and I'd lick his hole while he squirmed and panted like a dog in heat. Honestly, I'd never felt so close to someone, both physically and spiritually.

And it wasn't just about sex. He was someone I could talk with every day, someone to share meals with. So what if he ate like a horse? Living with him and his appetite was better than living alone, wasn't it?

Ummm…

I had friends come up for the weekend—an old coworker from Cincinnati who'd moved to L. A. with his girl—and we four hung out together. I mean, the apartment was small and we lived close, real close. My L. A. friend made comments about the kid: how the kid's shit was strewn everywhere like the apartment was his and not mine. How the kid did not help clean up. And then one night my friend—the guy from L. A.—said he did not think the kid was entirely innocent. For twenty-one, he seemed pretty shrewd, my friend said. And I tucked this observation into the back of my mind; I mulled it over and over.

That was another thing: the way the kid did not help out. I mean, he'd brought a limited amount of clothes with him, so they had to be washed every few days. I had a washing machine and it wasn't a big deal for me to wash his stuff along with mine. But one day I asked him to help with the clothes and he said, "I don't know anything about doing laundry. My mother does it for me."

I thought: *You're twenty-one years old and you don't know how to wash your clothes? And who am I, your goddamned laundress?*

I didn't understand his behavior toward his parents. A week into his stay, he hadn't contacted them a single time. One day, I said, "Don't you think you should call home? Just to let them know you're okay? You can use my cell phone."

He said, "My parents don't give a shit whether I'm dead or alive. They just don't care, and why should they? I'm not even their real kid."

Sad, eh?

Then there was his work. Like I said before, each day he'd spend hours and hours on his laptop, tapping away at the keys and staring into the screen with his brow furrowed. He'd only take breaks to smoke cigarettes or make a sandwich. Then it was back to work. Aside from our sex sessions, our visits to the supermarket and our evening meal, he had little time for me. I saw all the tourist stuff—the Golden Gate Bridge, Candlestick Park, Sausalito and Fisherman's Wharf—by myself. And he kept on eating those goddamned sandwiches and drinking beer. His shit continued to be strewn about my apartment, like flotsam after a shipwreck, and I grew damned tired of it.

Finally, one afternoon, I confronted him. He sat at the desk in his boxer briefs, tapping on his keyboard, his gaze fixed on the laptop screen.

I said, "Turn off that fucking computer. Let's talk."

He looked up. "About what?"

"Us," I said. "How come I'm spending so much time alone?"

Staring at the carpet, he hunched his shoulders. "I have a lot of work to do."

"You're at that keyboard twelve, fourteen hours a day, unless a soccer match is on. Can't you make more time for *me*?"

He jammed his hands between his thighs and didn't say anything.

"Come on," I said, "talk to me."

A tear spilled out of one corner of his eye. He blinked and another spilled out.

"What's wrong?" I said. "What is it?"

He leapt to his feet and the desk chair fell over. His face was distorted and brick red. He cried, "I'm doing my best here, but it's hard. This 'living together' business is new for me. I don't know who I am—not anymore—and I'm not sure *where* I belong."

I rested my hands on my hips and made a face. "I don't get what you just said," I told him. "Exactly what does that mean?"

Without answering, he ran into the bedroom and slammed the door shut.

I stood there shaking my head.

Human nature's strange isn't it? We want something—a new car, a piece of ass or whatever—and we crave it so badly we ache. But once we get whatever it was we wanted, the specialness fades and we take it for granted, like electricity or indoor plumbing. Then we start dreaming of something else: an item we don't already have, a thing that'll be tough to get.

After three weeks, that's the way it became with the kid and me. I mean, if I'd seen him on the street a month earlier, I'd have taken out a loan just to buy a night in the sack with him. But now, even though he lay next to me each morning, I didn't care.

I was tired of his shit everywhere, tired of looking at his damned hair gel and toothbrush on my bathroom shelf. I was sick of watching him devour the contents of my refrigerator, and weary of being ignored. Sure, he was cute as hell in his own way. Our sex was great, too. But I had reached the limit of my patience.

So, I brought up the subject of his departure with him, and when I did his eyes watered. He said he didn't want to leave. He said Willow Creek was a shit hole, that he hated living there.

"I prefer living with you in San Francisco," he said.

I sort of lost it, then. Words *spilled* out of me. I told him, "Look, this whole thing's not working. I want a boyfriend, not a part-time sex buddy. I need someone who'll take walks with me, watch TV with me, that sort of thing. It's what I expected when I invited you down, but it hasn't happened. Plus, this apartment's small, and it's always cluttered with your shit. You don't help me keep house—you haven't once washed a dish—and it's not fair. Why don't you take a bus back to Willow Creek and let your mom take care of you?"

He didn't try to argue. He only hung his head.

"Okay," he said, "I'll go, if that's what you want."

So he packed his shit into his computer bag and backpack. (How did he get it all in there? It had practically filled my whole damned apartment.) Then he stood at the front door, fresh tears glistening, and we traded the lightest of kisses before saying good-bye. Moments later, he descended the stairwell and entered the street.

I closed the door and pressed my forehead to it. I held the knob and shook my head, while my eyes itched and my stomach churned. *You blew it,* I thought. *Once again, you're flying solo. Is this how it's always going to be? Will you die a lonely old man in a nursing home? Why can't you be more flexible*?

I fought an urge to run downstairs, to chase the kid down

and tell him to come back. "We'll work things out," I'd say. But I didn't do it; I stayed put. Common sense told me things would never go smoothly between us, not unless he altered his behavior.

And leopards never change their spots, do they?

Summer drew to a close. I returned to Cincinnati and found work at a warehouse. I ran a forklift five days a week, had weekends to myself. Fall arrived early, and leaves on the trees turned shades of gold, brown and red. The air smelled fresh; it felt good on my face while I waited for the bus in the morning. The Reds played first-rate ball—they'd make the playoffs for certain—and I went to a few games. I painted all the rooms in my apartment, and this consumed much of my free time. I even volunteered at the Children's Hospital three nights a week, shelving books in the library.

Then, on a rainy Saturday afternoon in mid-October, my doorbell rang.

I crinkled my forehead. *Who could that be? A door-to-door solicitor? Someone looking for directions?*

The kid stood on my doorstep, soaking wet, wearing his usual clothing and backpack, and clutching his laptop computer bag. A raindrop hung from the tip his nose. His dark hair was plastered to his skull and stubble dusted his chin and cheeks. Behind him, rain clattered on the sidewalk; it sheeted off the eaves of my apartment building, creating quite a din.

His gaze met mine. "Can I come in?"

How could I say no?

Moments later we occupied my sofa. The kid had shed his wet clothing; he'd dried himself with a towel, and now he wore the towel about his waist. I studied his lithe physique, recalling our sexual encounters, back in San Francisco. Due to the gloomy day, my living room was full of shadows, but I didn't switch on a light; I wasn't ready for brightness. The kid's sudden appearance had caught me off guard. Why was he here? What did he want?

"I would've called," he said, staring into his lap, "but I was afraid you'd have told me not to come."

I didn't say anything.

He looked up and gazed into my eyes. "I've lived on the street in San Francisco, ever since I last saw you. It hasn't been easy."

I made a face. "Why didn't you go back to Willow Creek?"

He frowned. "I can't; I burned my folks' house down, the night before I met you. They weren't home—they weren't injured—but if I went to Willow Creek tomorrow, the sheriff would arrest me for arson."

I thought, *Holy shit.*

"How come you torched their house?"

He narrowed his eyes. "Think about it. You already know why."

I thought back to all he'd told me about them: his adoption, their secrecy about it, their constant criticism, and the beatings. *Of course,* I thought, *I know exactly why.*

He said, "I've done all kinds of things to survive: day labor, hustling, even stealing. I lived in a shelter, mostly. My lack of a home destroyed my computer business."

I nodded while licking my lips. "Why are you here?" I said.

He looked away then back at me. He said, "You're the closest thing to a family I've ever had and I've missed you. I want to live with you again, if you'll have me."

I shifted my weight on the sofa and chewed my lips. One side of me, thought, *Come on: give the kid a chance.* But the other side said, *Don't do it. He'll only disappoint you, like before.*

"Look," I said, "I like you and all, but—"

"I know I did wrong," he said. "I wasn't fair to you. But I've changed since then; I've grown up."

"How's that?"

"I quit smoking, for one. I learned how to do laundry—you wouldn't have to do mine anymore—and they taught me how to wash dishes at the shelter. I can clean toilets, too."

I couldn't help myself; I chuckled and shook my head, thinking of what an idiot I'd been, letting him go in San Francisco, just because he was different from me, *and* because I felt certain he'd never change his ways.

"What's so funny?" he asked.

"Nothing," I answered.

Then I ran my fingers through his damp hair.

That was a year ago.

The kid got a job; now he busses tables at Red Lobster while earning his GED. We split the housework fifty-fifty and take turns cooking dinner. Every evening, we do dishes together and he takes out the trash. Each night, we make love in my bed, and—

Oops: I meant *our* bed.

No, he's not perfect. He leaves wet towels on the bathroom floor and his shoes lie in the hallway each morning, for me to trip over. But that stuff's not as important as I once believed. I think if two people love each other and need each other, everything else becomes secondary in importance.

He's a good kid, and you know something? Maybe he's not the only one who's changed.

Maybe we're *both* leopards who've earned new spots.

# SPORN

Davem Verne

It seems like everyone is going gay these days. Celebrities and politicians, athletes and priests. Cultural synergy has finally caught up with the fact that it's okay to come out. But honestly, it's getting to be like the wild, wild west! Everyone wants to plant his own rainbow flag and marry a closeted queer.

I promised Evan that I would go gay soon, but I lied. I lied so he wouldn't annoy me with talk about his gay life and all his gay friends and fantasizing about me as his gay lover. If I let him, he'd plead my gay case to the Supreme Court and publicly out me.

"That will only backfire," I warned him. "You can only tame me with love."

He listened and took me to bed. And with my pants down to my knees, I reluctantly agreed to take that first step and tell a few friends that I liked boys.

But sadly, in the real world you can't make gay promises.

Being straight is all I have; it's all I'll ever have. Sometimes

I feel going gay is a social event hosted by a well-paid queen and I'm decidedly against showing up. I can fake it, no doubt. Get on TV; smile bright-eyed, wink and tell the whole world what a fabulous homosexual I am. But that's not me. Not the real me, anyway. I'm a straight boy. A pussy-bred hot rod with a breeder bone.

That's before Evan calls me.

"Hey, *baby maybe.* Are you ready for wedded bliss on my gay ass?"

I hesitate and reply, "Can we *fuck* it over?"

Later, sniffing between my legs, he growls and agrees.

Nature invented holes so wild boys can play. And I'm a holy fucker—while Evan is a soft sucker. But he's better than most girls I've dated. He takes smooth advantage of my straight meat by blowing me in the dark, on the sofa and in the bedroom where we can't be seen. It's all kind of passive aggressive and I feel mostly used, but I let it happen because I'm between girls these days.

"Get over here!" he growls on the phone. "And bring me a dirty dude magazine with a rated-X cover. I want you to squirm at the check out!"

He hangs up in hysterics.

My straight stars—another test!

I consider the task before me as a simple measure of my confused affection for him, so I halfheartedly agree—only because I know if I arrive at his doorstep bearing gifts I'll get two turns popping his ass, not just one.

Behind the gay magazine rack, a shelf full of boys stares back at me. *Freshmeat* this and *Boyhung* that. Porn rags are so inventive. They're hoaxes, of course. I mean, the models inside advertise themselves as *Chad here: suburban straight meat with a nine-inch boner ready to turn a trick.* Ha! Notorious cons, every one of them. They make up that routine just to get print space. In real life they're camped-up, five-inch suburban queers.

I flip through one and stop suddenly. I think that dude works out at my gym. Damn, he looks good in print! And I've definitely seen this one selling tickets at the multiplex. Can't miss those popcorn eyes! If I continue, I bet I'll find half a dozen boys from Evan's salon who've suddenly become "workout buddies" for the magazine royalties.

Now. Which magazine would I buy if I were gay?—and I'm not!

I think I'd go for the muscle hunks in the fitness rags. Oh, yeah. Text and testosterone on the same glossy page. That's what I like. But I'll have to pay extra attention and read between the lines. The magazine promises, *We'll train you to build your biceps and then show you how to mix protein drinks.* Ha! Another elaborate con. I laugh and shrewdly translate that to, *We'll train you to blow your own boner and then show you how to mix cum shots.*

I better not buy that. Too hetero on the surface and suggestive beneath. Evan likes to see guys who are opaque, thin and petite in the moment, not jock-strapped to the hilt. When the shirt comes off, he wants to see pretty gay-boy meat, not pumped-up man flesh.

In order to get off, however, I buy the fitness magazine with the half-nude portfolio in the back. Sports meets porn—*sporn.* Allow me to read:

*Here's how you get diesel, boys. Pump this up, drink that down, crunch here, curl there. Oh, and by the way, after your workout, there's a dirty little treat for you on the back page.*

I rifle through the pages.

A spread of buff dudes catches me salivating.

*Ha! Gotcha! We hang out in the back like bouncers at a club. You needn't look if you're not into sausage. But you did—queer!*

I swiftly complain, "But everyone looks in the back out of fitness *and* desire."

*Shove off, jerk! And put us back on the rack.*

Sporn magazines give men pleasure. They give boys pleasure. They're primordial and well produced. Our fingers dance along the fine edges of a choice bodybuilding magazine and a normal guy can't help but feel the pinch of a woody approaching. As I flip through one, I sense myself getting hard like the legions of straight guys who dumbly purchase these rags, then hurry off for solo action in the shower, thinking they're buff and beautiful and big like the guys in the centerfold. By their second fitness rag, and still too naïve to see the tease, their dicks are raging for a blunt cunt attack. Better take a piss in a cold shower, boys, and save that wad for later.

Knowing the ropes, I finger through a few more then notice some real dude scoping me out from behind the NASCAR rack. He's been standing there for an hour, unbuckling his belt like he was letting off steam. At the same time he's cruising me with his Motorola eyes. It seems we both enjoy sports photography, so I wave.

*Over here, gay guy! Isn't this what you want?* I call out—silently.

"Are you a member of my gym?" he asks politely.

His voice is convincingly masculine, but I know it's an act.

"You own a gym?" I ask.

He grins, "I'm Nate."

I grin, "I'm Bobby."

He likes the sound of that and five minutes later he's stroking me off in his car.

"Doesn't that feel hot, *Bobby*?" he asks, faking a testosterone tone.

His chest is suitably built, but I think he should shave. He spits on his mitt and lets me feel how swift he can jack off. My cock fills his hammered palm. He looks like a Hollywood boxer—the John Garfield type—but I know it's only makeup. He probably reads the same rag that my dad does, *Boxer Builder*.

Pretending his face has been punched in too many times, Nate frowns and slobbers over my dick. The cum in my balls leaks inside his grip. He sweeps his upper lip over my dickhead and fakes being too masculine to go all the way down. He probably suspects I might complain about his chapped lips scraping against my man-shaft, not to mention turning an innocent straight boy like me into a five-minute fuck.

"I'm going to cum!"

I yank my cock from his fist and haul it away.

"I could jack you all night, tough boy."

Oh, brother—smut dialogue. If he's serious, he'd shut up and give me head.

Please understand, I'm nutty about my junk. Many chicks have announced undying love for it. If I could, I'd sniff my balls all day and lie down on my dick just to see how the girls feel when I'm ready to explode.

But NASCAR *Nancy* is too anxious. He begins to beat my balls silly. He's desperate and doesn't know how to conceal it. I bet he'd lose control and kill me if I told him I was on my way to my boyfriend's. That would break his hetero delusion of me and send him packing to the next convenience store, flipping through the wrestling rags for a more appropriate mate. But right now, what he doesn't know excites him.

"I'm getting close," I say.

"Okay, stud. Time to taste it!"

He laps up my cock in his mouth. That makes him moan. I reach down and pinch my balls just to show him how comfortable I am handling my own meat.

"Better let me do that," he snarls. "I know my way around Boy Town."

Oh, Mary, quit with the speech writing!

One, two, three—he pummels my balls again.

"Just say when, little hot rod," he gasps.

His eyes gape over my sweaty head. His lips moisten. His hands whack me off and my dick nudges completely out of my boxers and into his mouth.

"Come on, come on, come on!" he growls, sucking in the air.

The dick juice splats all over the place. My hips thrust into his boxed-in mug. His face pinches. By the time I'm done, hot ball fluid is dripping off his cheeks and he needs three oil rags to clean up the spill.

NASCAR Nancy pants. His engines overheat. My fat head bubbles in his mouth. A mean amount of dick fluid leaks into his gut to cool off his cylinders.

"That was *boy*tastic," he finally breathes.

When he lets go, my straight cock retreats—another victim of drunken gay greed.

With the well dried up, he trembles and spits into the ashtray.

"Put that away before we do it again," he warns, exhausted. "'Cause next time it'll be on the sofa in my man cave. Yeah, wouldn't that make a picture? Me watching an old match, reliving the glory days, and sucking on your dick just as the wife walks in."

Hold on—did he say *wife?*

"I'm willing to risk some things," he adds, "but not that."

Wha-wha-*what?*

"Pack it up, sissy, and go back to your boyfriend!"

"Hey! You've got it all in reverse!" I say.

"You gay boys should stay in the bars where you belong, you know that?" He licks a permanent bruise. "You're going to ruin us regular boys and make us all go gay."

Huh? Does this dude think I'm gay? Did another straight dude just seduce me like gay meat?

I fold my cock over my balls and stuff them limply between my legs. I want to argue some more, make him sweat and steam that he just sucked off another straight brother, but NASCAR Nate drops me off outside Evan's door and burns rubber back to his suburban wife.

I have a two-second walk to contemplate our car jacking.

He was cruising me, right? He was jerking me? He swallowed me? *But I'm gay?*

Evan storms out the door in a huff. I drop my thoughts. His flat chest and lean thighs are visible through his robe. A peach-colored g-string bunches up his package.

"You better get in here and explain yourself, *baby*!" he commands, chasing my tail indoors. After a series of loud exchanges, we finally reach the bedroom where he draws the curtains and unzips my pants and peeks into my drawers.

"Where is it?"

"Where's what?"

"The reason why you're here, where is it?"

"It's there. It's just not hard yet."

"No, stupid. The dirty magazine."

Oops! I left it in Nate's car.

"They were out of your favorite, *Spoon*."

"Don't *Spoon* me. Why don't you just lie down and tell me you didn't wanna look," he spouts, then pouts. "I've been working all day, making myself look super-fabulous, and you don't even respect me."

"I do! I went and I looked, but I know what you like and they only had fitness rags. Honest. You know you don't like sporn."

Evan gags at the thought, but he isn't convinced. Neither am I. I can already hear his ass clenching and his crack sealing and his spine bumping me off the road. I immediately make plans to enjoy the first round on top of his ass twice as hard.

"Lie down," I say.

"Why?" he asks.

"Because I want to tell you something."

"Why do I have to lie down to hear your shit?"

"Because I want to fuck you, *then* I'll tell you."

My cock pulses out of my boxers and conspires with me. He sees the monster growing with abounding grace. Evan drops my drawers and shoves my dick in his mouth. He squeezes the meat with his teeth. I thrust it in, silencing his fears and begin fucking his face. The skyward arch of my dick rides into his mouth where it causes a little pain and I feel a teaspoon of jism shoot into the washer. Then a preliminary orgasm, one-fourth my usual force, breaks the golden gate and boy mix sears from my balls.

Evan goes wild as the precum ripples out of my nuts to the back of his throat. He grumbles and grinds and shudders with pleasure, turning pale in the face as he coaxes more out.

Dazed and amused, Evan slips off his robe and starts squirming on the bed. He's warming his butthole for imminent penetration. He's horny for it, having rehearsed all day with a jar of olives. He twists his nipples and covers his groin and prepares for the straight seduction.

The raincoat I yank out sends him into hysterics.

"Not another *shower*!" he shrieks.

"Yes, Spoon."

I slip it on and stand over him, sawing my prick across his face.

"This ain't a magazine!" I knock my canvassed dick against his brow. "You want me to leave in this state? You want me to go home and play fantasy football with the boys? Or do you want me to club you in the ass and get you all preggers?"

He doesn't respond. He turns into a silent movie star as I lumber over him. He crawls backward in bed. He reclines on his side, the way I like to fuck him, with his ass preening in the air. Against popular opinion, straight boys like to sidesaddle. With a captive gaze, Evan spits in his hand and slaps the edge of his hole.

"I gave you a blow job," Evan breaks his silence, "now give me a baby."

I lie on my side, too, and assume the position of warriors on a Monday night, who ride their sofas with a pillow on their knees and watch the gridiron boys hump each other between posts. I warm my crotch against his butt. I slide my cock high. And I bounce my balls up and down.

"Wiggle it, bitch!"

I ride his rump and find the hole.

Evan swoons. He peeks from his pillow.

"Turn around!" I bray. "You want to marry a straight boy, remember? Well, I'm going up your ass for as long as I want. This is our fucking wedding night. Say you want it. Say I do!"

"Get in there and get off, stupid!" Evan curses.

The gay hole inhales my cock and I abandon seduction for a raging screw. I stuff it in and find Evan hot. His ass captures my dick in an oily grip. We're going to have a slippery session, I can tell. It may not take an hour after all.

As I pump it, I recall the helpful hints inside today's sporn rag: *Massage your muscle. Expand your hips. Don't lock your knees.* I wrap my thighs around him for leverage. *Breathe deeply.* Our necks collide and we exhale at once. We almost kiss.

Suddenly, I lose it. I lose all control. I call out the names of the girls I want to fuck. All the bitches who chased me down this rabbit hole of super-straight-jerkdom.

"Liz! Liza! Joan!" I scream.

Evan shouts from his pillow, "Don't forget Lucy!"

That turns me wild. My frenzy ramps up. The pubes around my groin rip.

I dare to kiss Evan as we side-fuck, hips grinding and both holding back cum. I feel I'm ready for my first sporn shoot when in that moment I remember Nascar Nate, who whacked me off because I seemed the perfect buddy for his repressed desires. I remember the fitness boys in their sports rag, who sell themselves off for the masculine gaze. And I declare I'm straight like them—I must be straight like them—'cause all I do is *think* about them!

My rapid hump strains Evan.

He cries out, "I don't want an abortion! I want to keep it!"

My legs buckle. I cum fast. I throw it in his hole. My juice oozes into the condom squishing between his legs. I play dumb and pretend I hadn't cum just to get off one more time. And I do!

"I'm a man!" I declare openly.

"You're a queen!" Evan shouts back.

I keep pumping, straining harder, until my cock is ready to shoot a third load so huge and thick that I need to see it for myself.

"I'm all the way *in*!"

"You better *come out*!"

Evan flips on his other side as I unwrap the hose and spray a riptide of sperm across his chest. He basks in the shower. He shoots a load himself; I can barely see it. I wipe the last drop from my head and flog him in the face.

"There! Our honeymoon is done."

I crash on the pillow, moaning and aching because I came four times in one night.

My cock is spent. My balls are sore. I need to eat pizza.

"Sleep," I mutter, like a lazy straight bastard.

I lie there, impressed. I did everything right. I retained my straight dignity.

After a few minutes, Evan pokes me in the belly. He combs my pubic hairs and stares at my cock.

"What did you want to tell me, Bobby?" he asks. "Before we got busy, you said you had something to say."

I mutter, "I'm buying a car."

"Tell me you're gay," Evan insists. "It's all I want to hear."

I burp, or maybe fart.

"Tell me you won't read *Men's Fitness* or *Health and Fitness* or *Bodybuilding Fitness*," he pleads. "You know they're out of your league. Instead, you'll read *Out* and pick up the *Pink Pages* and buy me the *Advocate*."

I hold back, thinking how easy it would be to say yes, how easy it would be to cancel my sporn subscriptions and move in with Evan and follow him down the aisle and yell at the top of my lungs, *I've gone gay! See the ring? You should, too. Yada-yada-yada!*

Instead, I curl up like a brute fumbling an imaginary football.

"When will you come out?" Evan whimpers. "Everybody knows you like boys."

*You'll never tame me*, I muse—silently.

Then I add, whispering, "Pretty soon, Spoon. Pretty soon."

# COSBY KIDS

## Roscoe Hudson

We were the only black family in our subdivision. My parents and I moved in right after Mom got hired at her law firm, just about the time I started middle school. The house is a lot nicer than the condo we lived in back in the city, and the neighborhood is much safer, but everywhere we go we're surrounded by white people who give us phony smiles and suspicious looks. Dad was sure they were all racists. I didn't have trouble making friends, but I was ambivalent about my new environment. Though I went to one of the best high schools in the state and outperformed my peers scholastically and athletically, I missed life in the city, its vibrancy and diversity. That's part of the reason I applied to an historic black college in the South. I couldn't wait to get out of the suburbs.

There weren't many black students at my high school, but we managed to stay pretty close to each other. We were all from well-to-do families: our parents were CEOs, doctors, lawyers, engineers, professional athletes or professors. We lived in posh multistoried McMansions and spent our weekends shopping in the city while our parents worked sixty hours a week. The white kids at school called us Cosby Kids behind our backs. I didn't give a shit. Truthfully, we never had a problem with any of them. As for myself, I tended to be very popular with the girls. From the time my parents moved us out here I was surrounded by one Barbie doll replica after another. White Barbie dolls gave me blow jobs in the locker room after school, black Barbie dolls let me finger them in the backseat of my Lexus RX, Asian Barbie dolls let me suck their titties behind the bleachers after basketball games. And I didn't really want any of them, not so long as my homeboy Rod was willing to offer me his cock from time to time.

Rod and I convinced our parents to let us visit the college campus on our own a couple of months after my eighteenth birthday. Rod graduated from high school the year before, entered a local college in the fall and didn't return after winter break. His parents both had advanced degrees and six-figure jobs, were active in the NAACP, state and local politics. They couldn't understand why their son, who had grown up with every advantage, couldn't handle college. He had been working at his uncle Nate's used-car lot for the last three months. Nate let us borrow one of his used Ford Expeditions for the trip; I didn't want to put too many miles on my Lexus. But our SUV broke down in the last place two young black men want to be stranded: near the Mississippi-Alabama state line. The car sputtered to a stop on a deserted stretch of highway around noon on the second day of our trip. The area was so remote Rod and I couldn't even get reception on our iPhones. We got out, lifted the hood and looked inside.

"Know anything about cars?" Rod asked.

"I'm a Cosby kid, remember?" I said.

"Motherfuckin' Nate." Rod slammed the hood down and spit on the highway.

He and I both kept trying our phones but had no luck, so we decided to walk to the nearest town. We walked for nearly two hours before we came upon a dilapidated filling station not far from a swamp in the middle of a wooded area. A shiny cobalt BMW was parked beside an old red F150 and a row of rusted, smashed, broken-down cars, some of them decades old. When Rod and I stepped onto the property two angry pit bulls charged toward us, barking and snarling. If they hadn't been chained they would have ripped us apart. A stout white man, grungy and grease covered, strode after them wielding a leather strap.

"Get your asses back inside!" he shouted. "Get, dogs! Get!"

He was built like an action figure: broad with gigantic swollen slabs of muscle. And he was short: about five feet eight inches I guessed. Dad would have said he was built low to the ground. His blue coveralls were zipped up to the center of his chest; a pelt of burnished blond hair covered it. His craggy, sunburned face held deep creases and his eyes had the predatory glint of an eagle. The name TOMMY was stitched on his coveralls. Once the dogs retreated inside he gave Rod and me a suspicious look, then approached us.

"Here we go," Rod whispered derisively under his breath. He had been ranting about potential run-ins with tobacco-spitting rednecks since we got on the road. He kicked at the dusty ground and squared his shoulders as the mechanic stepped toward us.

"Fellas need something?" Tommy asked. His Southern drawl was so thick each word he uttered had an extra syllable. I could smell the spearmint gum he was chewing and the pungent odor of tobacco mingled with it.

"Yeah," I said. "Our car broke down a couple of miles or so up the highway."

"That's a bad situation. Walkin' in this heat... That sun got y'all soppin' sweat, sure enough. Y'all city boys must not be used to it." Two dimples punctuated Tommy's smile as he kept chewing his gum. He looked up at the empty blue sky. "Yep. Bitch of a day. Where y'all headed?"

"Why you wanna know?" Rod asked.

The dogs started barking again.

Tommy looked over his shoulder and bellowed, "I said cut out all that shit goddammit!"

The dogs became quiet again. A cloud passed, momentarily blocking the sunlight.

Tommy's face looked different in the overcast light, ashen and worn. His rusty blond hair was gray at the roots, and gray hairs coiled among the blond ones on his brawny chest. I looked lower and noticed a decent bulge in his overalls. His eyes, blue as the BMW and fierce, caught mine when I raised my gaze. He winked at me and popped his gum.

"We're on our way to Atlanta," I said, "and our car—"

"What y'all drivin'?"

"An Expedition. It just stopped—"

"Found On the Road Dead!" Tommy let out a hearty laugh and scratched his nuts. They looked like two tennis balls in his coveralls. "A new Expedition?"

"Used." Without thinking I gestured to Rod and said, "His uncle let us borrow it from his lot."

Tommy scratched his chest hair and spit on the ground. The clouds passed and the sunlight, bright and stinging, returned.

Rod had been lethally silent through the conversation, but he finally blurted out, "Look, man, you gonna fix my ride or fuck around all damn day?"

All the good humor drained from Tommy's face. "Guess y'all ain't got no manners up North, do you?"

"What we got is motherfuckers who don't stand around all goddamn day in the heat jibber-jabbering about bullshit. Now you gonna tow the motherfucker and fix it or what?"

Just then a pockmarked man around sixty, dressed in a business suit twice his size, stepped out of the garage. He stopped at the entrance when he saw us talking to Tommy and stared at all the three of us. He looked like a nervous mouse caught in a maze.

Tommy whipped his head around and looked at him. "Just some customers. Don't be scared."

"Guess y'all think we out to rob the place and shit," Rod said.

Tommy smiled again. "You funny."

The man in the suit, still staring at us fearfully, took a wad of money out of his pants pocket and handed it to Tommy.

"You like it?" Tommy asked him as he counted the money. "Told you that was some grade-A shit."

The man kept looking at us. He looked ready to run at the slightest movement from either of us.

Tommy lightly patted his shoulder. "Hey, man, it's cool. They giving me business."

The man said, "Sure?"

"You think I'm not?"

Once Tommy finished counting the money he said, "Thanks for the cherry on top, amigo."

"Sure," the man said. He stepped over to his car, the BMW, and got behind the wheel. Tommy waved to him as he drove off in a cloud of dust.

"Sorry fellas," Tommy said, "Another customer."

"Looks like you're backed up," I said.

"Who, him? Nah, he was here for something else. One of my

sideline businesses." He raised his eyebrows a couple of times and winked at Rod.

"How soon can you fix our SUV?" I asked.

"I can fetch it soon as Earl gets back with the tow truck."

Rod said, "We looking at ten minutes? Twenty?"

Tommy shrugged. "Ain't no tellin' with Earl. I s'pect he'll head on over to the Blue Bucket for some lunch and shoot the shit a while. Probably another hour."

"Shit!"

"Sorry homie, we're workin' men. A man's gotta eat." He turned to me, his eyes twinkling, and said, "Ain't that right?"

The bulge in his pants was getting bigger. If Rod hadn't been so mad he would have seen it too. Then again, I never knew him to be attracted to white guys.

"You fellas more than welcome to come on in and wait. I got air-conditioning and HBO."

"We got another fucking choice?" Rod said.

Tommy popped his gum and smiled at me. "I bet he's real funny on the road, ain't he?"

Tommy's dogs barked again as the three of us walked past and into the waiting room in the office of the garage. It was covered in faux wood paneling the color of buttered toast. Three red plastic chairs lined the wall opposite the door. An old floor model television with rotary dials stood in the corner by the door. A Chevy Chase movie was playing.

"Ain't this nice." Rod rolled his eyes and dropped himself in one of the chairs.

I stood beside Tommy in front of the television set. An ashtray full of cigarette butts and ashes rested on top of it.

"Sorry this ain't no Buckingham Palace," Tommy said to Rod. He snapped his gum loudly and scratched his right nipple, glowering at Rod the whole time.

Rod folded his right leg on his left knee and sighed. "I can't believe this shit." He took his iPhone out of his pocket and tapped on the screen. "Still ain't got no motherfuckin' bars out here. Fuckin' boondocks, man. Stuck out here with fuckin' crackers."

Tommy's ears and forehead reddened. A thick green vein snaked across his throat and his eyes widened. "Look here, I ain't got to take all this shit! You gonna come struttin' in my place of business talkin' shit and callin' folks names y'all can just hightail it on outta here, homie!"

"Listen to this country motherfucker," Rod groaned.

"Look," I said to Tommy, "he's just angry about the car. Don't mind him. He's just talking shit."

"You don't need to speak up for me."

"You want to get the car fixed or not?"

Tommy began chewing his gum again. He smirked, looked me over, cleared his throat and tugged at his crotch.

"Where's the bathroom?" I asked.

"Down there." Tommy pointed to one of two doors at the end of the small hallway.

I left the waiting area to go to the bathroom, trusting Rod not to say anything stupid while I was gone. There weren't any paper towels so I had to air-dry my hands.

I walked back into the waiting area and found him sitting in one of the red chairs. His coveralls were down to his ankles and Rod rested on his knees giving him a blow job.

Tommy rolled his head to the side, spotted me in the doorway, and smiled. "Come get some of this dick, boy."

I got on my knees beside Rod and put my lips on Tommy's big hairy balls. Only one could fit in my mouth. Rod, who had been so antagonistic toward Tommy only two minutes before, swallowed Tommy's dick like a glutton. His spit drooled down

Tommy's thick shaft and onto his balls. I slurped it up. Soon I felt Rod's hand squeeze my ass.

"Yeah," Tommy groaned. "Y'all boys like to play. Knew y'all liked dick. Sucking country dick, ain't you?"

Rod lifted his head and began jerking Tommy's cock while I kept licking his balls. "Fucking cracker," he called Tommy.

Tommy smirked. "You like swinging on a cracker's dick, don't you boy?"

Rod's nostrils flared; his eyes shined with rage. My tongue slid out of my mouth and flicked Tommy's right ball while I massaged his left one. Rod, still jerking Tommy's cock, spit on the helmet head before he swallowed the full length and buried his face in Tommy's lap.

"Goddamn, boy," Tommy groaned. He closed his eyes and started pinching his nipples.

I worked my mouth up Tommy's dick, slick with Rod's spit, and together Rod and I licked the head. I placed a hand on Tommy's hard, hairy thigh and gradually worked it up to his balls and massaged them.

Tommy breathed and moaned like a bull lowing during mating season. "Hell yeah, boy. Uhhh! Y'all get your clothes off. Goddamn!"

Rod was out of his clothes and straddling Tommy's lap before I could pull my jeans down. They slobbered each other's face with rough kisses while Tommy squeezed Rod's juicy high-yellow ass and Rod stroked Tommy's cock. Swirls of soft blond hair, like wheat pastures, nested at the base. They smelled of sweat, musk and laundry detergent. It was by no means the longest cock I'd ever seen—Rod and I had much longer dicks—but what Tommy lacked in size he more than made up for in girth. Getting fucked by Tommy's furry beer-can dick would be painful for even the most experienced bottom. Tommy and

Rod opened their mouths as wide as they could and twisted their tongues around each other's. I slurped Tommy's fat cock, savoring his precum and his ripe stench.

"Yeah. Get on that pig sticker, boy," he grunted.

My tongue ran the length of this prick before I angled my mouth toward Rod's asshole. He moaned when I slid my tongue inside his ass.

"Yeah, loosen up your buddy's ass."

"You gonna fuck me?" Rod asked.

"I'ma hurt that pretty butt," Tommy said, before I heard their mouths smacking again.

Tommy spread Rod's ass as wide as he could. I used my fingers to loosen up Rod's hole. I started out with two and held them close together, treating them like one instrument. I probed his asshole as deep as I could.

"You know you ain't got to be shy," Rod said. "Wreck my hole, bruh."

I took his cue and worked a third finger past his sphincter. Rod muttered, "*Mmm,*" and began to fuck himself on my fingers, his asshole gripping them as tight as possible. My fingers were so deep in him I could feel his prostate; I stroked it and Rod's moaning increased. Soon my whole hand was moving inside of him. The sound from his slicked-up ass was like batter being mixed in a bowl. I wanted to plunge my dick in that sweet hot hole. I took my fingers out and buried my face in his ass before I lowered my head and sucked him off. With my free hand I jerked off my own hard dick.

"You 'bout ready for some white dick?" Tommy asked.

Rod closed his eyes and whispered, "Ooh, Daddy, yes. I want some white dick."

He smacked Rod's ass a few times and chuckled like a villain in a cartoon.

I backed up and let Rod wiggle his ass onto Tommy's dick. He winced as he took Tommy's stout cock into his butt, gnashing his teeth as if he had cut himself with a knife. He bellowed. His body trembled.

Tommy's dimples reemerged as he pumped his dick into Rod. "Sweet black ass! Goddamn!"

The echo of their flesh smacking together bounced off the walls. Tommy kicked off his work boots and I pulled off his coveralls and tossed them over the television. Rod's eyes were shut tight. His moved slowly on Tommy's chubby cock at first, but he gradually increased his tempo and rode Tommy's dick faster than Tommy could thrust into him. But Tommy quickly caught up with Rod's manic pace and their hard muscular bodies crashed into each other with perfect synchronization.

"Going to town on my johnson, ain't you boy?"

"Oh, yeah, Daddy."

"Like gettin' off on redneck dick, huh?"

"Shit… Uhh! Uhh!"

"Hillbilly dick done made you a bitch, ain't it?"

"Hell, yeah."

Tommy forced Rod's mouth onto his, and they shared a sloppy kiss. I stood behind them jerking off. I stuck a finger in my mouth to get it wet then slid it up my own hole. I wanted a turn with both of them.

Tommy took a finger and started poking at Rod's asshole while he kept plowing him. Rod slowed his ride and milked Tommy's dick with his ass.

"Yeah," Tommy whispered between kisses, "you know what you doin'." He kept prodding Rod's hole until he worked his finger inside along with his thick dick. Rod didn't seem to noticc at first but when Tommy inserted a second finger and stretched his sphincter, Rod yelped.

"You feeling good," Tommy told him rather than asked him. "Gonna give you what you need, boy." He looked at me and gestured to Rod's dark round butt. "Get in this ass, boy."

He slipped out of Rod's hole just before I rammed my slick cock up his ass. Rod gasped. His buttcheeks quivered and his sphincter tightened around my dick. I didn't waste any time plowing his hole.

"Got a bull black dick slammin' up in your guts." Tommy jerked his cock and ran his tongue along his thin lips while I gave Rod's ass a thorough pounding. "We gonna breed you, boy."

Rod's ass felt so snug and wet around my dick I didn't think I could hold back my jizz another minute, but just before I was about to squirt inside of him Rod moved off my dick and squatted on Tommy's cock again. They fucked for a few minutes before Rod raised his haunches and let me slide my dick back into him. We went back and forth like that for about ten minutes before Tommy stuck his dick back up Rod's ass, looked at me and said, "You too. Stick that ass."

I thought Rod would resist but he didn't flinch at all when I began to insert my cock inside of his asshole along with Tommy's. I didn't think we could accomplish the task because of Tommy's large girth. I tried being gentle; I didn't want to hurt Rod. But his asshole wasn't able to stretch wide enough to accommodate both Tommy's beer-can cock and my ten inches.

"Just keeping workin' it," Tommy urged me. "This boy needs two dicks."

My wet dick slid against Tommy's as I worked to penetrate Rod's ass along with him. Soon I could feel the heat of Rod's asshole surround the mushroom head of my dick. He sucked in a huge breath and I saw him gnash his teeth.

"You takin' them dicks," Tommy demanded. His hands were still grasping Rod's ass, spreading his cheeks.

I kept pushing my cock in slowly until about a third of my dick, just over three inches, was inside of him.

Rod panted softly while he moaned, "Shit...shit...shit..."

The only other DP I ever had was with Rod and a white girl he had been messing around with named Hailey. I could feel his big dick sliding in her ass while I fucked her pussy. As good as it felt this was much better. Nothing separated my cock from Tommy's cock. They slid against each other while we stretched out Rod's hole. Rod moaned; his whole body became stiff and he dug his fingers into Tommy's chest just as Hailey had done to me. Gradually his moans became full-out screams.

"You gonna take it, boy," Tommy said. "Be a fuckin' man and take them dicks."

I stepped onto the couch, planting one foot on each side of Rod and Tommy, and I held on to Rod's shoulders to keep my balance. This allowed me to penetrate him deeper. Now I could get about half of my dick into him, which pushed out Tommy's cock. He pushed it back in, and when he did we both started thrusting in and out. Rod's screams quieted to muffled whimpers before he silenced completely. The three of us fucked quietly for a few minutes, breathing hard and grunting from time to time, until Tommy, in a low voice, asked, "You like it?"

"Yeah." Rod kissed him, then he raised his head so I could kiss his plump lips. My tongue traced his lips then slithered into his mouth.

Tommy said, "I'm lovin' your ass, baby. Like your big dick slidin' on my chest."

"Yeah, Daddy," Rod whispered.

"I'm your Daddy?"

"Um-hmm."

"You like a white Daddy and a black stud stretching you out?"

"Hell, yeah."

They kissed. Tommy and I had been moving in and out of Rod slowly but Rod began to hit his ass harder. Then so did I. I pushed into him as far as I could, and with my hands still holding on to his shoulders I forced Rod to bounce on our cocks. His big round ass jiggled a bit and his hole, slick from the mix of sweat, spit and precum, squished and farted as Tommy and I rutted deep inside him. I swung my ass back as far as I could and clenched it tight when I thrusted. My back, armpits and the backs of my knees were slick with sweat. Every muscle in my body ached and strained from holding my position in back of him so long. I wanted to stop and change positions but lust wouldn't let me.

"Want me to dirty up your hole?" Tommy grabbed Rod by the throat.

"Yeah, baby."

"Breedin' you now, boy. Fuck! Yeah!"

Rod's asshole became wetter and hotter. Tommy's body convulsed; he bellowed and choked Rod so hard he gagged. I continued fucking Rod, ready to reach my own orgasm.

Tommy pulled his dick out and drilled Rod's mouth with his tongue. He looked up at me and said, "You like sliding in on my cum?"

I smiled. "Makes his ass juicy."

"Make you wanna squirt?"

"Hell, yeah."

"Gonna get a double load today, boy," he said to Rod before he shot his gun-metal stare at me and barked, "Shoot that fuckin' load! Do it!"

It was like he pulled the trigger of a shotgun. I thrust into Rod one last time as far as I could and pumped my cum deep inside of him. Our bodies quivered. We groaned and struggled to breathe.

Tommy and I got up, but he told Rod to bend over the couch with his back arched, his beefy ass high in the air. "Got the best of both worlds today, huh boy?"

He patted Rod's ass a few times. Rod smiled wide and jerked his dick.

"Nice dirty butt."

Tommy squatted behind Rod and started licking his glazed ass crack. My dick, which was going soft, began to get hard again as I stood by and watched.

"Push, baby," Tommy said before he dug his tongue deep into Rod's glistening anus. He took it out and said, "Push out all that jizz."

He spread Rod's asscheeks and dug his tongue inside of his anus. I could hear his tongue working inside, the familiar sound of fluid sloshing between warm bodies. It was a sound as pulsating and erotic as the image of the felching itself. Tommy withdrew his face. "Push it out, baby."

Rod, still masturbating, closed his eyes and bit his lower lip. His anus, distended about three inches, emitted a big fart and then a large glob of semen, the combined result of Tommy's and my animal fucking, was expelled from his ass and projected into Tommy's mouth.

Tommy roared. "Yeah! Gimme more of that jizz, boy!" He gave Rod a good hard smack on the ass. "Squirt that cum."

Rod's asshole opened wide again and the rest of our cum leaked out of his hole. Tommy buried his face in Rod's ass again and gobbled it up. Seconds later Rod squirmed, moaned and tugged on his cock faster. Tommy placed his palm beneath Rod's cock and caught all four shots of cum that blasted from his piss slit. When Rod finished he brought his hand to his face and lapped up his semen, licking his fingertips and smacking his lips.

"Hot motherfuckers," Tommy said to himself. Licking his palm, he looked like a bear who had just reached his paw into a pot of honey. "My lucky day." His eyes shined like Christmas lights.

Once he was done eating he looked at me wide-eyed, as if it was the first time he had ever seen me. I was still jerking my dick, ready for another round of pig fucking. He sauntered over to me. "I ain't forgot about you, sexy." He wrapped his hands around my ass, rubbed my asshole with two fingers and clamped his lips over mine. The room tilted in my eyes and a small salty ball of cum rolled to the back of my mouth.

Hours later, after Rod and I had settled into our motel room near the university, I phoned my parents and told them I had already begun to get quite an education in the South.

# SNEAK THIEVERY

R. G. Martin

Blinker pretended to lounge on the porch where the college boys lounged. He was in fact watching the art store across the street—watching the owner, Lonnahan, move inside. Older guy. Handsome, broad shouldered, eagle eyed. When he disappeared, Blinker peeled himself up, slunk over and went in.

No, wait. He shucked his shirt and went in.

The store prole looked up. His face brightened. "Justin!" he exclaimed.

"Hey!"

The prole was balding but boyish and extremely, extremely nice. His shirt was filled with gay muscles. "How's it going?" he asked. "Here for that silk-screen kit?" he asked.

"Not yet. My friend got an airbrush and I was wondering if you have airbrush paint."

"Right over here."

Blinker already knew about the airbrush paints, although he hadn't swiped any yet. "Oh, wow," he rhapsodized. His jeans were tight and low, and he felt the prole's gaze deconstruct his waist, such as it was.

Skinny no-account redhead.

"Are they all two ounces?" he asked. "What if I needed something bigger?"

"How big?"

"Big."

The prole went back behind the counter and flipped through catalogues. "About eight," Blinker called as he stooped to pinch calligraphy nibs.

"Really?"

"Or a little bigger." Blinker joined the prole at the register, watched him try not to leer at his nipples. "Listen," Blinker said earnestly. "Is it a problem for me to be in here shirtless?"

Blinker spent a buck-something on a Flair. He left with the nibs and a bottle of India ink warm in his pocket, next to his junk.

Next time, Blinker kept the shirt. "What's up, Justin?" the prole asked.

"Just checking things out."

Checking out fresh opportunities—windows, hidey-holes, et cetera. The store was an old two-story house. It had a sales floor where a living room would be, and a hall leading to a door, a driveway and a garage.

Blinker dropped a blister-carded pen set down his shirt. "Hey," he called. "You know your back door is open?"

The prole shot to his side. "We keep it open. Sometimes people park back here."

"Nice lawn," Blinker said. "Listen, I don't guess you need someone to mow it."

"That would be great! But the owner does that."

"No way. I thought you were the owner."

Vamping the prole gave Blinker a hard-on, or rather the blister-carded pen set did. He left by the front, but doubled around and let himself in the garage. Place was like a damn hoarder's. Hot, ninety degrees. Boxes and boxes, nothing of value.

He walked toward an enclosed stairway, sidled up to the window and cranked his eyeballs outward. Oh, fuck. Lonnahan's hot car. Lonnahan himself, pacing with his phone.

Lonnahan was younger than Blinker thought, but not that young. He had a linebacker's build and sharp clothes. Blinker could see the sleeve creases from where he was standing, how the fabric hugged the man's lats. This was the man Blinker was sticking it to.

Lonnahan drifted out of sight. After a second, Blinker heard a creak, a rattle and Lonnahan's voice in the doorway, like God. "No, a dozen." Apparently dressing someone down. Apparently good at it. Blinker became one with the wall.

"I received a dozen. I was billed for a gross."

The door slammed. Blinker's sweat shimmied south, along with his adrenaline. He clutched the pen set. He flicked open his shirt and his fly. His erection dropped like a drawbridge. He grabbed it in the middle and pulled the skin back to the bush.

He knew this was a little gay.

"Do I have to show you the freight slip?" Lonnahan again, just outside. Blinker froze, with precum rolling through his slit.

Lonnahan paced before the window, tick-tock, tick-tock. He had a straight nose, a straight philtrum, a straight chin cleft. There was gray at his temples. His cuffs had two buttons, and that was annoying. Blinker began to slide his cock skin, tick-tock, in time with Lonnahan's pacing.

"Because I will drive up there."

Blinker knew nothing about dozens or grosses, but he could tell that Lonnahan was right, and that was also annoying. The corner of the pen set cut into Blinker's skin. His balls shot up.

"I will drive up there and show you the freight slip."

Blinker gulped aloud. He bit his wrist and jammed his thumb in his cum tube, which angled his cock down, and the pen set fell with a clatter.

Lonnahan stopped pacing.

Blinker's cock was sausage tight. The veins were blue. The lips were open. The underside pulled on the foreskin. Blinker's orgasm bit, right up the ass. His cum rained on the floorboards.

He shivered in the heat. He watched as Lonnahan headed for the store.

Blinker's victim. Blinker almost felt possessive.

Lonnahan ran laps in red split shorts that cost a lot of money. Blinker took to hanging out at the track, sketching with stolen materials. He enjoyed hiding in plain sight. One day, he nodded and Lonnahan nodded back, but with no juice.

So Blinker swapped his nine-by-twelve stolen pad for an eighteen-by-twenty-four stolen pad. Still no juice. At least the man made a good subject. Body out of *Anatomy for Artists*. Lips so handsome, it was like a joke.

Blinker saw a need to step things up.

He hit the store on the hottest day of the year, with a thin white T-shirt sticking to his tits. "Ninety-five degrees out there," he announced.

"I know." The store prole's own shirt was unbuttoned to the breastbone.

"I heard about block printing. Can you show me?"

"More than happy to."

The prole took Blinker to a nook beside a half-opened door. "Where does that go?" he asked.

"Upstairs. The frame shop."

"Oh." Blinker dug his toes into the prole's personal space. "You're always here alone."

"Well, summer is dead."

"Where's your boss?"

"Out. Here's the cutter set."

"Sweet." Blinker put his arm up, wafting melted deodorant and a young man's sweat, and dug in another quarter of an inch. "Listen. Is it hard?"

"Uh, block printing? I've never actually done it."

"What do you do?" Blinker dropped the cutter set. He bent to pick it up real slow. After a beat, he felt the prole's hand on his sweaty waist. "Hey!" Blinker hopped out of the prole's personal space *tout de suite*. "What's that?" Blinker fake demanded. "What, what, what is that?"

The prole turned melon pink.

"Do you do that a lot?" Blinker demanded. "I thought you were my friend."

"I'm sorry. I'm sorry."

"I thought you were interested in my art."

"I am. We are…friends. Aren't we?"

Blinker shook his head in fake disbelief. He ticked the cutter set between his thumb and index finger.

"Can I buy you that?" the prole asked. "As a peace offering?"

"Peace offering." Blinker let this settle in. "Tell me, how is the light in the frame shop?"

A minute later, the prole—dazed and terrified and hopeful—was unbuttoning his shirt. His chest was solid from armpit to armpit. His stomach was banded with muscle. All of it was thirtysomething and pale, pale, pale. Pink skin, pink nipples, sparse baby hairs.

"You work out," Blinker said, pulling out his cell phone.

"I try."

Blinker waved the phone at the prole's slacks. The prole said, "But the store…?"

"Summer is dead." Blinker loved wielding this power. He didn't want to overdo it, though. "I hope I look that good when I'm your age," he schmoozed. "I don't look that good now."

"You do, you do."

"Underwear too," Blinker said.

"But…"

"I told you, figure studies!"

The prole inhaled, dropped his bikini briefs, came up cocked. The shaft was a Lincoln log. Dime-tight, the foreskin encircled the slit. Blinker wasn't stimulated, but he was…something.

"Put your hand on it?" he said crisply.

Blinker got an image—more of a sensation. Him on his knees, smoking that thick, smooth… Just so this extremely nice man would keep thinking that Blinker was extremely nice.

Never going to happen. Blinker snapped the phone shut. "These are going to be useful."

"Useful?"

Blinker helped himself to the silk-screen set he'd wanted on his way out.

Blinker was on a roll.

He spent two days rendering the cumulative amount of his thievery in fourteen-inch numerals on the back of his sketchpad. He approached Lonnahan on the track, with the pad under his arm.

"Listen. I hope it's not a problem that I draw you."

Lonnahan, stretching, barely looked up. "Tell me why it should be." Blinker wished that he had sprayed the number on the garage.

He had planned to blackjack the prole, planned to be nice about it. But the prole was gone. In his place, a low-cut blonde with a blue blouse and blue toenails. Blinker made his eyes wide. "Oh, wow! I've never been here before! Can you show me around?"

She let him cop a feel beside the Conte Crayons. The relationship held promise, but in a week she too was gone. College started and the art store grew packed. Blinker kept tabs from the porch across the street, now full of shirtless college boys—

*"So what's this about you telling Jillian that I have high armpits?"*

*"I don't know what you're talking about."*

*"Oh, you know."*

—who either failed to notice that Blinker was not one of them, or failed to notice him period.

And Lonnahan was around all the time, all the time.

One day Blinker snuck in the back door while Lonnahan waited on people. Wet-palmed with fear, he inched along the wall behind the racks, flipped a window latch and fled.

He climbed in Friday night. The art supplies were in shadow. The floor caught the streetlamp darkly. The college boys stood on the sidewalk with signs: YOU HONK, WE DRINK. Blinker doffed his shirt. Anyone could peer in. No one would see. Now Blinker really felt like Blinker.

Cash register first. He was pretty sure he could get in. He patted around, but then the sleigh bell that hung on the door jangled. The lock turned.

Blinker bolted.

Lonnahan's voice: "Aidan, its Dad. This phone is about gone, so call me at the store."

Blinker hid behind the door on the stair landing. The register rang. Peering out, he saw red split shorts, naked lats, hot skin. Lonnahan, about to take the goddamned money.

Drawing back, Blinker brushed something. It skidded. He froze. He scrambled up the stairs and around the corner. He flattened himself against the wall. After a moment, footsteps. One, two, three...twelve in all. The light snapped on.

The phone rang.

The footsteps retreated. "Aidan"—Lonnahan's voice in the distance—"are you with your mom?"

The light was like needles. Blinker clutched his stomach. He'd have hurled if he wasn't in so deep. Off to the left was a room—a bathroom—a real one with a bathtub. Blinker crawled into it and cringed. At length, Lonnahan's shadow appeared on the floor. Then the light went out. Silence.

Blinker waited and went down to the store. The fun was gone, but it might return. He resumed shopping. He checked the register. *Cha-ching.* At least fucking Lonnahan had left some fucking coins.

Blinker heard a switch flip. Suddenly, light, and Lonnahan, with skin aglow and shadows coming off his nipple points. "Oh, you," he said as he shut the cash drawer. "Big surprise." He put his hands on his hips and turned into a barricade.

"You need security cameras," Blinker managed.

"No, I don't."

Lonnahan advanced. Or not, Blinker found it hard to think. If he could skate past, or barrel through, perform a crotch twist. They performed those in martial arts, probably. Blinker tried it.

It did not go well. His thumb closed around something as fibrous as bamboo, and his fingers around spongy bulk like avocado, and it was just terrifying. He found himself in a half crouch, inhaling oxygenized testosterone, with no way to save face.

"What's the idea?" Lonnahan clapped a hand on Blinker's junk. "*This?*"

"Yeow!"

He twisted. "Or this?"

"Yeow!"

"Or this?" He dropped to his knees, yanked Blinker's pants down and swallowed him to the root.

Stars flew in. Blinker saw them and felt them. The pleasure was a wire in his cock, coals in his balls. Incapacitating, and Lonnahan stayed parked—sucking, breathing through Blinker's orange pubic hair.

Blinker's tits popped, buzzed, pulled. Lonnahan started to move. His mouth became a potato peeler. Cars honked outside. Passing lights made Blinker's shadow spin across the wall. Anyone could look in. Anyone could see. Blinker covered his ass crack, as Lonnahan's mouth methodically shaved back and forth, back and forth, until—

"Uh!"

Lonnahan clamped him off.

"Urgh!" The blockage was a ball buster.

Lonnahan picked him up, dumped him on the sales counter. Blinker had to crunch into cashew shape or break his neck. Lonnahan yanked off his shoes, yanked off his jeans, yanked off his blue briefs, which were all waistband. Now Blinker was afraid.

"I'm sorry," he said in a small voice.

"Go to hell."

Lonnahan hoisted Blinker's butt and shoved his face up the crack. Blinker giggled. Lonnahan smacked him and set about ripping out crack fuzz with his teeth. *I could kick him in the face,* Blinker thought stupidly.

But Lonnahan was a shadow with light on his shoulders. He split Blinker's asscheeks. His tongue stamped Blinker's hole.

*Not for real*, Blinker thought. Tipped the balance, didn't it?

But by then the tongue was halfway up, injecting saliva.

Lonnahan stepped back, wiped his mouth and skimmed off the red split shorts. His cock popped up long and floaty, bobbing on its pins. He dropped spit on it. He stood for a moment, shining in his wonderful, terrible muscles.

He grabbed Blinker by the thigh and pulled his butt over the counter's edge. Blinker had to press down, push his trunk up, to keep from falling. Lonnahan slathered his thumb. He reached between Blinker's legs. Blinker felt the thumb tap around his crack and his pucker—

"Yeow!"

Lonnahan corkscrewed the thumb and then repeated the process with his cock.

"Yeow!"

"It is what it is."

Lonnahan pushed upward. Blinker stared down at his lower abs, with their sharp waist wings and the crunch crease that ran across his navel. The abs began to pump. The pain became a menthol throb that filled Blinker's crotch.

Lonnahan reached back. He flipped the light off. He picked up the phone. "Aidan, Dad again. Can you stay with your mom tonight? Yeah, I got stuck. Pick you up in the morning. Love you."

Lonnahan's torso, biceps, deep pecs, all flashed red and white from a cop car idling at the college boys' porch.

Oh, Daddy.

Blinker flung himself around Lonnahan's shoulders and mashed down on Lonnahan's cock.

He knew he was a bitch.

# GOING BACK FOR THIRDS

Hank Edwards

The bleacher beneath me is cold, hard and uncomfortable. I usually enjoy sitting on hard objects, but when the temperature is hovering in the forties and the object happens to be made of aluminum, everything changes. I shiver in a fresh gust of wind and wrap my arms more tightly around myself, wondering just why the fuck I had agreed to this in the first place.

On the field below, the players break their huddle and line up. I take a long, lingering look at the young, firm asscheeks hugged by tight-fitting uniform pants before the ball is snapped and the play commences. The quarterback falls back, searching for a viable target. He finds an open man, cocks his arm and sends the ball spiraling down the field to his teammate. The receiver catches it with ease, tucks it into the crook of his arm and sprints to the end zone as the crowd, myself included, gets to its feet screaming with joy.

The kid who just scored is my ex's nephew, Brady. He's attending college across the country from his family and, at my ex's request, I came to watch his game today. The first time I met Brady was twelve years ago at a Fourth of July gathering my ex, Robert, dragged me to. Brady was eight then, a stocky, sports-loving kid with a broad smile and more energy than two suns. He was the third of five kids pumped out by Robert's sister, Madeline, and her husband, Greg. Robert and I had been going out for six months and this was the first time I was meeting his entire family. A little overwhelmed and feeling put out of sorts by all the familiar conversation going on around me, I stepped out into the yard for a moment to myself. I found Brady punting a football, chasing it across the yard only to turn around and punt it again. The kid cajoled me into tossing the ball with him and we spent an hour laughing and playing catch until Robert stepped out on the deck and called us in for dinner. I saw Brady a few times after that, all within the year Robert and I dated. We bonded a little because we both felt like outcasts at those gatherings: him the middle child and me his uncle's reluctantly acknowledged male date.

And so here I sit, watching as Brady, now twenty and playing college football, struts off the field. I wait a bit for the stands to clear before I make my way down and into the hall outside the locker room. The place smells of college man sweat, soap, and fresh dirt from the field, a mixture that shoots straight to my crotch and gets me half hard in minutes. I may be forty-four, but the plumbing works just as well as it did twenty years ago.

I wait for half an hour, talking with the quarterback's parents, who are smiling so broadly I fear their faces may split in half. The door to the locker room bangs open and a muscular group of players pours out, yelling and whooping and punching each other as they head for the exit. They all smell of soap and cologne and, just lightly, of clean, fresh sweat. My cock swells even more and I turn to watch the group of them run off down the hall, squinting to see if Brady is mixed in with them.

"Mike?" The voice is deep, tentatively hopeful.

I turn and feel a flutter in my heart at the sight of him. Brady has grown into a hot young man. Wide hazel eyes; dark red hair; broad smile filled with white, even teeth; square jaw shadowed with stubble. He stands six-three, an inch shorter than me, but his shoulders are broader.

"Uh, yeah," I say, caught off guard by my reaction to him. "I'm surprised you recognized me."

"Are you kidding? You were my hero!" He moves up to throw his strong arms around me, hugging me tight. I hesitate then hug him back, my hands feeling the muscles in his back even through his jacket. He steps back and his eyes take in my face. "Wow, it's so great to see you. I knew you lived out here but never thought I'd get to see you."

I shrug, embarrassed and turned on and flustered. "Well, your Uncle Robert wanted me to come watch the game so you'd have someone representing your family here. No one back home could get away."

"Yeah, I was bummed about that." He takes a breath and turns to wave as a few more guys file out of the locker room and pat him on the back, then he looks back to me. "What are you planning to do now?"

I blink and stuff my hands in my pockets to try and disguise my erection. "Um, well, you know. Probably head back to my apartment and get some things done around the house. I'm sure you've got parties to go to; I don't want to keep you, just wanted to let you know someone from your past saw your amazing play."

He grins at me. "Well, there is a party later, but how about we go to dinner and catch up? It's been a long time."

I catch myself nodding without realizing it. "Okay, sure. Dinner would be great."

I drive us to a steak house and am amazed at how open and comfortable Brady feels around me. I only saw him three times the entire year I dated his uncle. Robert and I broke up with the mutual decision we made better friends than lovers and have kept in touch ever since. I had heard about Brady's exploits as the kid grew up, saw the occasional school photo framed on Robert's desk but never saw him in person again until today.

"When did you move out here to California?" Brady asks as he slathers butter across a thick slice of warm bread.

"About five years ago. I got a promotion and was able to transfer to the Los Angeles office. I miss Boston the city, but not the weather."

Brady grins. "I hear that." He tears the buttered bread apart, thoughtful. "So, do you talk to Uncle Robert a lot?"

I shrug. "Sure. We're still good friends. We decided we were better friends than..." I let my voice trail off, not sure how much Brady knows about his uncle's personal life.

He looks up with a smirk. "It's okay, Mike. I've known Uncle Robert is gay for a long time." He sits back as the waitress places a thick, steaming steak before him. When she leaves he looks me in the eye and says, "I really liked you. I was bummed when you stopped coming to the family gatherings."

I don't know what to say and struggle for words. "Well, sometimes things just don't work out between people."

"Yeah, sometimes." He carves into his steak and pops a piece into his mouth, closing his eyes and moaning. "God, this is so good. I never eat like this."

"Welcome to college, here's your boxed macaroni and cheese and pizza coupons," I say and he laughs.

"Yeah, really. That should be part of the orientation." He focuses on cutting his meat, quiet, then asks, "So, are you dating anyone now?"

My stomach clenches at the hint of interest in his voice and manner. What the hell is going on? Brady is twenty-four years younger than I am; I dated his uncle, surely that makes what I cannot help watching in the back of my mind like some kind of endlessly looping porn film somehow wrong.

"Um, no. No one special." I tuck into my own steak and we fall silent as we both eat.

Later, I drop Brady off at his dorm and hand him a card with my various phone numbers listed. "Here. If you need something, give me a call okay? I know it's tough to be so far away from your family."

He leans down into the car and smiles at me as he slides the card into the back pocket of his jeans. I envy that card for a brief moment, tucked so close to the firm swell of his ass, then turn my attention back to his bright, hazel eyes.

"Thanks for dinner, Mike. It made the game a lot more special knowing someone I knew was watching. I'll talk to you soon."

"Take it easy, Brady."

I watch him take the steps to his dorm three at a time and consider those long, strong legs wrapped around my waist as I drive myself into his tight, willing ass faster and faster.

Shaking myself from the fantasy, I shift into DRIVE and head for my apartment. The moment I let myself in the door I begin to strip and move right to the bedroom. My cock is at full mast, precum dribbling down the pulsing shaft. I lie back on the comforter, wrap my hand around my aching dick and begin to stroke furiously. Images of Brady's young, strong body flip through my mind as I reach down with my left hand and stretch my balls out between my legs. I can see Brady's tight, pale asscheeks spread wide as I bury my face between them, my mouth and tongue working over his throbbing anus. Flash to his hard, strong cock, standing tall and proud over his dark red bush. Runners of my spit glide along the length to pool on his balls and in his pubes as I suck him hard and fast. My cock, in turn, is stuffed in Brady's mouth, his full lips clamped tight around it as I thrust into his throat, fucking his face.

I grunt as my balls fire off their pent-up load and cum splatters over my flat, hairy belly and up to my broad chest. I squeeze the slick, fat head of my cock, milking the last few drops of my spunk from the slit.

Afterward, I stand beneath the hot spray of the shower and try to stop thinking about Robert's nephew, focusing instead on the pile of paperwork I brought home with me on Friday. The trick works; my erection fades and I turn off the water, determined to get my mind off Brady.

A few weeks later I find myself staring at the calendar in disbelief. Good god, how did it get to be the Tuesday before Thanksgiving already? I've been consumed by work and have not had a chance to attend any more of Brady's games. I have called his dorm room a few times, left a couple of messages on his voice mail and received messages back from him, but we have not yet been able to connect. As I contemplate the image of another lonely Thanksgiving dinner spent eating alone in a restaurant and maybe going to see a movie by myself, I keep thinking of Brady. The kid has to be lonely this time of year. He's away from his family, his old friends. True, he has new friends, but most college kids go home for Thanksgiving to be with their families. Unless their family lives thousands of miles away.

I shake my head as I open my address book, pick up the phone and dial his number. This is ridiculous. He's going to have plans already and I'm going to appear to be a pathetic and lonely old man, which, apparently, I have become.

"Yo, Brady here, bust me a rhyme."

Thinking it is the voice mail again, I pause and wait for the beep.

"Hello?" It's his voice, questioning but friendly.

"Oh, Brady?" I stammer. "It's Mike. Mike Nelson."

"Hey, big Mike! How's it going?"

The kid sounds excited to hear from me and the tone of his voice lends me courage. "I'm well, thanks. Look, I know it's short notice, but I just realized this Thursday is Thanksgiving and I wanted to check and see if you had made any dinner plans. Thought I might whip us up something if you didn't have anything else going on."

"Oh, wow, that would be great," Brady replies. "That's so cool of you to invite me over. All I had to look forward to was cafeteria food, and 'look forward to' is really a euphemism for 'Oh dear god, please let me die now,' you know?"

We both laugh then he tells me he'll grab a cab or a bus over and not to worry about picking him up. I give him my address and tell him I'll supply all the food then hang up, simultaneously cursing myself and looking forward to Thanksgiving.

Thanksgiving morning I start to make dinner. I don't normally cook a lot; being single makes it tough, but I'm no slouch in the kitchen. I lather a ten-pound turkey with butter and seasonings, all the while trying not to imagine Brady himself stretched out on rubber sheets and covered with butter. I busy myself even more, keeping my mind distracted as I whip potatoes, slide the yams in the oven and cut up bacon for the green beans.

Right at three p.m. the bell announces Brady's arrival and I buzz him into the building, popping the hall door open and returning to the kitchen.

"Gobble, gobble," Brady calls and I turn to take him in. He's the picture of young health, wearing his letter jacket over khakis that fit him like old denim, and a green button-down shirt left open to reveal tufts of dark red hair on his chest, the material's color bringing out the green in his eyes.

I swoon at the sight of him then smile as innocently as possible. "Hey there, Happy Thanksgiving. Come on in and make yourself at home."

Brady drops his jacket on a chair and comes into the kitchen to stand behind me, a hand pressed against my back as he looks down to where I'm cutting celery for appetizers. He places a bottle of wine on the counter and I narrow my eyes at him.

"How did you buy that? You're only twenty."

He shrugs and grins, snatching a piece of celery to munch as he looks around at the dishes I've dirtied so far. "I've got my resources. Jesus, did you use every dish in the place?"

"Not yet," I reply. "But it's on my to-do list."

Brady starts rolling up his sleeves and moves toward the sink. "Looks like I'll earn this dinner."

"Hey, Brady, you don't have to do that. I'll clean up later."

Brady shakes his head. "After dinner is for visiting and getting to know the host. I don't want a pile of dishes waiting once the tryptophan kicks in."

We work well together; Brady cleans each dish and utensil and places it in the dish rack to dry as I bustle around him chopping and basting and stirring. I try not to stare too often, but his ass is a thing of beauty snuggled beneath the light khaki material and I cannot help myself. Once or twice he catches me looking and I blush.

"Sorry, it's just that you look so much like your mother," I explain, which he does.

"Yeah, I get that a lot."

Dinner is finally ready and, as Brady is retuning the last

mixing bowl to its rightful place, I set the turkey on the table and light the candles. He stands beside me, his hand on my back again, and looks at the table setting with shining eyes.

"Mike, this is so great of you," he says quietly. "I've been feeling really lonely out here this year. For some reason, this year is worse than my freshman year."

"Well, don't worry about that today. You're with a friend."

He turns to look at me, his face serious, and he says, "Thanks, that means a lot."

I tear my eyes from his and wave him to a chair at the end of the table. "Please, sit. I'll pour us some wine if you'll carve the turkey."

The meal is delicious, more so than I had hoped, and between the two of us we devour the turkey and most of the trimmings. Conversation runs from my job to his classes to the goings on of his family back home, but never once does he mention a girlfriend or, for that matter, boyfriend.

We leave the dishes to soak in the sink and move into the living room. I light the gas fireplace and several more candles scattered around the room. Brady chooses classical CDs from my collection and loads them into my player and we both sit on the soft leather couch.

"So, anyone special in your life?" I ask, ignoring the warning bells going off in the back of my mind.

Brady grins and stares into his wineglass. "No, not yet."

"Haven't found the right girl?"

He shrugs, keeping his eyes from me. "Something like that." He's quiet a little longer then says, "It's hard to find the qualities I like in the people around me."

I raise my eyebrows at this. "Oh? Qualities like what?"

"Oh, you know. Stuff like life experience, maturity, personality." He glances at me then darts his eyes away. "Things that most college kids won't have for years."

My cock begins to harden at the ideas running rampant in my mind and I chug the last of my wine, getting up to pour myself another glass as I say, "Sounds like you're attracted to older women."

"You could say that." He downs his own wine and holds out his glass for a refill. I turn away to set the wine on the table and when I turn back he has moved closer to my spot on the couch. Not much closer, but enough that I can tell he has done it.

I sit in my same spot, aware of the waves of heat coming off his strong body. "Brady, let me ask you a personal question."

He puts his head back against the cushion and smiles at me. "Sure, ask away."

"Are you gay?"

He is quiet, his eyes staring right into mine, then he nods and looks away. "Yeah. But don't tell my folks or Uncle Robert. They don't know yet."

"You know, it's not such a bad thing."

"Oh, I know, it's just...they'd have trouble with it at first, and I want to get some more experience before I tell them."

"More experience?"

He nods, spinning his wineglass slowly in his hand, eyes watching the swirling liquid. "I've fooled around with a few guys, but I've never gone all the way." He looks back at me. "I've been waiting to do that with someone I trust. Someone I care about."

My cock is a raging spike of flesh in my pants, precum leaking into my boxer briefs and threatening to soak through my wool pants. I keep my eyes on Brady's face as I ask, "What are you trying to say, Brady?"

Instead of answering me, he slides quickly across the slick leather cushion and presses his mouth over mine. The stubble on his jaw scratches across my smooth skin and sends shivers down my spine. His tongue pokes roughly at my lips, begging for access, which I grant him, opening my mouth and taking it in. He groans and leans into me, his big hand falling into my lap where he encounters my rigid cock and gasps.

"Oh, fuck," he moans against my mouth, "you're so fucking big and hard. Oh, fuck."

I put my hands on his shoulders and push him back a little, looking him in the eye. "Are you sure you want to do this?"

"Oh, yeah," he says in a breathy voice, his pupils dilated and his lips slightly swollen from the force of our kiss. "I've been attracted to you since I was eight."

I shake my head. "I feel like the priest in 'The Thorn Birds,'" I mutter.

Brady frowns. "Who?"

"Never mind." I lean forward, slowly, and cup his face in my palms. "You are a very attractive and outgoing kid. You could have anyone you wanted. Why me?"

He shrugs. "I like older men. And you were always really nice to me at our family gatherings. You're very attractive, Mike. Come on, it's okay. I'm not going to change my mind once we start."

I take a breath then lean forward and kiss him, hard. My tongue fills his mouth, wrestles with his own, then eases back over my lips, inviting his in for more. We kiss for a long time, tongues battling back and forth, mouths gasping, practically chewing at each other. I feel the muscles in his back move with his body and then slide my hands around to his chest. Football has filled him out, built up his torso. I unbutton his shirt and run my hands through the dark red hair on his chest, over his square pecs to pinch his small, round nipples. They harden into points that I tug on as Brady gasps and moans against my mouth.

"Oh, fuck," he says, leaning back to allow my hands to caress him. "That feels really good."

"You've got an amazing body," I tell him, my eyes roving his pale, muscular torso. His stomach is flat and ripped with muscle, the hair narrowing to a happy trail that disappears beneath the waist of his pants. I plant my fingers around his navel and press down to open it up then lean forward, darting my tongue into its salty depths. Brady gasps and lays a large, warm palm on the back of my head as I lick and suck at his navel. I move my mouth slowly up his stomach to his chest where I take each hardened nipple between my lips. I suck them, hard, and tug on them with my teeth as he squirms and moans beneath me.

Brady, meanwhile, has pulled my shirt from my pants and unbuttons it, spreading it open and sliding his hands inside to massage my hairy chest and belly. His fingers twist my nipples and I grunt against his chest.

"You've got a hot body, Mike," he says. "You must work out."

"Gotta keep the goods in shape so they can be put on display once in a while," I reply and he laughs.

"Let's go into the bedroom," he suggests. "I want to see you naked."

My mind is no longer screaming for me to stop, throwing up warning klaxons and flashing neon signs; my cock has overridden whatever logic may have existed and guides my body as I push up from the couch, my shirt hanging open. I take Brady's hand and lead him down the hall to the bedroom where I switch on a couple of low-watt lamps in the corners and turn back to where he stands beside the bed, still clothed, waiting for me.

"You're gorgeous," I say as I step up to him, my voice quiet and eyes serious.

"Funny, I was just thinking the same thing," Brady replies.

"What, that you're gorgeous?" I murmur, running my tongue around his ear.

He chuckles. "No, that you're gorgeous." His fingers slide beneath my shirt and ease it from my shoulders to fall on the floor. He moves his hands down over my chest and belly, parting the hair before his fingers and stopping to twist my nipples and squeeze my pecs.

I mirror his move, sliding his shirt off and feeling his chest, and lean forward to kiss him, softly at first then more insistent. He wraps his arms around my neck and pulls our bodies together, his hips grinding against mine and pressing his firm cock alongside my own erection.

Unable to take it any longer, I break our embrace and fall to my knees before him. My mouth is dry as I fumble with the buckle on his belt, finally getting it open and undoing the button and zipper on his khakis. His pants fall around his ankles and I find myself staring at the overflowing pouch of a jockstrap.

"Oh, god," I groan. "That is so fuckin' hot."

"I thought you'd like it." He moves his hips forward, pressing the thin, stuffed cotton against my mouth. "I wore it while I was working out this week. Haven't washed it yet."

My own cock jumps as I open my mouth and run my lips and tongue over the sweaty pouch damp with his precum. I bite softly along the length of his dick, pressing my tongue against the straining cotton as I move up and down the shaft. He is at least seven inches long, and thick. I reach the top of his jock and find the fat, bulging head peeking up from beneath the waistband. The smooth, silky skin glistens with precum, inviting me to run my tongue across its surface. Brady groans, pressing his hands against the back of my head.

I peel the waistband of his jock down and release the confined serpent. His cock stands straight up along his belly, almost reaching his navel. The dark red bush around the base spreads out to a thick forest that runs down along his muscular, powerful legs. I stare at the gorgeous dick before me as I reach to lift each of his feet and pull the jock and his pants off. I then peel off his socks and run my hands along the tops of his large, handsome feet, up along the bulges of his calves, across the hairy expanse of his thighs until they meet at the *V* in his crotch. I tightly grab hold of his pulsing cock and pull down until it is pointing right at my face. Leaning in, I open my mouth and take him down my throat, tasting the slick of precum left behind along my tongue.

"Oh, fuck," Brady gasps. "You sucked that fucker right down to the root. Oh, god."

His hips begin to move and soon he is fucking my face, his fingers snarled in clumps of my hair. I reach down to free my own cock from its prison of boxer-brief cotton and stroke myself as Brady's dick slides in and out between my lips.

He grunts, a deep, animal sound that makes my balls clench with desire, and suddenly my mouth is filled with the sharp taste of his cum. He pulls my face in tight against his body, my nose buried in his sweaty bush, and empties his balls down my throat. I greedily swallow his load, relishing the taste of his spunk as my hand moves faster along my cock.

"Don't cum yet," he gasps. "I want you to cum on my face."

He slowly pulls his cock from between my lips and helps me to my feet. His hands push my pants down and I step out of them as he leads me to the bed where he stretches out on his back. I kneel on the mattress and position myself over him in push-up position, my stiff cock pointing down right over his open, eager mouth. I ease my hips down and he closes his lips around my shaft, sucking hard as I begin to fuck his face. He reaches up and begins to pull on my nipples, an act that pushes me even closer to the edge of orgasm.

Just as I'm reaching the point of no return, I sit up and back on his chest, pulling my cock from his mouth. He watches as I stroke my dick, slick with his spit, my eyes locked on his. His mouth, full lips wet and parted, is open, ready to take my load, and the sight flips my switch.

"I'm cumming," I moan and feel Brady's hands tighten on my thighs in anticipation. My stroking narrows to the magic spot just beneath the head of my cock and I aim it down just as the first surge of semen spurts forth. The shot splatters across his cheek and he groans. The rest of my load floods his mouth and halfway through I stuff my cock between his lips, leaning back as he suckles it greedily, eyes closed, fingers gripping my sweaty thighs.

A few minutes go past and I finally roll off him, reluctantly pulling my dick from his soft, sticky lips. I lie beside him, my arm around his shoulders as he rolls against me, his head on my chest and shoulder in my armpit. We are a perfect fit.

"Do you want to clean up?" I ask through a yawn. The turkey and the sex have ganged up on my middle-aged stamina: I am exhausted.

"No, I like the feel of your cum drying on my face." Brady kisses my chest and reaches down to squeeze my softened cock, pushing drops of clear fluid up out of it.

We fall asleep like that and lie peacefully until I startle awake several hours later. The room is darker, the sun has set by now, and I look down at Brady's soft, unlined face, so young, so open and calm in sleep. He stirs a little and his eyes blink open, confused for a moment until he raises his head and sees me, then he smiles broadly and my heart jumps in my chest.

"Hi," he says, running his tongue over his teeth. "How long were we asleep?"

"Awhile," I say vaguely. "Want to take a shower?"

He nods and follows me into the bathroom. I have a large, glassed-in shower with two showerheads and a built-in bench along the side. We step beneath the hot spray and take turns lathering each other up. His large hands, so nimble with the football, are soft and find all the right places to get me hard again.

I turn him to face away from me and run soap over his wide shoulders, down the ridges of his spine and over the round, tight mounds of his ass. I nudge the pulsing wrinkle of his anus with a soapy finger and Brady immediately lifts a foot to the bench, opening his asscheeks and allowing me access to his asshole. With slow, delicate movements I slide my index finger into him and watch as he tips his head back, the hot water bouncing off his firm chest.

"Oh, yeah," Brady groans. "Get it in deep."

I oblige, fucking his ass with my index finger as I reach up to turn his face so I can kiss him. We stay that way for several minutes, my finger pumping into his ass while our tongues grapple together between our mouths.

"I want you to fuck me," he sighs. "I want your dick to be the first one inside me."

Eager to satisfy his request and my fantasy, I switch off the water and grab two towels. We kiss as we dry off, our hands straying to touch, fondle, squeeze each other. My eyes devour the sight of his muscular, long-limbed body as my cock twitches and leaks precum.

Brady drops to his knees to suck my cock deep for a moment, licking it clean of precum. He gets to his feet, kisses me then leads me back to the bed.

"What do you want me to do?" he asks, his eyes glowing.

I do not hesitate. "Lie on your back and raise your legs."

He follows my orders and I lean down to feast on his tender, virgin asshole. My fingers spread his anus to allow my tongue admission to the hot, damp darkness hidden behind his beautiful rosebud. I lick and suck, spitting into the reddened opening and slipping one, two, then three fingers into him.

"Goddamn," Brady groans, turning his head side to side. "Get those fingers up inside me. Yeah, that's it."

"Ready for something bigger?" I ask, my voice deep with longing.

"Give it to me," he says and looks up at me. "I want your cock in me. I've fantasized about this for years."

I don't need any more convincing. I grab a condom from the nightstand and roll it onto my throbbing prick then squirt a large helping of lube across it. I pull Brady to the edge of the bed and take hold of his ankles, pushing them back over his head to lift his hips and bring his asshole up to the height of my crotch. Brady reaches down to take hold of my cock, wraps his fingers around its girth for a moment before directing it to the spit-slippery threshold of his body.

I take it slow, pressing firmly into him for a few moments then pulling back, feeling his body gradually relax around my invading member. Brady keeps his eyes on my face and concentrates on loosening the muscles in his rectum as I slide slowly in and out of his hole.

"Does that feel okay?" I ask.

"Yeah, it feels good. Go deeper."

I press harder on my next thrust and stop three quarters of the way inside him at a muscular blockade. Brady gasps and closes his eyes then laughs a little.

"Sorry, I guess I wasn't ready."

I pull back, the head of my cock just inside his sphincter, and ask, "Ready now?"

He nods and closes his eyes as his fingers tighten their grip on his legs just above the knees. "Yeah. Drive that fucker in."

Slowly, very slowly, I penetrate his spreading sphincter. His rectal muscles part before the rounded head of my cock and, with a last, deep push, I am embedded completely within him.

"Oh, fuck," he says. "You are fucking huge. Oh, god!"

I pull back and begin to fuck him, my hips starting slow but picking up speed until I find myself banging his ass like some kind of porn star. Sweat flies from my forehead and I watch his balls bounce with each of my thrusts. Brady takes the brunt of my fucking with his mouth gaping open, eyes closed, hard cock bumping up and down along his flat belly.

"Oh, god," he moans again. "You're fucking the cum right out of me. Oh, fuck."

I look down to watch as his dick jumps and cum sprays up to his chest. He has not touched himself; his hands are still clasping his legs. The sight of his hands-free cum shot gets me going and I throw back my head to groan as I plow deep between his round, pale asscheeks and blow my load into the condom buried high up inside his ass.

I lean my head against his leg as we catch our breath, then I slowly pull out of him. His asshole is red, gaping, and I hold his legs up to watch it slowly close as I peel off the condom. Brady finally lowers his legs and pulls me down on top of him, his cum and our sweat mixing together. We kiss for a long, slow time, and then he runs his hands through my hair and smiles up at me.

"Happy Thanksgiving, Mike."

I laugh and kiss him. "Happy Thanksgiving, Brady." I get up and lead him back into the bathroom where we shower quickly. Afterward, I loan him one of my terry-cloth bathrobes and we sit on the floor by the fire eating pumpkin pie with real whipped cream.

"Thanks for inviting me over for dinner," Brady says around

a mouthful of pie. "My bird really needed to be stuffed. I can't wait to do it again."

I shake my head and grin at him. "Are you sure you want to pursue this?"

He nods and sets his plate aside then gets to his knees and walks to me, untying his robe to expose his erection. "Oh, yeah. I'm sure."

I open my mouth and start to suck his cock once more, trying to remember the last time I'd gone back for thirds at Thanksgiving.

# SOMETIMES SEX JUST...HAPPENS

Daniel W. Kelly

Hey, Kooky," Scott greeted Tim, with a big bear hug and one of his varying pet names.

Comfort washed over Tim as he was taken into the strong arms of his towering friend, whose masculine voice exuded honest adoration.

When the two had met through a mutual friend three years ago, the summer right before Tim began college, they had clicked immediately. Scott, more than a decade Tim's senior, had been single, but Tim had been in a committed relationship with his high school sweetheart since day one of his young coming out.

Tim was innocently flirty, had a rambunctious personality—due in part to the A.D.D. he chose not to have diagnosed or treated—and loved to get playfully under the skin of anyone who could handle his hyperactive nature. Scott's thirty-four years of life experience, his time in the bear and leather scene and his stern look that clashed with his gentle temperament, easygoing ways and heart of gold, had awoken Tim's curiosity, respect and desire.

Had their circumstances been different when they'd met, their relationship would have been different, too. Neither had any problems with pushing the envelope, teasing and arousing the other with words and playful feel-ups. Theirs was an extremely physical platonic friendship.

Now, circumstances were different, but once again, not in favor of the sparks that burned between them. Tim's one and only relationship had come to an end recently. As it had been taking a downward turn, Scott had met Ken, his boyfriend for almost a year now. Other men imagined spying on them while they were in bed together—which spoke volumes to how perfect a package they were.

Scott's sparkling blue eyes were deeply set into his square-cut features. He had short-cropped dirty blond/graying hair, and was currently sporting a full, neatly trimmed beard. His barrel chest, thunder thighs, bulging stomach and swelling back looked more like the results of laboring as a lumberjack than actually going to the gym, and his thick layer of body hair was somehow darker than that on his head.

Tim walked the edge between pretty boy and cub. His dark looks were intense, his high cheekbones and dark eyes captivating. He usually did the whole gold hoop earrings, slick spiked hair and sleek clothes thing. Occasionally, he dabbled in his bear potential, throwing on jeans and a flannel shirt and sporting scruffy facial hair while close-shaving his head, but one could still detect the fun-loving young soul hidden right beneath the manly surface. Because of his young age, the dark coat of body hair he sometimes exposed when wearing a tank surprised and delighted bear hunters.

Scott placed a soft kiss on Tim's lips—he was one of only

a few people Tim would be so intimate with, usually turning the cheek to lip-obsessed acquaintances—and playfully pinched Tim's nipples.

"Aaah!" Tim giggled, pulling away and covering his chest.

"How you doing?" Scott asked.

"Better now that I'm with you." Tim fell back into Scott's arms.

"Awh...you're so sweet," Scott cooed as he held his friend tightly in his bulging arms. "I'm so happy to see you."

Scott kissed him on his head and they stood there for a moment longer before Tim's anxious personality kicked in.

"Where's hot Ken?" Tim moved over to a rack of DVDs, dividing his attention in order to look through them for any new ones.

Scott was in the nearby kitchen area, pouring Tim some lemonade as he answered, "He's upstairs just finishing his shower."

He handed Tim the beverage.

"You guys didn't shower together?" Tim put his lemonade on a small table beside an easy chair, grabbed the remote and began flicking through the television stations without sitting down.

"Not this time. We would never have finished before you got here."

"What the heck? You know how much I want to watch you two shower together," Tim feigned annoyance. "You always promise."

"Hey, Scotty? I need to borrow a shirt," a voice said from the next room.

Ken entered in only a pair of sweat shorts, showing off his stocky but defined build—as wide and powerful looking as Scott's, but a bit more polished. He had warm brown eyes, short but thick mahogany hair, and a well-groomed goatee. His body hair formed itself in tight curls on his chest, arms and legs.

"Hey Tim," he said, moving to hug the new arrival. "I didn't know you were here already."

Tim felt the coolness of Ken's freshly showered body, savored the hard muscle that pressed against him and inhaled the sweet scent of herbal shampoo. "Hey, hottie Ken."

"How you doin', kiddo?" Ken asked. It had been agreed there would be no detailed breakup discussion tonight.

"I'm okay," Tim said.

"You look cute as always," Ken commented.

Tim, always quick to warm up to people who were special to the people who were special to him, had won Ken over the night Scott had first introduced them.

"So, what do you want to do? Go out to eat? Or get pizza and stay in?" Scott asked.

Tim shrugged.

"You don't look so up to going out." Ken noted the somewhat subdued manner of the usually vibrant younger man.

Tim shrugged again.

"Kooks, this is your night," Scott said. "Whatever you want to do."

"I'd kind of rather stay in," Tim admitted.

"That's fine. No need to get all dressed up then." Scott was wearing just a wifebeater and shorts with a string tie. "Huns, you can grab a shirt from my middle drawer," he said to Ken, giving him a smooch on the lips and rubbing his bare back.

"If we're staying in, I'm okay like this," Ken replied.

"Yes! So glad I decided we should stay in," Tim cheered, breaking out of his shell a little.

Ken blushed as he took a seat on the plush couch in front of the TV. He was more sexually reserved than Scott, not wanting to step on anyone's feet by being overly flirtatious, which is why he was always entertained when Scott and Tim derived pleasure from creating an almost tangible sexual tension between each other, and always turned red when Tim flattered him.

"Uh-oh," Scott rolled his eyes and rubbed Tim's head. "Someone's horny."

"I'm always horny," Tim dropped to the floor and grabbed a hardcore leather magazine from a pile on the coffee table.

Scott joined Ken on the couch. "So what are you doing? Looking at the porno mags or watching the video channel?" he provoked Tim. "Focus, focus."

"Both. That's the point of my special talent," Tim replied smartly as he flipped through the magazine. "Ooh. Yummy. Look at this."

He held up an explicit spread.

"Yes, I've seen it. And I thought of you and which of those three guys you'd like to be when I saw it."

Tim gave a devilish look. "I already know who I want the other two guys to be."

Ken laughed self-consciously, which was Tim's cue to start causing trouble. He crawled across the floor on his knees, threw his arms around Scott's waist, and dropped his head into Scott's lap, pressing his cheek to the warm bulge.

Scott instinctively began rubbing Tim's back and neck affectionately.

"How many times am I going to have to beg you guys?" Tim asked, looking with bedroom eyes over at Ken's bashful smile.

"Hey, he's the boss," Ken patted his boyfriend's head.

"Come on, Scott. Be the boss," Tim said. "Boss me around. I'll do anything. And tell Ken what to do to me."

"Oh, please. You're all talk," Scott said as he massaged his friend.

"Just let me watch you guys together. It would be so hot."

"For you maybe," Scott smirked.

"Why are you always so mean to me?" Tim acted like a hurt little brother. "Come on. Whatever it costs, I'll do it."

"Please. You're too innocent to do anything."

"No way! I can be a pig." Tim was bouncing his upper body on Scott's lap.

"You *wanna* be a pig," Scott corrected. "But you'll never go through with it."

"Pleeeaaasse!" Tim begged, shaking Scott to annoy him. He reached his hands up and tried to snatch hold of Scott's large nipples, permanently swollen from years of tugging, as they practically burst through the material of his wifebeater.

"Uuugghh! This one's gonna drive me to drink," Scott groaned, wrapping his hands around Tim's wrists, dwarfing them in the process. Tim tried to pull away, with no success. He was wriggling all over Scott's lap, and Scott began to laugh, looking to his boyfriend. "What can we make him do?"

"You're asking me? I don't know." Ken sat there in his typical serious manner, and then suggested, "Our dirty jockstraps are on top of the hamper in the bathroom."

"Aha! That's a good idea. They're still nice and smelly. We were at the racquet ball court right before you came over."

"So what am I supposed to do with them?" Tim gave Scott a mock submissive look as they continued their little tug of war with his wrists. "And what do I get in return?"

"What do *you* get in return? One of these days I'm gonna have to teach you the rules of being a little bitch. But, you want something?" Scott asked, and Tim nodded. "What you get depends on how far you go. How about…"

"What? Dare me, and I'll do it."

"You so wouldn't do this," Scott thought aloud.

"I so will," Tim challenged.

"Okay. Go upstairs and come down with one of our dirty jocks in your mouth."

"Ugh," Ken cringe-giggled.

"He so won't do it." Scott rubbed Tim's head.

"I totally will," Tim insisted, standing up. "They're in the hamper or on top of it?"

"On top," Ken said.

"Wait, there's more." Scott stopped Tim from walking boldly from the room.

"Oh, boy," Ken said, knowing how much his boyfriend loved to see just how far he could get Tim to go.

"What?" Tim asked.

"You have to *wear* the other jockstrap, and nothing else."

Tim hesitated for a moment but didn't really have time to let the new challenge sink in before Scott continued, "*and*, you have to come down here on all fours like a dog."

"Scott, don't make him…" Ken was the voice of reason, but Scott frowned with furrowed brows at his boyfriend, shaking his head in a *he'll never do it* gesture.

"I'm *so* doing it," Tim contradicted Scott's nonverbal comment as he left the room.

"He's not gonna do it," Scott promised Ken.

"You've known him longer than I have, and *you* don't think he'll do it? He's still getting over his boyfriend leaving him, and he's so frisky as it is…."

"Well, it wouldn't be such a bad thing seeing him crawling around in a jockstrap, would it?" Scott pointed out.

"No…it really wouldn't," Ken admitted.

Upstairs, Tim found the two jockstraps right where Ken said they would be. His heart was pounding in his chest as he removed the clothes he'd thrown on less than an hour ago. His nipples quickly shrunk to points. His dick was already at full attention—had been since he'd begun taking orders from Scott.

He pulled on one jockstrap (it was still sort of moist, perhaps from the condensation formed after his two friends' showers?) and then moved the other toward his mouth. He smelled it first. It was musky...definitely the rank odor of crotch sweat. He thought of putting it in his mouth, considered what it must taste like, considered carrying it in his hand until he was right near the den where the big guys waited, realized his mouth was totally watering and then pushed himself to the edge—as always.

He bundled the jockstrap into a ball and wrapped his lips around it. For a moment, he thought the taste of the sweaty cloth was going to make him gag, but he swallowed hard, and allowed his salivary glands to become accustomed to the spice. Mouth full of man crotch remnants, he got down on his hands and knees, shivering as air crawled into his ass crack.

"Uh...I think I hear someone coming," Scott was saying on the couch as he was flicking through the television stations. "Did he chicken out?"

Scott and Ken looked to the doorway. The first thing they saw over the armrest of the couch was Tim's spiky hair rising up.

"He seriously did it," Ken said in awe as the nearly naked Tim crawled up to Scott.

"You little bitch whore," Scott laughed with impressed shock at his daring friend, who waited at his feet with the article he had fetched, to either be let off the hook or instructed further. "You like that?" Scott petted his head then grabbed the jockstrap and began playing tug of war. Tim fought back with his teeth, which sunk firmly into the fabric.

"You wanna come up?" Scott patted his lap.

Tim obeyed. He made his way around the coffee table, and

stepped over Ken's feet as Ken tried to move them out of the way.

"You two are unbelievable." Ken giggled in awe at what he was witnessing.

Tim climbed his way onto the couch and draped himself over Scott's lap. Ken couldn't disguise his appreciation of the swelling ass that protruded from the jockstrap, revealing two furry cheeks and a fur-filled crack as Tim's calves landed on his muscular thighs.

"This little bitch is in heat," Scott giggled as Tim served himself up. "Look at his ass begging for some attention." He placed one large hand on Tim's butt and rubbed his cheeks lightly. "You want me to spank you, don't you?"

Tim nodded. He'd spent pretty much the whole of their friendship hounding Scott to administer the spanking he so deserved. Scott had often described in detail his participation in spanking sessions, knowing how hot it made Tim.

"You think he needs a spanking?" Scott asked his boyfriend, making sure the man he was in a committed relationship with wouldn't object to a little play.

"I'd say so," Ken shrugged.

Scott gave the round surface a good swat. Tim barked through the saliva-soaked material in his mouth at the unexpected sting. Scott couldn't help but giggle as Ken rolled his eyes and shook his head. A slap on the other cheek, and Tim's grunt ended in a muffled sigh.

"Ooh...he likes it," Scott said, rubbing Tim's cheeks before administering another echoing, open-handed blow.

"You're making his ass red," Ken pointed out from his close-up spectator's view.

"He can take it," Scott reassured Ken. "I think he probably wants you to teach him a lesson, too."

"I can't, Scott," Ken begged off. "He's not as close to me as he is to you."

Tim's ass shook in disagreement. Scott smirked at Ken, and Ken turned red as he bit his lip in hesitation.

"Just do it," Scott sounded almost childish.

Ken brought both hands down on Tim's rump. Tim moaned. Ken left his hands on each cheek.

"His ass...feels so good," Ken confessed as he glanced into his lover's eyes.

"I know," Scott nodded. "I've always loved his ass." He took hold of Ken's hands, and they rubbed Tim's butt together, leaning in and sucking on one another's lips as they did so. Scott slowly coaxed his lover, bringing their fingers through the jungle of hair that exposed itself as Tim brought his hips up to open himself to the possibility of exploration. Scott gently pulled Tim's globes apart, and said in a hushed tone, "He wants more."

Ken gave his lover one last look and kiss, then turned his attention to Tim's hairy mounds. He used his fingers to burrow his way toward the center, searching for the prize.

Scott, meanwhile, wrapped his massive arm around Tim's head, and tucked it safely under his armpit, saying, "Just relax, cubby bear. Tonight's all about you. Whatever you want. There's nothing but love in this room."

Tim had his arms around Scott's thigh, and he gave it a tight squeeze to signal that he felt safe. He *was* getting what he really wanted...Scott was making him relinquish control and have someone else call the shots for a change.

Ken exhaled in wonderment as he parted tufts of hair and found the tightly drawn pink curtain that was Tim's asshole.

Scott placed his free hand on the back of Ken's head and lowered him toward the waiting orifice.

Ken felt no guilt as he placed his tongue in the most private spot of a man other than his lover. His cock pulsed with loving warmth as he recognized that, even though Scott and Tim didn't see each other that often, their bond was so deep that they were like an extension of each other. Making Tim feel good tonight was going to make his lover feel good. He began to lick and sample Tim's slit like it was Scott's. Love and permission coursed through him as Scott stroked his hair. His testicles were burning from the intense passion.

"That looks so beautiful," Scott was whispering above him.

Tim's fuck hole came alive as it was exposed to the conflicting texture of Ken's silky wet tongue and gruff, prickly goatee.

Ken came up for air and glanced lovingly at Scott. Their mouths and tongues connected. Scott ate Tim's lingering taste from Ken's mouth as their locked lips hovered above the saliva-soaked asshole that Ken still held apart. Scott gently pushed Ken's face back into Tim's crack and then lifted his arms to pull his wifebeater off over his head.

Tim, head free, finally dropped the jockstrap from his mouth and lunged for the nearest distraction—the bush of hair under Scott's raised arm. He licked and slurped at the light moisture that had gathered there since Scott's shower.

Scott tossed his shirt across the room and kept his arms raised for Tim. But Tim's attention didn't linger too long on the armpit. He craned back so he could reach the closest nipple and attached himself to it.

Scott heaved with pleasure and closed his eyes. Then he felt another mouth nipping at his other nipple. He opened his lids and watched as Ken took a break from dining on Tim's ass to join in the nipple play. Each of his gorgeous men was licking and sucking on the protruding mounds, taking flesh and chest fuzz into their mouths. He wrapped his massive arms around them and kissed the tops of the two thick heads of hair that were making his nipples—and cock—throb.

Tim was in heaven, with Scott's cock poking into his gut and Ken's rock-hard pecs pressed against his asscheeks, as Ken leaned over him to suck Scott's other nipple.

But the experience had just begun. Scott and Ken flipped Tim onto his back on Scott's lap and removed his jockstrap. Tim lay completely naked in front of the two big bears, his cock sprawled across his lower belly. Ken got on all fours at the end of the couch and hunkered down to take it into his mouth. Scott used his big hands to rub the layers of hair on Tim's torso.

Tim closed his eyes to focus his mind on the physical sensation. As Ken moistened his cock, gliding up and down on it steadily, Scott plucked at his nipples, using each index finger to circle Tim's rather large areolas, then bringing index finger and thumb together to gently squeeze and twist each one.

Tim's head began to roll from side to side, and his body convulsed. His groin started to grind into Ken's mouth automatically. Scott, playing Tim's chest like it was some sort of instrument, half smiled through his golden beard, watching Tim fuck his boyfriend's mouth. His heart fluttered as he ogled the two men that he loved opening up entirely for each other.

Tim began to whinny like a horse, his body spasms deepening as all his internal erogenous nerves were pushed to the edge and, for a change, he was faced with more stimulation than he knew what to do with.

His mouth still around Tim's dick, Ken brought his brown eyes up to Scott's face, wondering if they should give Tim a moment to recuperate. Scott nodded. Tim's fantasies were all filed in Scott's mind. He would never forget the second time they'd met, while at a party, and Tim, probing him with explicit questions, had brazenly asked, "Do you have a hairy ass?"

Scott had just as boldly turned around, stuck out his bulbous buttocks and pulled down the waistband of his pants as just a tease, showing Tim the hair-covered muscle underneath. Tim's reply had been a wide-eyed, "If you ever need a place to sit..." as he tapped on his lips.

Scott pushed the coffee table out of the way and instructed his boyfriend to put his knees on the floor and bend over the couch cushions. Ken did as he was told. Scott grabbed the top of Ken's shorts and yanked them down and then out from under his knees and feet, revealing a meaty, muscular ass covered in mahogany curls. He pulled off his own shorts and straddled Ken, bringing his ass right over Ken's and lying across Ken's back. Ken looked up over his shoulder and the two began to kiss.

Scott did not instruct Tim in any way.

Tim stood completely hard and completely stunned at the stacked asses on the couch. His eyes followed the two perfectly aligned hairy cracks that traveled from Ken's balls up to the treasure trail at the small of Scott's back. He swallowed hard and then, anxious, lowered himself onto his hand and knees. He was so excited—and nervous—that his arms were shaking, making it hard to hold himself up. He crawled closer, leaned down farther, stuck out his tongue and licked his way up from Ken's scrotum.

With the first contact of Tim's tongue, Ken got goose bumps and groaned into Scott's mouth. The groan transferred from Ken's mouth to Scott's and then back again as Tim traveled the long slot, starting his journey all over from the beginning once he was done—giving new meaning to the term *doing laps*. His initially slow exploration of their assholes soon grew more frenzied. He began licking his way up quickly, not knowing where to focus first. Ken and Scott both felt Tim jumping back and forth, drilling his face between each of their asses, munching and slobbering all over them. The two stopped kissing for a moment and laughed softly as they felt the furious attack and Tim's saliva soaking every strand of hair sprouting from the area surrounding their assholes. It got to the point where Tim seemed to forget that the puckers he was feasting on were attached to men.

It was finally time for another major shift in the action. Scott and Ken dismounted, and Scott bent Tim over the couch in the exact spot where Ken had just been. Tim immediately arched his back in anticipation.

Scott leaned over him and whispered in his ear, "You stop this at any time if it's not right for you."

Tim's only response was to kiss Scott on his bearded cheek. The go-ahead shot through every nerve in Scott's body.

Scott dropped to his knees and gulped down Ken's swollen cock. Ken watched as his boyfriend coated it with gobs of glistening spit, then turned his attention to Tim's raised cheeks. He dug his face between them and quickly lubricated him orally as well. Tim was watching this entire process over his shoulder. Between his legs, a long stream of precum poured forth.

Scott moved aside and separated Tim's asscheeks. Ken dropped down and placed the head of his soaked cock into the opening. Hands free, he simply pushed forward, spearing Tim slowly.

The fucker and the fuckee vocalized in unison, Ken exhaling his appreciation while Tim gasped his. Ken looked down and took in the visual of his cock embedding itself into the hairy crevasse his boyfriend held open for him. Ken rebounded as soon as he was all the way in and immediately began riding Tim's ass.

Scott massaged Tim's glutes, separating and bringing the cheeks together in time with Ken's thrusts. He and Ken sucked face while Ken kept up his pelvic motion. Ken thought it incredible to be experiencing the joy of his lover's kiss while his dick was being engulfed by Tim's tight, warm insides.

"It's good, right?" Scott asked him. "He's got a beautiful ass."

"He's fucking gorgeous," Ken confessed.

"Fuck me, hot Ken," Tim said softly.

Tim reached his hands back and placed them on his ass, finding Scott's hands. Ken placed his hands there, too, and the three intertwined their fingers. Tim was put at ease by the gentle contact of the two men he was completely opening himself up to, and he felt a lump in his throat. Ken was only the second man who had ever entered him...and it seemed more intense than his relations with his ex. There was something magical about giving in to a man based on absolute trust in another man's judgment of character. If Ken was wonderful for Scott, then he was wonderful for Tim. And from the more lustful perspective, it was just hot permitting the use of his fuck hole to two hairy hunks as he played a side role in their love for each other.

Scott stood and inched his cock into his boyfriend's mouth so Ken could prep him for his turn. When he was good and wet, Ken pulled out of Tim and stepped aside. Scott swiftly mounted his friend, and then just stayed in his anal embrace for a moment. He draped himself over Tim's back and whispered in his ear, "It's me, kooky bear."

"Make me feel good, Scott," Tim requested.

With total understanding, Scott took things up a notch, not holding back as Ken had. Tim wanted to be fucked by a bear. Fucked good and hard. Scott began pouncing on him, nailing his body into the couch. Fucking like an animal, basically.

Tim began whimpering as he felt his tunnel being intruded mercilessly. Scott's cock was creating a burning friction within him. He'd wanted this for so long, imagined sacrificing himself to Scott, having Scott's solid furry frame plastered to his. The combination of Scott's sexual experience and knowledge of Tim's desires were making for a fuck Tim had never fathomed. He was on an emotional and physical high, and his balls felt like they were on fire.

"Oh god Sco-oo-oo-ot, that's so-oo-oo-oo go-oo-oo-oo-oo-od!" Tim nearly sobbed as he edged toward emotional and erotic euphoria, his sustained tone skipping with each of Scott's repeated crash landings on his pelvis.

Behind them, Ken witnessed about four years of pent-up barbaric hunger being unleashed, and it was breathtaking. He began to masturbate.

"I want to look at you," Scott finally broke in as Tim's cries of pleasure reached a fevered pitch. Scott pulled out, and got onto his back on the couch, with his legs hanging off the edge. He held his cock up.

Tim climbed on, slipping all the way down to Scott's balls, then tightened and loosened his anal muscles without moving. He reached out and stroked Scott's beard.

Scott smiled without saying anything. They just stared at each other, not allowing any awkwardness to creep in. Tim dropped onto him and held him. Scott could feel tremors running through Tim's small physique.

Ken positioned himself behind them. He'd smeared his own precum over the head of his dick. He got down, lifted his partner's legs as much as he could without interfering with their positioning, and licked Scott's asshole a few times. Then he placed the head of his cock against Scott's pulsing opening, and allowed it to slip in. He slowly fucked Scott, lying on Tim's back as Tim and Scott began to share their deepest, longest kiss ever.

Tim reached in between his and Scott's stomachs so he could

masturbate. The sweaty, hair-matted torsos of both bears were sandwiching him together, and with Scott parked way up inside him, he had never felt such ecstasy in his life.

"I love you so much," Tim said to Scott, and then panted with each expulsion of cum that landed on Scott's belly—and as far up as his chin.

"I love you too," Scott responded, and as Tim's ass clamped down with each ejaculation, Scott let his own climax pour forth, filling Tim.

Ken withdrew from Scott, and without removing himself from Tim's back, he yanked himself to climax. His cum spurted onto the top center of Tim's parted cheeks and slid its way down and around Scott's cock as if to cement it within Tim's opening.

The three lay crushing each other, syncing the rise and fall of their breathing, sucking in the damp scent of sweat and sex.

As the silence descended, Tim suddenly spoke. "I can't believe you two would take advantage of me at such a vulnerable time in my life." His charming mischievous grin spread across his face.

Scott looked over Tim's shoulder at Ken, and they both grinned.

"He's such a little bitch," Scott panted.

None of the three was ready yet to get out of their cramped, sticky situation. They wanted to linger in the memory of what had just...happened.

# SPIT SHINE

C. C. Williams

"What's the matter, Dan?" Ryan paused the Xbox, stilling a zombie in mid-explosion. "You're pacing like a caged lion." His blue eyes gleamed, filled with concern. At twenty-one, Ryan was really still just a pup, growing into his paws. And like a puppy, he was young, adorable and eager to please—or to follow any command I might give him.

I grabbed a handful of his straw-colored hair and messed up the carefully faux-hawked look, making him appear even more irresistibly boyish.

"It's nothing." I ducked, evading his attempt at revenge. "Just the usual Sunday evening blues: I'm thinking about the Myerson prosecution and really *not* looking forward to heading into the office tomorrow."

"Then don't think about it!" He shrugged, turning back to the undead invasion. Employing a machete and Uzi, he cleared the level. "You want to fuck?"

Slightly amazed, I looked up from the crossword I was trying to finish. "Ryan! For crissakes! You spent half of the night handcuffed to the bed, and I screwed the living daylights out of you in the shower this morning! How much more sex can your ass take, anyway?"

Ryan shot me a bad-boy leer. "My ass can handle anything you can dish out, stud. What do you say we put in some porn? I got a new DVD with those hot Czech twins! Yummy!"

Over the years I've found it rarely pays to let your lover get too cocky. "Maybe later." I pretended to stifle a yawn. "I've got to polish my shoes for the morning."

"I'll get the polish," Ryan offered—a hint of mischief sparking in his eye. Something was up—Ryan and manual labor rarely occupied the same piece of space-time. Abandoning the video game, he vanished from the family room. Returning from the bedroom, he confirmed my suspicions—he'd changed out of the jeans and button-down shirt he'd worn to brunch. Dressed only in a torn, gray T-shirt, white Jockey shorts, and a pair of dirty gym socks, he looked hot as hell.

"Something tells me—"

"Shh!" Ryan held a finger to his lips. Favoring me with a view of his tight ass, he rummaged under the kitchen sink and came up with the cardboard box I keep filled with various pastes and waxes. "One shoeshine coming up!"

He beamed, quite pleased with himself. After spreading out some old newspapers on the kitchen floor right under my feet, he searched through the shoeshine box for the black polish. "You might have to remind me how this is done," he warned me. "It's been a while."

Curious to see just exactly where all this was leading, I decided to play along with his game. "All right, first you have to get all the dirt off."

Immediately, Ryan dropped to his knees and began licking my black penny loafers.

I watched silently, not sure how to respond to him on all fours giving my shoes a thorough tonguing. We'd never done anything like this before—role-playing had always struck me as silly. Still, the sight of my boyfriend, wrapping his hot, wet tongue around my size-thirteen loafers, his Jockey-clad butt sticking straight up in the air, was proving to be a major turn-on for me. I rubbed the growing bulge in my jeans with the palm of one hand while my other hand inched its way underneath my T-shirt toward my left nipple. I was seriously aroused.

Ryan lapped at my shoes, working for a good five minutes. "Guess they're clean now, huh?" As proof, he stuck out his tongue. The sight of his luscious mouth, now black with grime, drove the air from my lungs and all my blood to my crotch. Instantly, my dick was rock hard and filled out the tightly packed crotch of my jeans.

"Now I suppose I apply the polish." Ryan grinned up at me, his head cocked to the side. *What a pup!*

"Dry them off first," I ordered. "Otherwise the polish won't adhere well." I figured what the hell! If we were going to do this, we might as well do it right.

Grabbing hold of his tattered shirt, Ryan ripped the T-shirt off, exposing his tanned smooth chest. Tearing the grungy rag into thirds, he went to work, drying my left loafer while I worked my right foot up between his legs. His cock stood upright, stretching the pee-stained cotton of his shorts. I pushed my heel firmly against his stiff dick.

Ryan moaned softly. "Yeah, work my dick for me!" He pressed his crotch even harder against the sole of my shoe. It was a ball buster for me to see the fucker so horny. I was only too happy to oblige.

Still, a little discipline never hurt anyone. "Keep your mind on your work, boy," I warned, removing my foot.

I allowed him to dry off my right shoe while I searched out his asshole with the tip of the other. Ryan loved nothing more than getting royally fucked and he ground his ass against the toe of my loafer, trying his best to get his butthole to accommodate my shoe. He would have managed it if only his underwear hadn't been blocking access to his hole.

"Enough!" I roared. "Get out the polish!"

Like a good little sub, Ryan obeyed instantly, climbing down off my shoe and breaking open a brand new tin of polish. Taking a scrap of his T-shirt, he dipped it into the can and wiped a large gob of the stuff on each shoe.

"Not so much," I reprimanded. "You'll make a mess."

The tension in my balls was getting to be too much for me. I ripped open the fly of my Levi's and freed my cock and balls. My dick—eight and a half inches of manmeat—dripped precome. Using my spunk for lube, I began stroking the shaft slowly, thoroughly enjoying myself.

Ryan, realizing what I was doing, looked up expectantly, as he spread polish across each shoe. He eyed my hard-on, licking his lips. "How about letting me spit-shine *that* thing?"

"Not a chance," I replied. Sadistically I held out on the boy, teasing him first. I stroked toward him, letting my hard cock snap back against my abs. "First you have to finish the job you started!"

"Bastard!" he jeered with a cocky smile. "All right then, what do I do next?" Ryan, who has spent his entire life in sneakers, honestly didn't know.

"Next you take a rag and buff them. That takes off the excess polish and brings up the shine."

He started to reach for another strip of his T-shirt but then stopped. Holding himself up on his hands and toes like he was doing push-ups, he maneuvered his Jockeys directly over my shoes. Very slowly he lowered his crotch onto the wax-covered leather.

"Let me know if I'm not doing this right," he whispered. His voice took on that deep, husky quality that meant he was really turned on. Then the fucker started humping my shoes.

Christ, what a hot sight! My blond bottom ground his dick all over my big feet, his bubble butt twisting every which way in an effort to reach every square inch of leather. His hard-on pressed against the arch of my foot, and his breathing grew more and more labored. He was really getting into it.

Ryan's arousal fired mine even more. My cock was so stiff that it hurt.

"Get up, boy!"

Instantly he complied, standing only inches from where I sat with my dick in my hand. His rock-hard cock tented the front of his briefs, trying to pierce the polish-stained fabric. The gray cotton stretched to the point where it looked like it was ready to burst. His shorts were filthy. Smears of shoe polish covered his belly and thighs as well. My slave boy looked disgusting—and extremely fuckable. "You did a good job, boy. Now I want to get off. Go get a condom."

Ryan bent over, reached into one of his socks and pulled out a package of condoms.

"Smart boy! Go ahead and slip one on me."

Tearing open the packet, he rolled the latex down over the head of my swollen dick. Once the head was covered, I pushed his hands away and shoved his head down into my crotch. "Roll the rest of it down with your mouth, boy. That shouldn't be a problem for you—you've got one hell of a talented tongue."

Dropping to his knees between my legs, Ryan did as he was told, taking almost all of my cock down his eager throat with no sign of discomfort. It was only the last half-inch or so that gave him any trouble.

"Come on, my little cocksucker," I urged. Holding his head down with my hands, I wasn't about to let him quit at this point. "Just relax and take it nice and slow. Let it slide right down. Easy does it. There you go."

After a couple of minutes, he got the hang of it. I let him deep-throat me, relishing the feel of his tongue as it teased the base of my shaft. After a while I pulled him off and made him concentrate on my balls.

"Yeah, lick my balls. Wash those nuts real good for me. Make 'em shine, fucker. Goddamn, you got one hell of a mouth on you, boy. You really know how to get me off."

It took some doing, but in time Ryan managed to ease both of my aching balls into his mouth. I let him enjoy himself until I decided it was time to change course. I grabbed him by his hair and yanked his head back until he was looking me straight in the eye. "Back on your feet," I ordered.

He knew what was coming, and he scrambled to obey me.

"Turn around and bend over, boy."

"Yes, Sir!" he cried, turning his back and spreading his legs especially wide. His melon-shaped buns screamed for attention—I couldn't resist.

Pressing my face down into his crack, I inhaled deeply, taking in his scent. Fresh sweat from his body and stale BO from his Jockeys wreathed me, triggering some primal piece of my brain. Salivating, I chewed on the thin cloth and began to eat his ass through the smelly shorts. Fucking him with my tongue, I dug as hard and as deep as I could through the funky cotton, getting him good and ready.

Ryan moaned and groaned, pushing his ass hard against my face. I could tell my boy was having one hell of a good time and was all set for the main event.

I stood up and grabbed hold of his waist, pulling him hard against me. My dick pressed right up against his asshole. "You're going to get screwed, boy, and you're going to love it. Is that understood?"

"Yes, Sir!" he replied, squirming with anticipation. "Please, Sir, fuck the hell out of me!"

I reached for the waistband of his shorts, but paused. Those sweaty, piss- and polish-stained briefs were really turning me on and, I strongly suspected, Ryan as well. Why take them off? Feeling out Ryan's hole, I dug into the fabric with my fingers and ripped a hole just large enough for my cock. Perfect.

Leaning forward I rasped in his ear. "I'm giving you a choice: spit, shoe polish, or no lube whatsoever. What's it gonna be?"

I hoped to god he'd have the sense not to choose the polish. I didn't want any of that messy crap on my dick.

Ryan deliberated. "Spit," he decided with a nod. "Polish might lube it up too much. I earned this fuck. I want to make damn sure I feel it—every goddamned inch of it!"

I slapped his asscheeks with a resounding smack. "Don't worry about that," I assured him. "You're going to feel this one for sure!"

Spitting a gob of saliva into the palm of my hand, I allowed most of it to drip through my fingers and down onto his thighs. I rubbed the very last bit into the crack of his ass, being careful not to let any of it get too close to his pulsing hole.

"All right?"

"Aw, no, please!"

"What's the matter?" I jeered. Reaching around, I started twisting and pulling on his sensitive nipples. "Afraid you can't take it?"

"You bastard! I said I wanted it to hurt a little—not put me in the hospital! You could at least stick a finger up there first!"

"Aw, don't be such a crybaby!" Without any warning, I grabbed hold of his hips and plunged my cock straight through the rip in his shorts and deep into his un-lubed asshole.

Ryan howled with pain and made a desperate attempt to break free of my grip. I wasn't going to have any of that, however. Wrapping one arm tight around his waist and pressing my other hand between his shoulder blades, I kept him bent over as I started to fuck his ass.

"You fucker!" he screamed. "Come on, Dan. Pull out! God damn you! You know my ass can't take that dick dry!"

"You can take it all right," I shot back. "In fact, you don't have any choice in the matter. Now beg me to fuck you! Come on, I want to hear you beg for it."

"No fucking way!" Ryan continued to resist, struggling against my grip. "You son of a bitch! Ow! Cut that out, man! Shit!"

Moving a hand to his groin, I wrapped my fingers around his nuts and pulled tight, stretching his ball sac by a good inch. "Beg for it, fuck face, or you can kiss these balls good-bye!"

"Shit, man, let go! Honest! All right, anything!" Ryan panted, his voice rough. "Please! Please fuck me! Fuck my poor ass! Plow it! God, anything, just let...go...of...my...balls!"

I released my grip on his sack, rolling his balls around the palm of my hand. "Grab your ankles, boy, and hold on tight. You're in for one hell of a ride."

Groaning heavily, Ryan did as I ordered.

Slowly I pulled my dick out of his ass, relishing the friction of his muscular ring against my cock. I positioned my swollen cockhead against his hole. "Beg!"

Ryan hesitated. I gave his balls a reminder tug. "Please, Sir, fuck me," he moaned. "I need your dick—bad! Fill my hole!"

He didn't sound very sincere. That was all right—I wasn't

feeling very particular just then. I shoved my cock in all the way to the root and ground my bush against his ass, wriggling my cock around nice and good for twenty or thirty seconds, then roughly yanked all the way out again.

Ryan gasped.

"Once more!" I ordered.

"Fuck me, Sir!" he cried a little louder and without delay this time. "I gotta have it!"

I pressed my swollen head into his ring, plunging deep inside him; moved it around, feeling his warm insides; and pulled out fast, gasping myself at the sensation.

This time he didn't have to be told. "Fuck me!" he screamed, half in pleasure, half in pain. In truth Ryan likes his sex raw and rough. And if I do say so myself I'm damn good at delivering.

Again he begged, "Fuck that ass as hard as you can, you fucker!" I could tell my boy was enjoying himself, and it made me work all the harder to pleasure him.

Over and over again we repeated the sequence. I shoved my fuck pole into that poor boy's butt while his thighs bucked wildly and he held on to his ankles for dear life. Every time I pulled out, he begged louder and louder for me to plug up his hole again.

I rode his ass like never before, filling his chute with a hefty serving of cock, roughing up his hole in the process. I didn't really give a shit about anything except my own need to get off.

I felt that tightening deep inside my balls as they got ready to erupt. "Fuck, boy, get ready! I'm coming. I'm gonna shoot. Take it, you little shit! Take your daddy's load!"

Suddenly Ryan twisted around, wanting to watch my face as I shot. My next thrust missed his hole completely, and I shot thick, creamy come into that damn rubber until I thought it was going to burst from the pressure.

"God damn!" he cried in desperation. "Shove it back in!

Quick! I want to jack off with you inside me. Please, Dan!"

I didn't care for his ordering me around, so I smacked his ass, hard. Put off balance by the slap, Ryan tumbled to the kitchen floor.

There he lay, sprawled out before me, his torn Jockey shorts soaking up the puddle of our sweat that had streamed off our bodies. I sank down to my knees between his spread thighs, grabbed the condom by its tip, and yanked the rubber off. Holding the condom up in the air, I let my come slowly drip out onto his back. There was more than enough fluid to write FUCK ME across his broad shoulders. *Jesus, he looked hot!*

Finished with my graffiti, I collapsed on top of him. He felt exactly like a man ought to feel: sweaty and sticky and, best of all, still horny as hell.

"Shit, why couldn't you have just stuck it back in me?" he complained. "You know I love having your cock deep inside me." He wiggled his butt against my still stiff dick. "It always feels s-o-o-o good, having your cock up my ass."

I laughed. "You whore!"

Still, it's nice to be wanted; but I'd just gotten off and was feeling very content—I didn't want to move a damned muscle.

"Tell you what..." I moved up a little and nestled my cock and balls in the puddle of jism that had pooled in the small of his back. "Let's wait a couple of minutes. Then you can go get me a washcloth. After you've cleaned me up—"

"Aw, come on, Dan, no!"

"Shush! After you've cleaned me up, you can fix us some dinner. Then maybe, if you're really good..."

"Yeah?"

"Well, I was thinking—my cowboy boots are awfully scuffed up."

"Yeee-fucking-haw!"

# THE DEVIL TATTOO

Jonathan Asche

As soon as I got home from work I went to my bedroom, unbuttoning my shirt as I walked down the hall, eager to get out of my office drag.

Parker smiled when he saw me. "Hey, bro. How'zit goin'?" He was sitting on the edge of my bed, turning a DVD over in his hand—a title he'd taken from my porn stash in the cabinet beneath the nightstand. He was in his underwear.

My greeting wasn't so casual. "When the *fuck* did I *ever* say it was okay to come in here?"

"Easy, easy. Just needed to borrow some lube. Figured you'd have some." He squeezed his crotch; his smile became a sneer.

Two months ago my niece Shayla called, saying she'd applied for a job at a nursing home in Sarasota and wanted to know if she could stay with me—temporarily, until she had the funds for an apartment—if she got it. Shayla looks like she stars in vampire porn. I agreed to let her stay, confident no nursing home would hire her. Five weeks later I learned just how badly I misjudged Shayla's employability.

She didn't say anything about Parker until she showed up with him on my doorstep. He was her fiancé, though Shayla might as well have introduced him as her future ex. He was young, a mere twenty-three, though still an older man in my nineteen-year-old niece's eyes. There was plenty of hard living in those twenty-three years; the crude tattoos on his arms and the scar across his forehead were at once badges of honor and warning signs. He was out of work, but Shayla assured me he was hunting for a job. In the past week I hadn't seen much evidence that he'd looked any farther than my refrigerator—or, apparently, my porn collection.

"You could get Shayla to get some lube on her way home from work tonight."

Parker chuckled, bringing a muscular leg up on the bed and leaning back against the pillows. "Shayla...shee-it, she's fine an' all, but"—another crotch squeeze—"I'm horny *now*."

My anger wavered, like he knew it would. "Shayla tells me you're queer," was Parker's ice-breaker when we first met, though he assured me that "it ain't nothin' to me you like suckin' dick." But I expected him to be uncomfortable in my presence, at best; hostile at worst. I was prepared to—eager to—evict him in either case. Instead, he provoked me in a wholly unexpected, and more confusing, way: seldom wearing a shirt, often lounging around the house in his underwear; not bothering to close the bathroom door completely when he showered, as if daring me to step inside for a better view. "Goddamn, Parker, put some shorts on," I overheard Shayla chastise him one morning. "What if Uncle Marty saw you? You know he's..." Like seeing Parker nude would drive me to rape.

Seeing him on my bed now, I thought her fears might be justified. He had the rippling torso worthy of a gladiator.

Despite the ink coverage on his arms, back and calves, his torso was only covered with hair, save a rendering of a cartoon devil just south of his belly button, peeking over the waistband of his white briefs. *Lucky devil.* His right hand rested over his crotch. I resented that hand for what it covered up; just the thought of the bulge beneath made my cock tingle. Compounding my resentment was my suspicion he'd put it there deliberately, just to fuck with me.

"Too bad for you I got home early," I said, trying to look him in the eyes; trying to keep an edge to my tone.

"Maybe," he said. "So this the kinda' shit you're into?"

Parker held up the DVD case: *Hot Cream Topping* 2, one of the nastier titles in my meager collection. The picture on the cover showed a rugged muscle-bear type licking a cum-covered cock nestled between a pair of plush asscheeks. "It was on sale," I offered. "You wanna borrow it?"

He shook his head, chuckling ominously. "That's good," he said, dropping the DVD on the mattress and getting to his feet. Standing, he stretched his arms over his head, letting me see his muscles flex, letting me get a good look at the bulge his hand had covered up. By the time he dropped his arms he had a smirk on his face. When he walked toward me I unconsciously took a step back.

"Shayla don't know this, but when I was livin' in Atlanta this dude paid me fifty bucks to video me naked." His hand went to his full basket on the word "naked." Still heading toward me, he continued: "Paid me another fifty bucks to jack off."

*You could've held out for two hundred*, I thought. I would've said it except now he was directly in front of me, so close I could feel his warm, smoky breath when he asked, "What would you pay to watch me jerk off, *Marty*?"

The collar of my shirt suddenly felt two sizes too small.

"How 'bout suckin' my cock? One hundred? Two hundred? I'll even come in your mouth for free."

My response sounded like a death rattle. "I don't intend to pay you anything."

"That right?" His arms were suddenly around me and I inhaled sharply, bracing myself for violence. I had twenty years on Parker and my body wasn't as ripped, but I'd maintained a solid physique. Still, I'd cultivated my muscles for show, not self-defense.

Parker squeezed me against his chest, rubbing his crotch against mine, the gesture more joking than erotic. His hands went down my back. "I see you lookin' at me, checkin' out my ass, trying to see my dick through my drawers. Bet you jack off every night thinkin' 'bout sucking my cock."

*Not* every *night*, I thought.

His hands rested on my ass, squeezing it as if he were testing it for ripeness. But it didn't matter if his intent was to mock. For the briefest moment I reconsidered my refusal to pay for the privilege of blowing him.

Parker withdrew his hands from my backside, keeping my wallet as a souvenir. I shouted at him to give it back to me, but he jumped away and onto the bed, bouncing as he hit the mattress.

"Let's see if you can afford me," he cackled, opening up my wallet and rifling through my cash. "Only thirty-seven bucks? You won't get much for that, Marty."

I pounced, landing on top of him. I got the satisfaction of knocking the breath out of him, but Parker quickly recovered, forcing me off him and rolling on top of me. "Give me back my money and get the fuck out of my house," I hissed through gnashed teeth, reaching for his throat. Brawny as he was, Parker was surprisingly agile, quickly getting astride my chest and pinning my arms to the mattress with his knees, ripping a sleeve of my shirt in the process. Nevertheless, I bucked and kicked and flailed beneath him, determined to regain the upper hand and my wallet.

"Whyn't you calm down dude, an' I can make this fun for both of us," Parker drawled.

That's when I became acutely aware that his crotch was inches from my face. Also, I had a hard-on.

"You want this?" he asked tauntingly, holding my wallet over my head. "Or do you want *this*?" His other hand slipped inside his underwear and grabbed his cock.

"Get off me, you fuckin' redneck," I spat.

"How'd you know I like dirty talk? Tell me some more, like how bad you wanna suck my cock."

"You seem to be the one wanting it."

"What guy don't like gettin' a blow job? 'Specially from someone really likes suckin' dick. Don't get me wrong, Shayla's a great girl an' all, but she gives head like she lost a bet. But I can tell by lookin' at you, you know how to appreciate a cock." His hand reached deeper into his briefs, pulling the waistband down to expose his bushy brown pubes, as well as the devil tattoo. Satan was winking. The musk of his balls reached my nostrils, weakening my resolve.

He tossed my wallet over his shoulder. "I'll let you get that if you're nice to me," he trilled. "You gonna be nice?"

My eyes were on Parker's hand moving inside his underwear, manipulating his cock and balls. I was hypnotized; I was powerless. I nodded. "I can be nice," I said.

Parker chuckled, and then pulled out his dick. My opinion of him of him went up several notches—make that several inches. It was a stunning penis, with a meaty shaft and a full, succulent head. I don't claim to be a size queen, but his cock was long enough to make my mouth water, and it wasn't even hard (yet). As much as I wanted this shiftless piece of white trash out of my house, at this moment I wanted him in my mouth.

Parker leaned forward, his knees digging painfully into my arms, bracing himself against the headboard with one hand. The other hand held his cock, batting it against my lips. I raised my head off the pillow trying to capture his dick in my mouth. He jerked it away, cackling, then dipping his cock toward my face like it was a chew toy and I was an eager puppy. And like a puppy, I lunged, my tongue seeking and rewarded with a taste of his dick. Parker let his cockhead linger on my tongue, letting me trace the rounded edge of the crown and press into the piss slit, only to pull away, laughing as I strained to follow it.

"You want it *bad*," he said.

My head fell back into the pillow and waited. Seeing the way he was pulling on his swelling dick, I knew he'd want it worse, and he'd want it soon.

Parker pushed his semi-hard cock down to my mouth. My tongue made tentative contact, prodding the underside of his cockhead, tracing the seam up to the dewy slit. He was still smirking, but the coldness in his eyes was melting. I opened wide and seized Parker's cock between my lips, again raising my head off the pillow to take as much of that meaty prick into my mouth as I could—quickly, before he could snatch it away. Parker let out a guttural groan: "Aw, *shit*." His smirk was gone. He let his cock remain where it was.

My tongue followed the engorged veins on his shaft as Parker fed his dick deeper into my mouth. I didn't care that my arms, still restrained by his weight, were becoming numb, or that the muscles in my neck were knotting up, or that a searing pain was burning across my shoulders, I was determined to swallow Parker's cock all the way to the root.

Parker's pelvis dipped and rolled as he fucked my mouth, the movements of his body making the mattress rock and creak rhythmically, creating a backbeat for the wet slurping of his cock sliding between my lips. Adding to the soundtrack was Parker's breathing out obscenities like they were erotic mantras: "Oh fuck shit yeah goddamn fuck yeah." It was all music to my ears.

But I had to stop. "Get off my arms! I think they're turning blue." *Like my balls.*

He climbed off. I immediately got up, making him suspicious. "Where the fuck you think you're goin'?"

"Not going anywhere," I said, my tingling fingers fumbling with the buttons on my shirt. My arms felt like rubber. "You'll still get what you want."

Parker's suspicions weren't calmed when I took off my pants. "I didn't say nothin' 'bout returning the favor."

My cock felt foreign in my still-sleepy hand. "Relax," I said, stroking my pulsing hard-on as I approached the bed. "You won't have to do a thing."

I'd be lying if I said I didn't like how Parker flinched when I climbed back onto the mattress, or how he scooted back as I crawled toward him. "What're you afraid of?" I chided. "I just want to suck your cock."

He let out a relieved sigh as I lowered my face between his legs. His stiff cock, harnessed at the base by the waistband of his cheap white briefs, throbbed against his belly, spitting out precum that collected in his navel. He giggled and convulsed beneath me as I dipped my tongue into the salty, syrupy pool, and loudly sucked up his juice. His body jerked when my mouth moved to his cock; he gasped sharply when I swallowed his prick whole. He placed a hand on top of my head, combing his fingers through my salt-and-pepper hair as he whispered more amazed obscenities: "Oh dude fuck oh shit yeah."

I pulled on Parker's underwear. "I want to lick your balls," I rasped.

He helped me strip off his drawers, eyeing me with equal parts anticipation and mistrust, leaving me to wonder when he threw his underwear in my face if the gesture was playful or contemptuous. Regardless, I held the briefs to my face, inhaling the scents trapped in the fabric: the cloying artificial fragrance of detergent unable to hide the natural, manly smells of musk, sweat and just a hint of piss. "Dude," Parker said, aghast at my excitement in sniffing his underwear, though I wouldn't be surprised if he tried to sell them to me later.

Tossing the briefs aside, I dove back into Parker's crotch. While mouthwatering on its own, Parker's cock looked more delectable with his balls exposed (I prefer seeing the cock *and* balls, which was why glory holes, so often created for the dick only, never fully excite me). Though Parker didn't bother with manscaping, his nut sac, now drawn tight over his balls, wasn't overly woolly. I playfully jostled his egg-sized testicles as if testing their weight on my tongue, then, finding them sufficiently heavy, licked his ball sac all over, until the curly hairs were slicked down flat by my spit and the thin, sensitive skin of his sack was wet and glistening. All the while Parker was moaning drowsily, as if about to drift off to sleep. I sucked one of his balls into my mouth and tugged, jolting him out of his reverie. "Oh, dude, *fuck*!" His cries became louder when I returned to his quivering cock.

"God*damn*," Parker gasped, again grabbing a fistful of my hair, holding my head as his dick disappeared into my gullet. His other hand pounded the mattress, as if the pleasure was too much to bear. I reached between my legs, tentatively stroking my dripping cock and shuddering. If Parker was close to coming,

I wasn't far behind. As sweet as a mouthful of Parker's load would be, I thought he should get more than the best blow job of his young, delinquent life.

The devil above his cock was giving me a thumbs-up.

My lips traveled down his shaft and over his balls. I slipped my hands under his thighs and tried to lift his legs. Parker resisted.

"Whoa, what the fuck? I didn't say nothin' about touchin' my ass."

"I'm not going to touch it, I'm going to *eat* it."

"I...uh, don't know." But I could tell he was intrigued.

"C'mon, Parker." I tried again to lift his legs. "You can't tell me you get rim jobs on a regular basis. Most straight guys have to pay hookers extra for what I'm going to do for free."

His smirk returned. "Maybe I should charge you."

My tone took on an edge. "Bring that ass up here," I ordered.

Parker kept his defiant smirk in place, but pulled his knees toward his chest, bringing his ass sunny-side up. A furry valley divided his hard, round cheeks, and at the base of that valley, almost hidden in the forest of curly hair, was a tight set of tan lips with just a hint of pink at the opening. I wet an index finger and traced his cinched-up ass-ring, feeling the sphincter throb to my touch. Parker protested, making another halfhearted attempt to assure me he was straight, but his cock, twitching and drooling against his abs, begged me to continue.

My tongue followed the path of my index finger, gently circling Parker's hole, teasing the opening. He made a noise that was part giggle, part sigh. With the tip of my tongue I pried open his asslips, worming my way into his chute. Parker's deep groans urged me on, and I continued burrowing into his hole, fighting his contracting sphincter for every advance. I used my fingers to stretch his hole wider, exposing more of the dark pink entryway. I buried my face in that trench, luxuriating in the feel of his crinkly hairs against my face and the smell of his musk, and flicked my tongue into that entrance. I quickly became less delicate, stabbing into his chute in hard, decisive plunges, pausing only to nibble at his ass-ring.

Parker was no longer moaning and groaning; he was howling. When I finally came up for air, he had the slack-jawed look of a drunk. His bobbing cock was leaving snail trails across his stomach. My spit was coursing down his splayed ass and dripping onto the bedspread. His butthole puckered as if blowing me a kiss. It was a kiss I wanted to return, but I wanted something else more.

The devil peeked around Parker's dick, grinning conspiratorially.

I hooked my hands behind his knees and leaned into him, my stiff cock sliding between his moist asscheeks. Letting his legs rest on my shoulders, I moved quickly to secure his wrists. Parker squirmed beneath me. "Naw, naw, naw," he said, jerking his head from side to side. "No way I'm lettin' you fuck me."

"I'm *not* fucking you," I said calmly. "Just rubbing against your ass, is all."

"Don't care. You're not—"

I grabbed his cock. That shut him up.

"That's it," I hissed, pressing my cock into his wet crack. "Just shut up and enjoy it. I'm making it fun for both of us, like you wanted."

I pulled on Parker's prick, simultaneously grinding against his asshole. With each stroke his cock would pulse in my fist and dribble out more precum. My cock was pulsing, too, and it took a lot of effort to maintain a slow, steady pace, to not hump that ass until I shot my load, though each slide through his sopping trench eroded my self-control.

Parker was even closer, grunting like a rutting pig. His eyes were half closed, his lips pulled back against clenched teeth. Any second he'd be covering his bulging muscles with cream.

What happened next wasn't a conscious decision on my part. I thought about it, sure, but only as fantasy; not something I expected to happen. I did not think that Parker, because he was so close to coming, would fight me, and therefore this was the perfect time to strike. No, when my cockhead pressed against his asshole and wedged those rubbery lips apart, it was purely by accident. When I kept pushing—well, *that* was intentional.

Parker launched into a sputtering protest. He tried to push me off him, but I still had his dick in my hand, stroking him into submission.

"Easy, we're almost there," I cajoled, inching my way a little farther into his ass. "Don't fight it, just enjoy it."

His response was a string of unintelligible noises, forced from between gnashed teeth. His face was red and his eyes crazed. His hands went to my throat.

Parker's grip wasn't tight enough to kill me, but it was making me light-headed. I fought back with a sharp stab, impaling him on my steel-hard cock. We cried simultaneously, he from the shock of penetration, me from the rush of pleasure of sinking my dick in his tight hole. Parker's hands went slack around my neck; his cock stayed hard in my hand.

The rage in his face twisted into an agonized expression. A deep, jagged roar filled the room as he came. His cock painted thick, white stripes up the length of his torso; a splat of splooge even hit his stubbled chin. If he were a boyfriend or a trick, I'd kiss that splat away, but Parker was neither. Kisses were out of the question, but I had nastier answers.

I raked a hand across his cum-stippled torso. "You ever taste your own load?" I chided, thrusting into his chute for emphasis.

"Fuck you."

I found his retort funny, given that my dick was still buried up his ass. "Of course you have," I went on, bringing my loaded hand toward his face. "Now I want you to taste it again."

Parker slapped my hand away. "You want it so bad, *you* eat it."

Chuckling, I looked him in his wild eyes and put my cum-coated fingers in my mouth, noisily sucking them clean. The taste of his spunk was almost as satisfying as the shocked expression on his face. "You freak," he gasped.

"You should try it," I said, patting the side of his face with my sticky hand. "You taste much sweeter than you look."

He called me a faggot. I laughed, stroking his sensitive dick. Parker thrashed and begged me to stop.

I fell on top of him, my body moving like a wave as I pumped his ass in steady thrusts. It was a gentle fucking, all things considered. Each time I jabbed my cock into his chute I told him it wasn't the savage pounding he deserved. "This is nicer than what you'd get in prison," I snarled. And then I roared, my body jerking violently with each heavy spurt fired into Parker's hole.

The stillness that followed, when we lay together in a spent, sweaty heap, was brief. "Get the fuck off me," Parker snapped, simultaneously pushing me away and rolling to the side. My cock popped unceremoniously from his ass. My load leaked out of his hole and onto the bedspread.

I sat up and waited, anxious about what Parker would do next. He lay there, facing the wall, brooding. Then he stood up and stretched. The sinking sun cut through the blinds, glimmering against his skin. The devil now looked at me from behind a milky veil of cum.

"Need to take a shower," he said. On his way to the bedroom door he stopped, bent down and picked up my wallet. In seconds he'd removed the bills from it and tossed it onto the bed. "Lucky I don't take the credit cards."

"You mad because I fucked you or mad because you liked it?"

After a beat, Parker said: "You won't tell Shayla?"

"You think I'm stupid?" I chortled, shaking my head. I felt a twinge of guilt at the mention of my niece's name. Parker's betrayal seemed a given; mine was not so easily dismissed.

"Well, try and fuck me again and I'll kill you." His lips then pulled into a lopsided smile. "But you can eat my ass anytime."

I stared at the bedroom door several seconds after Parker left, his parting words and pert butt lingering in my mind. He was trouble and it was stupid to let him stay. I knew this, just as I knew I'd be seeing more of that devil tattoo before I told him to go.

# THE OTHER SIDE OF THE FENCE

Logan Zachary

Casey, where the hell is the keg tap?" I hollered up to the open window overlooking the frat's backyard.

"Isn't it on the bar?" Casey poked his head out of his bedroom window and looked down at me from the second floor.

"If it was on the fucking bar, would I be asking you for it?" I slammed the doors closed and rested my hands on my hips.

"Well, Brandon, who used it last?" he asked.

"You did, Sunday night for the barbeque."

"Oh. Yeah. We iced the kegger in the bathtub Sunday. Shit. Hang on." Casey pulled his head in. A minute later, his arm and the tap thrust out of the window. "Here, Brandon, catch." He threw it at me, but he overshot.

Tubes and pipes spun over my head. The metal tube that sucked the beer out of the keg hit the top of the twelve-foot fence behind my head and flipped the plunger and the tap over into the neighbor's yard. Thick vines and vegetation covered the fence like a jungle, and tendrils reached up and made a canopy over the neighbor's backyard.

I held my breath as I heard it clatter to the ground on the other side. "Nice going, asshole," I called.

"Fucking butter fingers," he shot back at me. "I can see why you're on the football team."

"I never touched the damn thing. You overthrew it. Now, get your ass down here and go get it."

"I'm not going over there. That guy's crazy. Mr. Abbott will blow my head off with a shotgun."

"I'm gonna blow your *balls* off with a shotgun. That was the only one we have. No tap, no fucking beer, dipshit. I want to go wild tonight, damn it."

"You go climb over the fence and get it."

I looked at the ancient latticework atop the fence. It would never hold my weight, and the grapevines were so thick, they looked like something the Addams family had around their house ready to eat intruders. "I'm not climbing over." I looked at the ground and saw it was a thick, impenetrable jungle. "Or crawling under."

"Go knock on the fucking door and be neighborly. You're the new golden boy at this wild frat."

"You threw it over there." I motioned to the fence. "You get it."

"I have to pick up the beer. Duh."

"Then get another one at the liquor store. Duh."

"They're too fucking expensive, double duh, and I doubt they even have any in stock. We had to special order that mother." He pulled his head back into the house and complained to whoever else was in the room with him.

"You have to do something, asshole." I called up to him.

"I'll see if I can get one at the store, but you need to get your ass over there and retrieve it, one way or the other. You're pledging this frat, and you're not in yet, golden boy. You can't afford to fuck up this party."

"Shit, shit, shit." He had me there. Fuck, fuck. *Fuck*.

I knocked on the front door.

No answer.

I rang the doorbell.

Nothing.

Did anyone even live here? I had never seen any lights or movements in this place, but I had only been at the frat for two weeks. Looking around the side of the house, I saw the fence ran right up to the wall, and I couldn't get into the backyard. The other side was the same. My only chance was getting in the front door or over the back wall.

I turned the knob, pushed, and the door opened. "Hello, Mr. Abbott," I called into the house. Dust swirled in the rays of sunshine that slipped between the blinds. The air had a stale smell. I doubted a window had been opened in this place in years.

Could the place be haunted? Stepping inside, I felt the floor with my foot, testing to see if it would hold my hundred-eighty-pound footballer frame. The wooden floor squeaked, but held. Another step inside and the front door slammed behind me.

My instincts said to get out of there. I'd seen this sort of situation in movies and it never ended well. I *knew* I needed to grab the doorknob before I was locked in, but I ventured farther inside. "Hello, anyone home? I live next door and something fell into your backyard that we need."

That sounded lame.

The living room had a grand piano and several framed prints of operas and Broadway shows. The walls were lined with over-stuffed furniture.

A formal dining room held a table for twelve and opened up into a huge kitchen. In the other direction was a sunroom that faced the frat house, too beautiful a room to be overlooking the ramshackle frat.

Walking by a potted tree and many plants, I headed to the backyard. A fountain burbled in one corner, birds perching on its levels to bathe and drink. Grapevines grew over and through the fence, a thick barrier of privacy.

Where had that fucking tap landed? Nothing black or metal was to be seen against the green of the vegetation. I pulled on the branches as I scanned the wall, but couldn't find anything.

"Looking for this?" a male voice said behind me.

Startled, I spun around and saw a man sitting in a wheelchair holding out the beer tap. "You scared me," I admitted.

"You're not used to breaking into someone's house?"

*Yikes.*

He was seated in the shadows and appeared to be old and gray, but as he rolled forward into the sunlight, the years dropped away. Decade upon decade disappeared and a man of thirty looked up at me. He scanned my body from head to foot.

"Mr. Abbott, I knocked but...no answer."

"So that gives you the right to come in?"

"The door was unlocked."

His eyes narrowed as he nodded. "An unlocked door is an open invitation? An invasion of privacy? Why don't you take your clothes off. And you can call me Kevin."

"What?" My body tensed.

"You may call me Kevin," he said.

"No, the other thing."

"I know you heard me. Take off your clothes. If you feel free to come in and see all my stuff, I should be able to see all of your stuff."

"You're welcome in my room anytime," I joked.

He pulled the beer tap onto his lap. "If you want this back, you'll strip."

"I'm not stripping for you."

"You strip for your football team, you shower with all of the guys at the gym, why so shy here? No one will see you, only me."

My cock start to swell in my shorts, and I wasn't wearing underwear.

"I doubt you have briefs on underneath there," he observed.

My groin warmed under his gaze, and my erection grew harder.

He smiled. "I see that you aren't."

I wanted to cover myself, but I didn't want to give him the satisfaction.

"All you have to do is kick off your sandals, pull your shirt over your head, drop trou, and your tap will be in your hand, and you'll be out the door."

I looked behind me in the frat's direction.

"Time is flying, tick-tock. Show me your cock."

I slipped out of my sandals and pulled my shirt over my head. My hairy legs were long and strong, my chest was broad and furred, I was deeply tanned from the shirtless workouts in the sun and I was chiseled from gym workouts and football practice. I unbuttoned my shirt to stall for time.

"I see you work hard on your body."

My baggy shorts flapped just above my knees as my cock strained against the nylon material.

"One more article of clothing and the tap is all yours." Kevin pointed to my shorts.

"I'm not wearing underwear."

"I can see that."

*Fuck*. A rivulet of sweat ran down my back and funneled into my crack. My balls were moist and my dick wanted to be free.

"Come on, wild boy. Show me what you got." He pulled up on his wheelchair's armrests and swung them to the side.

"What are you doing?"

"Come closer."

I stood where I was.

He wheeled forward. He pointed to my shorts again. "And I want a lap dance."

I didn't move. I couldn't.

"The longer you take, the more I'll want..."

I pulled my shorts down with one hand and covered my cock with the other. I stepped out of them and my balls swung free.

Kevin smiled and wiggled his finger. "You're covering yourself up. Don't hide your light under a bushel—though your basket looks mighty fine so far."

My cock leapt in my hand, and precum oozed down my wrist.

"Are you wet?" He motioned for me to move closer. "Come, sit on my lap." He rolled closer, until his footrest tapped my hairy shin. "Spread them." He rolled forward again.

The wheels nudged my bare toes. I widened my stance.

He wheeled forward again, forcing me to leap, and my bare ass landed on his lap.

I relinquished my cock as I reached for him, to stabilize my position. My erection bounced, and precum dribbled down my shaft.

He ran a finger along my dick and through the clear fluid and brought it to his mouth. "Salty, sweet." He reached around me and grabbed my ass. "Where's my lap dance?"

"I don't want to hurt you, your legs."

"I'm fine, even better now with you here." One hand grabbed my dick and stroked.

I thought I was going to shoot all over him.

His other hand cupped my hairy balls and squeezed. "Nice and full and not shaved; you are such a good boy, so handsome, hung and hairy."

My cock slipped easily in his grasp, and my head fell back as I enjoyed the sensation. My butt slid over his lap, and his cock started to swell underneath, to press between my cheeks. Not everything was paralyzed down there.

"Do you want to ride it?" His finger slipped between my cheeks, to my tender opening. His rough tip circled around and around seeking entry. His other hand jogged my body and encouraged me to press down harder. "I know how wild the parties are next door, so whoop it up." He slapped my ass.

The sting burned, but excited me, too. I reached between my legs and unbuttoned his pants and worked his zipper down. A crest of thick pubic hair rose above his underwear's waistband. A huge bulge strained against white cotton and a wet spot spread, making it sheer.

"Do you think you can handle me?" Kevin looked deep into my eyes, his own hazel eyes glowing golden in the afternoon sun.

My hand rubbed over the hot lump and felt the dampness. "I wouldn't be here if I couldn't."

"You needed the tap; you didn't plan on me." He stopped stroking me and had me stop. He bent forward and licked the tip of my cock. A pearl of sweetness rested at the opening and he spread it around the fat head, before sucking it clean.

More clear liquid oozed out and ran down my shaft. I threw my head back and savored the feeling.

"You like that? Do you want me to take it all the way down my throat?"

"Yes," I croaked through dry lips. I licked them to moisten them, but he saw my tongue and pulled my head to his and kissed me deeply, his tongue dueling with mine for control. I tasted myself on his tongue, salty sweetness.

His teeth trapped my lower lip and rolled it in his mouth. He sucked down hard on it, pulling it in as far as he could.

My lip stretched to the point I felt a slight pain.

I tried to catch his lip, but he was too quick. I licked his upper lip and felt the rough stubble of his moustache. He tasted like sweat, minty toothpaste and testosterone, all male.

Kevin released my lower lip, but held on to my biceps. "Let's head to the backyard to enjoy the sun and heat."

Panic raced through my body. The frat boys would see me, my naked ass, my cock, this wheelchair-bound man fucking the shit out of me.

He read my expression. "No one will see us. You've never seen me, now have you?"

I searched my memory, but I had only been there a few weeks.

"Oh, that's right, you're fresh meat. Transfer student from Michigan."

"Are you a mind reader?" I stared at him in amazement.

"I wish, but no, you guys are very loud."

"Sorry," I looked down at the floor.

"Don't be, I enjoy the excitement and the music. I know more about what's going on in your house than you do." Kevin rolled his chair to the sliding door and opened it. He motioned for me to go out.

I looked around. The vegetation was so thick I couldn't see into our backyard. I stepped outside. It felt great to be naked outside, unashamed of my nudity.

He pushed his wheelchair over the door runner, wheeled to a small table, and locked his brakes. He pushed his pants down below his knees, exposing hairy legs, not as withered as I expected.

Walking over, I knelt and moved his leg rests out of the way. My fingers walked up his legs and found his waistband. They dug underneath and pulled. His raging hard-on escaped and I gasped. He was huge, bigger than me, and perfectly shaped. His heavy, furred balls rolled out of the briefs as his underwear slipped down his legs.

Voices and music from the frat house filtered through the fence, and I suddenly felt exposed with my ass in the air.

But as his cock swelled, I forgot about my frat brothers. Any concern over being seen vanished as desire took over. I licked the tip of his cock and explored the hole, lapping out his precum. Opening my mouth wide, I swallowed him whole. As Kevin's pubic hair tickled my nose and his balls bounced against my chin, I inhaled musky, male sweat. He tasted like a real man.

His hands combed through my hair as he guided my head to the speed he liked.

I sucked and swallowed; his dick teased my tonsils. Drool ran out of my mouth and down my neck. The patio's rough tiles hurt my knees, but pleasure vanquished the pain.

His hands slowed my rhythm on his cock and forced me to look up. He guided me back to my feet. "Turn around." He pulled a small drawer open and pulled out a bottle and a condom. "I have a new plan for your ass."

As I turned away, I flexed my buttcheeks at him. He inhaled deeply at the sight.

"Back up," he said, as he ripped open the condom and quickly rolled it down his shaft. He lubed his hand and slipped his fingers between my cheeks.

Pressing back, I felt his lubed finger brush my pucker.

As soon as he found the hole, Kevin pushed into me. Sweat

and lube gave him easy access. He wiggled his finger, trying to relax me and spread me wider.

Two fingers slipped in and explored.

My legs started to collapse.

With his other hand, he grabbed my hip and pulled me in front of him. "Come back." His hand cupped a cheek and pulled me on top of his cock. The fat head slid along the greased pathway and into my expectant hole. I pushed back with my legs, and the length of his cock entered my asshole.

He rocked his hips, and the pain became pleasure in one thrust. I repositioned my feet to assist his thrusts.

He reached around and grabbed my dick. Warmth and wetness engulfed my rod as Kevin pulled me down.

I twisted my head to the side as he kissed along my neck, his tongue licking the sweat from my skin.

One of his hands released my cock and slid up my hairy torso to a nipple. He pinched it gently first, then twisted it firmly; his other hand jacked me harder and harder.

I rode him like a cowboy, filling my ass with every inch he offered. Lube and sweat allowed for a wild ride. Faster and faster, the frenzy of joy intensified. His wet tongue laved my ear, and that was all it took to launch my balls into orbit. The orgasm hit me so hard, I thought for a flash that I'd skyrocket off his cock. Hot cum sprayed my chest, slowed, and then my muscles constricted when the next spasm hit. My butt squeezed his dick, pulse after pulse of his cum filled the rubber and his spasming cock slammed into my prostate, sending another gush of spunk out of my junk.

Kevin let go of my cock, which slapped my belly as a final arc of cum followed. Stickiness coated my lips, and I tasted my own juice. My body slumped against his; we were both drenched with sweat and cum.

His hand ran up my torso and scooped up all it could and he brought his fingers to my mouth and played with my tongue. Who needed shots of tequila? I was ready for this frat party.

He held me close for a minute until I slowly disengaged from his lap. His cock popped out, like a cork from a bottle.

"I'll get you a towel." And he rolled away, before I could say anything.

I stood dripping cum and sweat on his tiles, taking in my surroundings—a hot tub, a barbeque grill, the fountain, a full bar, a table and chairs: paradise.

My erection still stood loud and proud when he returned. He was dressed once again and groomed as if nothing had happened. He handed me a fluffy towel.

Wiping away the afternoon's fun, I looked into the house for my clothes.

"They're right where we left them."

I entered his home, still holding the towel. He followed close behind, and, sure he was gazing at my ass, I wiggled it. He laughed. I stepped into my shorts and turned to face him.

"Sorry for the interruption."

"It was all my pleasure." His eyes scanned my chest. "You missed a spot," he said pointing to my right pec.

"Thanks." I wiped the cum away and handed him the towel. I stepped into my sandals and pulled my shirt around my shoulders, but left it unbuttoned. I retrieved the tap and was ready to leave.

As I turned to go, Kevin took my hand. "You're welcome over here anytime. If you need to get away from the chaos," he motioned to the frat with his head. "And if you need an excuse"—he pointed to the fence—"you can always throw something over."

# RED RIGHT

Dominic Santi

"You have a beautiful butt, Sir."

I concentrated on my hand, thrusting again, waiting until Martin's asslips snugged up tight around my wrist before I answered. "You think so, punk?"

"Yes, Sir," he gasped, shivering appreciatively as I carefully turned my fist.

Martin's hot young body was pure eye candy, especially when he was stripped down to just a leather harness, his combat boots, and the gold bar in his right nipple. I knew he was legal—I'd made him show me two IDs our first time together. But his curly brown hair and big brown puppy-dog eyes, and my knowing he worked as a bicycle messenger, kept me very aware of the sizeable difference in our ages.

I hadn't restrained him this time. I wanted to see if he could hold himself in place with just a voice command. He'd made me proud. I pressed deep again. He groaned, gripping the chains suspending the sling. His legs were spread wide, his puffy asslips glistening under a heavy frosting of Elbow Grease. The room echoed with his guttural cries each time my fist slid over his prostate. His biceps strained, hard and sexy, as he held on, dripping sweat, his eyes closed tight.

I eased my hand out, quietly fingering him while he caught his breath. We'd been playing all evening. Martin's low purrs told me he was getting tired. His soft cock rested contentedly on his belly. He never got hard when my hand was in him. As usual, my dick was so hard I hurt. I'd considered having him suck me off before we called it a night. But his comment got me thinking. I had an inkling this particular punk was not all bottom.

I moved to the side of the sling. Martin dropped one hand and tentatively reached toward me. When I nodded, he brushed his fingertips lightly over the smooth leather of my chaps. I tried to hide my shiver as his hand glided up my thigh and burned onto my hip. His fingertips were hot, the way I liked a man's hand to feel sliding over my ass. Martin didn't know it, but this particular daddy was not all top.

"Wow, Sir. Your skin feels great. Smooth and hard and kind of, you know, silky." Martin blushed at the unaccustomed flowery words. His voice was a firm, steady tenor. He'd be able to do a lot with it when he learned how.

"You think so?" My eyes wanted to close, to sink into the sensation of those powerful fingers curling around my ass. Instead, I slowly worked my hand back inside him.

"Yes, Sir." Martin breathed with my strokes for a while, clenching my asscheek instead of the chain. When I rested my hand, his fingers slid down into my crack. Touching. Feeling. Learning me. His fingertip brushed lightly over my asslips.

"Your ass is hot, Sir."

I nodded, not trusting myself to speak. Martin had a firm,

steady grip. And for the first time, his cock was filling with my hand inside him. I watched as his flesh grew harder and longer and redder than I'd imagined it could. His balls tightened as I almost imperceptibly turned my fist. I twisted, pumping slowly, rubbing his prostate and reveling in his groans. I shifted my weight, moving my left leg to the side, spreading my thighs for him. The cool air fluttered against my asslips as they kissed his fingertip. My own dick got painfully harder.

"So hot, Sir—unh!" Martin clutched my asscheek hard, staring wide-eyed as a translucent pearl oozed from his piss slit. He looked down at his dick like he couldn't figure out who it belonged to.

"You like that?" I tried to keep my breathing steady and almost managed it.

"Yes, Sir," he whispered, grinding his shoulders against the sling. I wasn't sure if he was talking about my touching him, or his touching me. I didn't think he knew.

Then his eyes widened as his brain registered what his fingers were feeling. I'd greased myself. I always did—a throwback to the old days. It was plain Vaseline. I hadn't been fucked in years, and my dildos didn't mind if the rubbers broke. My asslips could kiss against each other all evening as I fisted my unsuspecting bottoms.

But something flickered in this one's eyes. As I curled my fist against his joyspot, another tear of precum leaked out of him. He grimaced, a cry breaking from his throat as his dick jerked. His whole body stiffened, clamping around my hand. In that same breath, Martin shoved three fingers up me, all the way to the knuckle. I arched forward, gasping at the pain and the burn and the unexpected stretch. The sensations rippled through my ass, and with no warning, my untouched cock spurted jizz onto Martin's belly, the long white ropes mixing with his as he threw back his head and howled out his climax.

I leaned my forehead against a leg chain, willing myself to hold still, trying to catch my breath as my heart pounded in my ears. I couldn't decide whether to beat Martin for his insolence or kiss him in relief.

He didn't give me much chance to think. I was still panting when he pulled his fingers out of my ass and stroked my asscheek.

"I'm sorry, Sir," he smiled, wiggling his butt at me and failing miserably to look repentant. "But I really want your ass. If I mind my manners, will you teach me?" He groaned as I took a deep breath and started carefully working my hand back out of him. "Please, Sir? Unh!"

"Let your body finish enjoying the trip," I growled, pulling my fingers free. "There will be years and years for you to work this side of the fence." His hole purred so appreciatively, I couldn't be mad. My fingertips stilled as they kissed over his puffy lips. I took a deep breath. "Saturday night, punk. If this is what you want, I'll be ready for you then."

"Yes, *Sir*! I'll be here, Sir!"

I'd resigned myself to being a top years ago. It seemed part of growing older, and I loved giving pleasure to other men. Deep inside I still saw myself as a slutty bottom. But no matter how I felt, the mirror still showed me a "mature" face. Short-cropped, steel-gray hair. Icy blue eyes. Sleek, black chest pelt touched with silver that rippled smoothly when I flexed. I prided myself on having maintained my physique, but I wasn't foolish enough to think I still had the body I'd had at twenty. Or thirty. Or even forty, dammit. My dick still looked good, though, nicely proportioned with a thick mushroom cap. My hand and I made sure it stayed in shape, even when I took a break from prowling the bars. And my balls hung lower now. I liked that—it made them look bigger.

My asshole was in fine shape, too. I treated it to a good workout with a dildo at least once a week. But I hadn't been fisted in almost twenty years. And in all that time, I hadn't called another man, "Sir." I made a ritual of getting ready. On Saturday, I dutifully lubed up a small plug and stuffed it up my ass, switching to gradually larger ones as I spent the morning scrubbing the playroom until it was sterile enough for surgery. That afternoon, I went into the bathroom and cleaned out in a way I hadn't done in a helluva lot of years either. Martin was due at 4:00. I finished up by putting on a plain white jock and the leather chaps he liked so well.

Martin was punctual, as usual. I recognized the sound of his boots on the sidewalk. This time, though, his sharp knock was decidedly arrogant. As I started to open the door, he barked, "Turn around and close your eyes!"

"Yes, Sir," I smiled, obeying at once.

The door closed in back of me. His backpack thumped on the floor, amid a shuffling of clothing, zippers and snaps.

"Okay. You can look now."

I did. My little bottom punk stood there wearing his boots, new chaps with a leather codpiece, and a new leather vest that showed off the shiny gold bars—in both his nipples!

He grinned as he saw where I was looking. "You like?"

"Very becoming," I laughed.

"Thanks," he blushed. "I wanted to do something to mark the occasion."

I leaned forward, toward his chest, then caught myself. "May I, Sir?"

"Um, it's still too sore to touch."

"I'll be careful, Sir."

When he nodded, I bent my head and placed a gentle circle

of kisses around the tender, swollen peak. I could almost taste his pride, in himself, and in the beauty of his proud, erect young nipple. I traced the outline of his pecs with my tongue, reveling in the sleek strength of his smooth, muscular chest and the light dusting of young fur. Then I turned my attention to his other nipple. I tugged lightly on the bar with my teeth. He gasped, his hips arching forward, his cock swelling as hard and fast as my own.

His hands didn't come up to hold my head, though. Martin stood there, hands obediently at his side, the way I'd taught him. I realized I was going too fast. With a final kiss, I took his hands in mine, and dropped to my knees.

"Thank you, Sir." I pressed my forehead to his hands. "You have beautiful nipples."

"Thanks, Sir. Um, I mean, you're welcome, S— I mean..." he stopped, flustered, breathing hard. "Give me a sec. I'm a little confused right now, S—Karl." Martin moved one hand tentatively out of my grip and put it on top of my head. "Just wait a minute."

"Yes, Sir." His cock was pressing hard against the codpiece, right in front of my face. But I didn't make a move toward it. He hadn't given me permission. Besides, with an erection like that, I knew that sooner or later, he'd open the pouch. Eventually, his hands moved down, massaging my shoulders, my back. The lower they went, the more my asshole itched to be petted.

"I've been thinking about this all day, Karl." Martin seemed to enjoy trying out my name, rolling it around on his tongue as he talked. "I probably shouldn't tell you this, but I've wanted your ass for a long time. I can hardly believe you're giving it to me." He pulled me to my feet, wrapped his arms around me and hugged me to him. I hugged him back, leaning carefully to the side so I wouldn't press against his sore tit. He seemed too excited to notice.

"I beat off this morning thinking about how good your ass was going to feel around my fingers." I jumped, partly from his words, partly because just then, he squeezed my asscheeks. Suddenly, he laughed. "I wasn't worth shit at work today. And now that I'm here, I'm hard all over again. I can hardly wait."

"I spent all day with butt plugs up my ass, so I'd be ready for you, Sir." I lowered my eyes respectfully as I spoke, gasping as his finger slid over to rub my asshole.

"Fuck, Karl." The finger sunk in. "Wow, you feel good. You're going to make me come in my pants if you keep saying things like that."

His finger was going to have the same effect on me if he kept up what he was doing. Martin didn't know how to pace himself yet. I tried to buy us some time.

"Would you like something to eat or drink first, Sir? I made lasagna if you want dinner." I knew if I didn't ask now, I might be too distracted to offer later. I didn't want him to get accustomed to bad manners in a bottom. "Or we can go straight to the playroom."

His hand cracked down hard on my left asscheek. I jumped, staring up at him in surprise. Martin's eyes absolutely sparkled. His grin was domineering and bossy and filled with lust.

"I'll decide when we go to the playroom." He squeezed my butt, just hard enough to emphasize the new heat burning there. "I want ice water, with a slice of lemon in it. Now!"

"Yes, Sir!" I said, my dick pressing hard against the jockstrap. Martin was doing just fine. Five minutes later I carried both our glasses down the hall.

I'd put on a different music mix than I usually used when we played together. I hoped that would help us both feel fresh. Martin took his time looking around, checking the setup, inventorying the supplies. Finally he nodded at me. "Looks like everything's in order. Good job, um, punk."

I bowed my head, hiding my smile as the unaccustomed word worked its way past his lips. "Thank you, Sir. I've had some practice."

"Yeah," he grinned back, his eyes flicking across the room to the case of Elbow Grease I'd opened at our last session. Then he put his hands on my shoulders and got very serious. "I really want to do this, Karl. The way your ass responded when I put my finger in you, that was so hot, Si—." He blushed. "Aw, hell. You know what I mean. When I realized you'd greased yourself, I about blew my wad right then."

"You did blow your wad." I kissed him. Impudent, but I couldn't help myself. Martin didn't notice. He was grinning again, eyeing me up and down, nodding approvingly at my attire.

"You were hot. Now strip to your jock and get in the sling. Punk!"

He helped me lie down, steadying the chains as I moved into position. Suddenly he put his hand on my leg.

"You've done this before, haven't you?" When I nodded, he sighed heavily. "Good. I'd assumed so, but I just realized I should have asked—in case this was your first time, too. I don't think it's a good idea for us both to be virgins at a time like this."

At the word "virgin," I burst out laughing. "Martin, it's been a long time, so I'll probably be tight as hell. But I have definitely done this before. And I love it." I settled back into the sling and lifted one leg toward its strap. "Think of me as a very experienced virgin."

He grinned all through adjusting my feet into the straps. He was still smiling as he walked around to my head and picked up a wrist shackle. "Give me your hand."

"What?"

"Give me your hand. I'm going to restrain your arms."

I froze, my guts suddenly clenching. I hadn't expected that. For some reason, it made me, well, if not afraid, anxious. "Why?"

"Because I want to." The puppy-dog eyes had taken on a distinctly wolfish cast. "I want you completely at my mercy. I'm going to make you come the way I've always dreamed of making a bottom come."

He waited. Patiently. His eyes locked on mine. When I finally, slowly, reached up, he took my hand and squeezed it, waiting for my answering grip. It was such a familiar motion between us. Yet from that angle, it felt surprisingly new. I could see how closely he was watching me, learning my body language as he buckled my wrist into the cuff.

"Tell me to stop anytime you want, Karl. Just regular words, so I don't get confused." When I nodded, he lifted my other arm. "I want to go nice and slow. Get your ass as loose and hungry as you get mine. Then I want to fuck you with my hand until you come." He tugged on the cuffs, testing them. "I can't climax with a fist up my butt, but I think you can. Right?"

"Yes, Sir." My mouth was suddenly very dry. My asshole twitched with his every word.

"I hope you're not in a hurry. It's going to be a long time before you get to come."

I groaned as my cock again pressed up into the now-damp cotton of my jock. Martin moved between my legs and started petting my thighs, getting me accustomed to his touch, himself to my responses. The friction over my leg hair made my skin feel alive. I lay back and enjoyed watching Martin learn my body. His hands were firm and strong, his nipple bars gleaming in the soft lights as he ran his hands up and over my asscheeks, gradually moving toward my crack. He was a beautiful bottom. He was also a beautiful top.

I jumped when he snapped on the glove. The smell of lube filled the room. A cool glob touched my asshole, and his hand slid up and down my crack. I moaned contentedly. His large circular motions gradually became smaller, until eventually he was concentrating almost exclusively on my hole. I sank deeper into the sling, my shoulders relaxing as he massaged me. He took his time, letting me savor each touch as first one finger, then another, worked its way inside and started tugging—long, slow, sensuous strokes that loosened me to my bones as he stretched my slowly opening asshole. I closed my eyes, lost in the sensations.

"Do you use these toys on anyone but yourself?"

"Huh?" I opened my eyes, blinking up at Martin as his question pulled me out of my reverie. I'd put out my own toys for him to use on me, but I was suddenly embarrassed to realize he was thinking of my having had them up my ass already. "Ah, just on myself...Sir." I blushed.

"Good. I like thinking about you being fucked."

I arched up as a greased plug slid up my butt. My ass tightened down hard. Martin grinned nastily. He alternated between dildos and plugs, stroking them in and out, letting the vibrating ones loosen me for him as my cock drooled and he ran his hands over my body.

"Mmm," he whispered, kissing my navel. He was fucking me with a particularly large dildo. "Your belly's telling me it wants me to fill it up with something even better than this fake dick—something alive and warm."

"Uh-huh." I gasped. My greedy ass was in heaven, my dick twitching every time the huge toy stretched me. I was sensitive in a way I didn't remember being the last time I was fucked.

I'd been used to it then. Now, everything felt new. I shivered as the dildo slid out. Then Martin's fingers kissed my asshole. I knew what I must look like, stretched open, glistening with lube, slightly puffy from the toys.

"I need more room." His pocketknife flicked out. He snipped one leg of the jockstrap, then the other, yanking the remnants off me. Then his fingertips were teasing over my asslips. "So pretty, Karl." He leaned over and kissed my thigh, licking softly. "I want to suck your dick, but I'm afraid you'd shoot."

My cock oozed at his words. "Sorry, Sir," I panted. "I probably would."

"That's so hot," he laughed. His hand pressed. He had four fingers in, and was going for the thumb. He stuffed gobs of lube in front of himself, methodically greasing his way in.

"Unh!" No matter how much a toy stretches me, the first push of a man's hand is always harder to take. But it's so fucking much better than any toy could ever be.

"Easy," he whispered. "Open for me. That's it. Just a little bit more..."

Martin was using all the tricks I'd used on him. Holding his hand against me with a steady, unrelenting pressure. Making my asslips beg for him, making them stretch and suck him in, making them kiss their way up his hand. I gripped the chains hard, groaning as he slid on the cool layer of grease, his knuckles pressing against me. The friction burned as I stretched, wider than my sphincter thought it could go. I wanted to scream—couldn't stop the cry that worked its way out of my mouth. It hurt so fucking good.

"Open for me, punk..."

I yelled as his knuckles slid in. My sphincter screamed at the burning stretch of his hand. My asshole snugged up around his wrist, and as he made his fist, the orgasm washed over me.

The waves spread out from deep inside me, and my jism spurted uncontrollably through my cock. I could hardly breathe. My whole world revolved around the fist that filled my guts with another man's hand, with the touch that wouldn't let me close him out.

Martin stayed stock still, holding me steady, keeping me from hurting myself as the climax tore through me and my whole body shook. Eventually, my breathing slowed.

"Fuck, Martin," I panted. "I'm sorry. I thought I was too old to do that." I took a couple of deep breaths, trying to regain control of myself. "Fuck, your hand feels good."

"I almost came watching you." His face was flushed. He was breathing as hard as I was. "I felt you come, Karl. Your ass pulsed and grabbed me, like it wanted more and more of me. Shit, I wanted to push my arm all the way up inside you." He shuddered. I looked down at his crotch. His dick was so hard it was stretching the leather.

I relaxed back in the sling and I started to laugh. In relief. At the pleasure, the release, the sight of the beautiful man standing between my legs with his fist up my ass and his raging hard cock straining to be free. "Martin, unsnap that thing before you hurt yourself."

"Huh? Oh." He smiled sheepishly. He reached down and yanked the codpiece off. His cock sprang free—dark red, the tip drooling a thin line of precum down toward the floor. He sighed contentedly as he stroked his free hand over himself. "Thanks."

"You have talented hands." Then I remembered myself and blushed. "I really am sorry, Martin. I mean, Sir. A bottom shouldn't come without permission."

"I know," he said, turning his head and kissing my calf. "I should probably beat you or something. But that was still the hottest fucking thing I've ever seen. I've heard some people could, you know, come just from being fisted. But I've never heard of anybody coming just from a fist sliding in."

"I used to do it all the time," I laughed shakily. "Took me a helluva lot of beatings to learn to control it. That and a top who pinched my dick to keep me from coming."

"Well, this time, you came on *my* fist." He slapped my ass, then rubbed at the sting. Suddenly he stopped and looked down at me. "Do we have to stop now? I mean, I don't think I could take having somebody's hand in me after I came."

As he spoke, he moved his hand slightly, twisting it gently inside me. I cried out, arching toward him, suddenly very glad he'd restrained me. It was nice not to have to hold myself still, to be able to lose myself in the burning pleasure/pain in my asshole and the pressure in my gut. It was embarrassing, though, to realize one of my punks was seeing me be such a slut. I looked up to see him smiling at me.

"We don't have to stop." I gasped, shuddering as I looked down at his straining cock. "Just go slow and use lots—and I mean *lots*—of lube. I'll be sore, but you should have plenty of time to come before I need to stop."

He raised an eyebrow. "You sure are bossy."

I blushed. He was right. "Sorry, Sir. I was just noticing..."

"You're noticing too much." I jumped as he draped a folded towel over my eyes. "Today, I'm topping you. So shut up, close your eyes and be a pig while I fist you." He swatted my ass, hard enough to really sting. "Unless you have to tell me something for safety's sake, the only words I want to hear out of your mouth are 'yes, Sir' or 'no, Sir.' Do you understand?" He punctuated his question with another resounding smack on my ass.

"Yes, Sir!" I said, half laugh, half groan. This punk was too smart by half.

"All right, then."

I groaned as he slowly withdrew his fist from my ass. Deprived of my sight, I finally relaxed and gave myself up to the feelings. A cool glob of lube touched my asslips. I moaned, loudly, as his hand slid in again. This time, I didn't come, but the sensations were so wonderful they were almost too much to process.

"That's better," he laughed. "You have a nice butt."

I didn't answer. He hasn't asked a question. I lay back and enjoyed the heaven of another man taking my ass. Martin twisted and explored, slowly and carefully. Letting me feel his steady, relentless strength. Letting me give up control of my body. Letting me make myself vulnerable enough to trust—to float, wallowing in sensation. My whole world was my ass. I squeezed back in pure bliss each time he checked my firmly restrained hands. He ignored my dick. That made me feel like even more of a hole.

Each time Martin's hand slid in, his breathing quickened. I imagined his shaft, hard and red and ready to shoot, the way it had when he'd had his finger up my ass the other night. With a start, I realized I was going to come again, too. The feeling was building, slowly and steadily, but it was there, and it was growing. My dick had stretched out hard again. Each time his fist twisted in me, the awareness of an impending orgasm grew stronger.

"You like that, punk?"

"Yes, Sir," I whispered. The coolness of more lube slicked into me.

"You have a beautiful ass." His fingers stroked my asslips. I could feel how puffy I was. "You feel good around my hand. Warm and silky and hungry." I groaned as his fist slid in. He rocked it slowly, side to side. "I think your ass likes being fucked by my hand."

"Yes, Sir." I groaned as he pressed firmly on my prostate.

Fluid I hadn't expected to be there slipped down my cocktube.

"Your dick looks pretty hard, too." He pressed again. I shook as another drop slid through. "Bet I could make you come again, punk."

Fuck. Oh, fuck, it was going to happen again. "Yes, Sir," I gasped.

"Real soon."

"Yes, Sir..."

He was fisting me hard now. Deep, slow, steady strokes. Each one causing a mini-orgasm to reverberate from my prostate.

"Gonna come..." I gasped.

"I know you are, punk," he growled. "You're going to come because I'm going to make you." His breathing was heavy now. "I'm going to make your beautiful punk ass come all over my hand, gonna make your dick shoot because your ass is coming."

My whole body was ready to erupt. I couldn't talk anymore. Nothing but embarrassing grunts left my lips.

"Fuck, oh fuck, yeah," he gasped. "Damn, Karl, you are so fucking hot. Do it!"

His hand slid in again. I cried out, uncontrollably, as the spasms started. Hot juice again sluiced through my cock. This time, the pleasure consumed me. My whole body shook as every nerve exploded. I yelled. I couldn't stop yelling.

"Yeah, man, let it happen. Fuck, you're beautiful. Your ass is coming on my hand, Karl. It's making me come. So good, it feels so good... Oh, *fuck!*"

I felt the tremor through his hand as his body tensed. He roared out his climax. My ass wrapped itself around his fist as spurts of his hot cream splattered against the back of my thigh. He shuddered above me, panting and shaking, straining as he held his fist rock steady in my ass.

When I could breathe again, I became aware of Martin's face

resting against my calf, the fine stubble of his evening's beard scratching against me as he started to laugh.

"Damn, Karl. That was the hottest thing I've ever done in my entire fucking life." He kissed me, tonguing his dripping cum off the back of my leg.

I wasn't quite ready to talk yet. My whole body was exhausted. I winced contentedly as he slowly worked his hand out of me. When his fingers were free, he patted my asslips, carefully tracing the outline of my hole. I was sore now. I knew I'd be more sore later.

"Thank you, Sir," I sighed contentedly. "You sure know how to make a bottom happy."

He pulled the towel off my eyes. I blinked, slowly adjusting to the light. His sparkling brown eyes were the first things that came into focus.

"Will you do that for me next time?" he said. "Come just from being fisted?"

My guts clenched in response. "I'll try anytime you want, Sir."

"Next weekend." Martin tossed the glove and gently smoothed his palm over my asscheek. "You have a beautiful butt, Sir." He paused then grinned. "Now I'm hungry for lasagna. Let's go eat."

# MR. LEE'S MEN

Joe Marohl

Mr. Lee tells Kent to go wash the blood off his face. Kent walks down the hall, me trailing behind. He lowers his face to the sink and splashes water on his lips and chin. I stand behind him, rubbing my fingers down the ridge of his backbone. Specks of Kent's blood circle the drain like Arabic consonants and then disappear. Maybe he looks like he's been crying when he walks back to the workout room. I don't know. That's what I tell myself when Mr. Lee glances up at him and then over at me with furious eyes. "Proud of yourself?" he asks.

I really don't know what he's talking about. Kent is tough as nails, I say. I've never seen him even wince.

"I ought to kick your ass myself, punk," Mr. Lee growls, scratching the sandpapery whiskers where his jaw takes a sharp turn up to his earlobe. Anger for him is a performance. Always. He plays with his natural intensity like a toy.

I tell him to go ahead if that makes him happy. I don't care. Then I add a provocation, "Or you can *try*."

Mr. Lee ignores me. His fingers are on Kent's face, turning it one way and then the other, like he's inspecting it for scratch marks. Then he pushes his lips against Kent's freckled forehead. Kent grunts. He isn't supposed to talk today, so he grunts and points at things with his nose. Mr. Lee touches him behind the ears, and Kent looks down, averting his eyes. Mr. Lee's hands slide down the boy's neck to his shoulders and give them a reassuring pinch.

"Sweet," he says, with minimal expression. Kent is pleased with himself. I can tell by how his eyelids fall slowly like the last snow and then open just as slowly. Not a blink but a drowsy gesture that conveys total trust in the man touching him, joy in the man's lavish attention. Mr. Lee has about twenty years on us both, not that either of us knows his age exactly—or much of anything about the man. He is our trainer and our protector. When I first met him, he told me he was an artist. He took my chin and held my face to the light, leaning in to examine its lines. "You'd make a good subject for my next project," he told me, his eyes on the cigarette he was stubbing out against the wall. I didn't say anything, but I wondered what kind of project—a statue, a painting, a porn film? I wondered what this tall and distinguished man did for money. But something convinced me I could rely on him, and I didn't ask questions. That's not like me, not to be suspicious, not to hold back, but such was the sway Mr. Lee held over me from the start.

This is February. I have been in this house for two years. Kent has been with us ten months. Before Kent, Mr. Lee and I would work out together five times a week, and twice a week we'd fight. At first it was sparring, with gloves, as Mr. Lee taught me how to defend myself, then how to put up a strong offense and finally how to hurt a man if I ever had to. Kent's a few inches taller than I, but we're the same weight. Kent's black hair is shaved to the skull, which looks like a knob or a lightbulb or a potato. Kent is from Derry, but his family moved when he was little. His cargo shorts ride low on his hips, exposing the waistband of his striped boxers. He's got a long, lean torso and the most nearly perfect iliac furrow I have ever seen. The hair on his chest feels like loose threads at the bottom of a silk pocket. His belly slides out and in as he breathes. His pale skin shimmers with perspiration. Mr. Lee tells Kent he is the most beautiful boy in the world. He *is* the most beautiful boy in the world, too, and what makes it weird for me is that he knows it and it does not make any difference to him. Kent acknowledges his beauty but ascribes no importance to it. That knocks me out.

Outside, the trees are bare, their twisted branches scratching at the silver sky like trees in a spooky cartoon. Our house, Mr. Lee's house, is a six-bedroom, four-bath Carpenter's Gothic with three working fireplaces. Mr. Lee has the master bedroom. The next room is a library, full of old first editions, a few pieces of samurai armor and a table covered with fossils and tiny meteorites on clear acrylic stands. The third room is the one Kent and I share. The fourth is the workout room, where Mr. Lee puts Kent and me through our paces. The fifth and sixth are for out-of-town guests, friends of Mr. Lee. In the winter the house smells smoky, with the muddy smell of old wood underneath. Today it's just the three of us in the house.

Mr. Lee kisses Kent on the lips. He runs his fingertips against the stubble of Kent's buzz cut. He speaks to him in hushed tones, almost cooing: "Show him no mercy. None. The blond punk needs to be taught a lesson for what he just did to my Kent-boy." Mr. Lee will not speak my name today. I have stringy white hair that touches my shoulders. When he says "the blond punk" he is talking about me. "Fuck the blond punk up. Will you do that for me, boy?"

Kent grunts, a grin flickering at the corners of his lips.

I sneer: "Fat chance."

Mr. Lee's head swivels and his flashing eyes lock on mine: "Shut your hole, or I will shut it for you!"

I lick my lips and poke my hand up my T-shirt to rub my smooth stomach muscles. My nut sac tightens, pushing my cock forward against my loose shorts. I tell Mr. Lee I would like to see him try. I really would.

Mr. Lee stares at me in silence. Then he half-whispers to Kent, "Somebody needs to take this piece of shit down a peg or two." Kent grunts. His lips widen, and his white teeth flash.

Kent smacks his right fist into his left palm, looking straight at my eyes. My boner stirs. Mr. Lee unsnaps Kent's shorts, and they slide down the boy's hairy legs. He breathes through his nostrils; long, steady inhalations that whistle through his nose hair. He slowly (*slooowly*) tugs Kent's boxers down the thighs, the knees, the calves. Kent's purple cock slaps up against his appendectomy scar, and his smile widens at a slant to reveal his canines. He steps onto the pile of futons Mr. Lee has stacked on the hardwood floor. A bead of sweat untangles itself from his armpit hair and glides down his rib cage, disappearing close to the hip bone. Not once does Kent break his steely gaze.

"Strip!" Mr. Lee commands. I make a spectacle of loosening the drawstring, inserting my thumbs in the elastic band and peeling my shorts down to my ankles and then kicking them off. I shed my purple T-shirt last. I step onto the futons and stand, legs apart, arms loose at my sides, fingers spread, a couple of feet from Kent. Mr. Lee turns his attention to me. I'm naked and he still pats me down. His hands are rough. He pokes and pinches like he's inspecting a goat he means to buy. His thumb brushes the blunt head of my penis. I stare at the chest hair through his open shirt and the constellation of honey-colored freckles revealed by the peninsular recession of his hairline. I'm conscious of my breathing now and the steady glare of Kent's eyes on me. His inspection complete, Mr. Lee looks into my eyes and says flatly, "Now he's going to kill you."

I can't help but smile, but the look on Mr. Lee's face is so severe the smile dissipates in half a second. I bend my head toward him. "Kiss your pretty boy good-bye," I tell him. "There won't be much to look at after I'm done. I'm putting him down."

Mr. Lee frowns, his eyes narrow and he backs off and takes a seat in the corner. Kent licks the cut on his lip I gave him in Round One. He and I face each other; our best blank looks say we mean business, and we take each other in with our eyes until Mr. Lee commands us to start the fight.

A fight is a fight, and there's not much you have to say about it. Kent starts it off with a slap across my mouth. It's a hard slap, nothing stagy or held-back about it. My cheek holds the feeling of that slap the way a cymbal holds a sound when it's struck. It's as if the blood in my face is swarming. The slap is meant to pull my full attention to Kent and rile me up, and it does that. I slap him back, and the cut on his lower lip burns bright red again. "More where that came from," I tell him, clenching my fist and hurling it to his ribs. The blow shoves him back a step, but he flies right back at me, grabs my head and drags me down.

Kent flips me over his body, snags my leg in his and crawls on top of me, huffing. His hairy thigh brushes up on mine, and I feel his breath hot and wet on my cheek. I squirm, but his body bears down on me, the tight muscle restraining me, smashing me to the floor. Deep down, my lungs let loose an exasperated "Ha," and I thrust, arching my back, raising my ass off the futon. Kent pounds me back down. His boner swipes up against mine, and my balls seize, sending a cool, rippling wave up my spine to spread like wings across my shoulders. I try to twist, but he's got me. His teeth click against my earlobe. His cock steels up, so that it no longer feels like flesh. He grabs a fistful of platinum-blond hair and thumps the back of my head on the floor. The blunt pain blurs my vision for a second. I reach up and claw at his face, fingers snagged on a nostril and the corner of his mouth. I dig my pared-down nails into his sweaty skin. He grunts and starts hammering me with his whole body. The constant blows wear me down, and my hand falls from his face.

"Attaboy, Kent." I hear Mr. Lee's strong voice behind me, over my head. "That's how I like it. Kill the shaggy punk. Show him who's boss."

Kent rolls me over on my side and starts slapping my bare ass. Hard, stinging smacks, like he means to raise welts. The guy's a dick when he has the upper hand, but, then, who isn't, right? Far be it from me to judge. He's in on me tight. I feel his breaths like huffs of steam against the back of my neck, and I reach down deep to my core, trying to bring up the fight from inside myself, while keeping cool, or at least staying as composed as can be with Kent's boner jabbing between my buttcheeks. I rear back, thrusting my elbow into his rib cage. He groans and pushes off. We roll away from each other and spring to our feet, fists cocked in front of our chests.

I glance at Mr. Lee. He's hard as a railroad spike. I smile to myself. He's busy pulling his shirt off, eyes glued all the while on the shiny wet orbs of Kent's pale ass, glutes tightening and relaxing as he dances on the balls of his feet. Mr. Lee has a good upper body for a man his age: a chest covered in ginger hair, and a respectable flat gut that bulges slightly when he inhales, showcasing a well-shaped navel, taut and round. For the first six months, he and I shared a bed. Then he set up a room for me. Then Kent moved in. Sometimes Mr. Lee videos our fights, just so we can watch them later, with an icy beer bottle in one hand and the other hand down the waistband of our shorts. He looks over at me, and our eyes meet. His flash angrily at me, and his upper lip curls. "Get him, Kent, get him," he commands his pet. I throw a fast right that lands on Kent's mouth. I smirk as the boy stumbles back, his shoulder blades smacking the wall. I dash in and ply his long, slender belly with punches. He takes the blows without much expression, except for the breathy grunt each time my knuckles make contact. Kent bends down, arms forward, trying to block my jabs. I grab him by the head and haul him away from the wall to the center of the makeshift mats.

It's not exactly what you think about Kent and me. We're not killers or ninja assassins. We're not fighting over Mr. Lee's affections like a couple of bitches either. The three of us hold to each other like family—like a wolf pack, looking out for each other, playing rough to keep ourselves tough so we can protect each other and what we've made of ourselves here together. Kent and I fuck all the time. Sometimes Mr. Lee calls us into his room, and the three of us pile on to each other, staying warm on body heat through a bitter winter's night. Rarely, too rarely, Mr. Lee fucks us, or lets us fuck him. He's not so much into fucking these days, but he lets us know that he is looking out for us all the time. We play these games of anger and rage more for therapy than for any other reason. They're like primal screams, "human spirit games," Mr. Lee likes to say. It's our way of pushing past eighteen years of social conditioning to be servile, repressed and oblivious like the rest of the world, commodity fetishists every one. Sometimes I jokily call Mr. Lee "comrade" and ask him when's the revolution starting. Sometimes I ask him if he's practicing psychotherapy without a license. Sometimes I pretend he is holding Kent and me for ransom. He doesn't answer remarks like these. He looks me firmly in the eyes for half a second and then looks away, way off into the distance; then sometimes he chuckles softly to himself.

Some people have God and religion. Kent and I have Mr. Lee and our tight three-man pack. Our master requires no worship, only strength, discipline, curiosity, reason and camaraderie. His hand on the back of the neck, or on the wrist, or on the small of the back is our smalltime version of grace. The bond among us is our refuge from a world gone blandly mad. It isn't a religion, it isn't a cult and it isn't a secret conspiratorial cell. We have no cable or satellite connection to the world of homogenized fantasy and desire. We make our own movies. We play instruments, making our own music. I play the banjo. Kent plays the recorder. Mr. Lee pounds on a drum. We dance. Evenings we huddle together and read aloud to each other—*Candide*, *Leaves of Grass*, *Typee*, *The Tale of Genji*, *1001 Nights*, *Don Quixote* and other books stacked high in the library. We eat and drink simply, at home—steak, green vegetables, bread, beer, coffee, olives and grapes, a lot of grapes. On alternate days, one of us will not speak all day, communicating only with his hands, by touch, by gaze; sometimes, it seems, by fluctuations in body heat. We entertain ourselves by fucking and fighting. Fucking and fighting bring us together at the same time as they set us apart as singular persons.

I'm squeezing Kent's head between my bicep and ribs. His buzz cut chafes against my skin. Pretty Kent grabs my cock and balls, and all at once I feel like I stuck a fork into a light socket. He jams his shoulder into my midsection and lifts me off my feet. I hear Mr. Lee's hands pound the floor with enthusiasm. "You got him now, Kent-boy," he hollers. Kent flips me over on my back. Then he falls back on me with an elbow drop. His sweaty body covers and clinches mine like an anaconda on a capybara, his hairy forearm smashing my nose and mouth as we roll three times across the futons, struggling. The hard scramble stiffens up the both of us. Kent's on my back, his boner gliding up and down the small of my back, his right forearm mashed against my nose as he jerks my head back. I hear my heart pounding in my ears. I feel the pulse of Kent's body up against mine. The pressure on my spine is unbearable. I scream through gritted teeth, my lips sloppy wet with spit and snot and sweat. "Now finish him," Mr. Lee barks out. "Knock the punk out."

Right then I sink my teeth into Kent's wrist and chomp down hard. Kent yelps, and his sweaty body goes suddenly cold. It tenses up and shudders, and then I flip him over, onto his back. He hits the mats with a grunt. I twist his arm up between my thighs and into my armpit. I stretch back and thrust my midsection up, amplifying the pressure on poor Kent's shoulder. Kent thrashes for a second and then freezes up, realizing resistance only makes his situation even more painful. My eight-inch cock is like an unsheathed dagger, thumping the skin below my belly button. Kent's cock stands tall, manically wobbling back and forth like a white flag. The mineral tang of his blood wets the tip of my tongue. Here's the second time I've made him bleed today. I've got him wrapped up, conquered. He can't move. His muscles go slack in my grip. His heels slide on the broadcloth fabric of the futons as his legs unbend. With his free arm, he taps my shin in submission.

I don't let him go. I rear back again, bending his arm backward, wanting to hear him yelp one more time. Kent knows what I'm after, and he struggles to deny me that base satisfaction. I respect that. But I want to feel him go all tense and limp again against my body, to feel the surge of raw power, like a runner's high, but, oh, much more ecstatic! His lips purse and clamp tight over his clenched teeth. The veins of his neck stand out. His skin blushes deep red from his forehead to his sternum. I raise my leg and bring it down on his chest. A shudder passes through him, and he gasps, a high-pitched squawk, eyes brimming with tears. Without releasing the hold, I turn my head toward Mr. Lee. The expression on my face is cocky and wicked. His pale-blue eyes relay an amalgam of contradictory messages that are nonetheless crystal clear. First, there are pity and horror. The boy is, after all, his pet, and though my surfer-boy looks exude sex appeal—long blond hair, honey tan and smooth muscle—I know Kent's uncomplicated beauty surpasses mine. Next, his eyes express his shock and rage that I, someone he cares for, would so willfully extemporize on his script and push the limits of the game, twice in a row now, to hurt, really hurt, an opponent I love as much as he does. But behind those emotions lurks something else—fascination—a terrifying nexus between him and me—a guilty recognition of the erotics of pain, control and humiliation—morally suspect, without a doubt, but genuine, raw, the uncouth bedrock of our being. It's his tongue darting out to lick the outline of his lower lip that gives it away, our collusion at this moment, though strictly on an emotional level, and our secret, lurid, but no less tantalizing appetite.

I keep my eyes on Mr. Lee's as I loosen my hold on Kent. Kent and I are sweat-soaked, and as soon as the exertion stops, as soon as we stop straining against one another, we feel the wintry chill in the air. I roll over on Kent. He lies on his back, shoulders scrunched against a futon, elbows pinching his ribs, hands open and outstretched melodramatically, like a transverberated saint. His bent knees bow apart, and his cock protrudes shiny and reddish blue, a lush, alien quartz. I crawl on top of him. His averted face looks softened by the fight. I kiss the corner of his mouth. I lick his sweat. I press my dully throbbing cock on his.

I bend his slender penis up against his hairy tummy. I mimic the rhythm of his breathing so that our bodies synchronize—one vigorous heartbeat in two persons. I press my hips onto his. He turns his face to mine and nibbles the tip of my earlobe. He raises a hand to run his fingers through my hair. I push, deliberately slow, unnaturally slow at first, gradually building momentum. He moans. Out the corner of my eyes I detect motion, as Mr. Lee stretches back against the wall, kneading his swollen crotch. A sudden red blindness forces me to sink into myself, my mind submerged in dark, ropy viscera—I am all touch and motion—slick, groping, exposed and vulnerable as a beating heart in a surgeon's hands.

Kent shoots first. His cum paints a warm slash across our stomachs. Immediately, there's the sensation that he's falling away from me, and I clutch him mechanically, still thrusting, now more feverishly than before. Then the crescendo release. My body shivers. The pressure behind my eyes subsides, and I blink like a moviegoer facing the sun after a long matinee. Things stay unfocused for many seconds, as I rise and fall gently to Kent's respiration. Then I feel the palm of Mr. Lee's hand on the small of my back.

# ABOUT THE AUTHORS

**JONATHAN ASCHE**'s work has appeared in numerous anthologies, including *Afternoon Pleasures*, *Brief Encounters* and *Erotica Exotica*. He is also the author of the erotic novels *Mindjacker* and *Moneyshots*, and the short story collection *Kept Men*. He lives in Atlanta with his husband, Tomé.

**MICHAEL BRACKEN**'s short fiction has been published in *Best Gay Romance 2010, Beautiful Boys, Black Fire, Boy Fun, Boys Getting Ahead, Country Boys, Freshmen, The Handsome Prince, Homo Thugs, Hot Blood: Strange Bedfellows, The Mammoth Book of Best New Erotica 4, Muscle Men, Teammates* and many other anthologies and periodicals.

**DALE CHASE** (dalechasestrokes.com) has been writing male erotica for more than a decade with numerous stories in magazines and anthologies. She has two story collections in print: *If The Spirit Moves You: Ghostly Gay Erotica*, from Lethe Press, and *The Company He Keeps: Victorian Gentlemen's Erotica*, from Bold Strokes Books.

**MARTIN DELACROIX** (martindelacroix.wordpress.com) has had stories in more than twenty anthologies and has published four novels—*Adrian's Scar, Maui, Love Quest* and *De Narvaez*—and three single-author anthologies—*Boys Who Love Men*, *Flawed Boys* and *Becoming Men*. He lives with his partner, Greg, on Florida's Gulf Coast.

**LANDON DIXON**'s writing credits include *Options*, *Beau*, *In Touch/Indulge*, *Three Pillows*, *Men*, *Freshmen*, *[2]*, *Mandate*, *Torso*, *Honcho*, and stories in the anthologies *Straight? Volume 2*, *Friction 7*, *Working Stiff*, *Sex by the Book* and *Ultimate Gay Erotica 2005*, *2007* and *2008*.

**HANK EDWARDS** (hankedwardsbooks.com) is the author of the Charlie Heggensford series: *Fluffers, Inc.*, *A Carnal Cruise*, and Lambda Award Finalist *Vancouver Nights*, as well as the novels *Holed Up*, *Destiny's Bastard* and *Plus Ones*. *Bounty*, a paranormal romance, and story collection *A Very Dirty Dozen*, are available at Amazon.

**ROSCOE HUDSON** is a creative writer and academic whose work appears in *Best Gay Erotica 2012*. He lives in Chicago.

**DANIEL W. KELLY** (danielwkelly.com) is the author of the erotic horror collections *Closet Monsters* and *Horny Devils*. His short stories have appeared in the anthologies *Manhandled*, *Dorm Porn*, *Just the Sex*, *Bears* and *Best Gay Erotica 2009*. He also writes excessively about horror, movies and pop music.

**JEFF MANN** has published three poetry chapbooks, three books of poetry, two collections of personal essays, two novels, a collection of memoir and poetry and a volume of short fiction. He teaches creative writing at Virginia Tech in Blacksburg, Virginia.

**JOE MAROHL**'s previous story appeared in *Muscle Men: Rock Hard Gay Erotica*. To pay the rent, he teaches writing and the naughty parts of great works of world literature. His blog, Ringside at Skull Island, is a hangout for men who get off on wrestling and pugnacious fun.

**R. G. MARTIN**'s stories have appeared in *Best Gay Erotica*, *Playguy*, *Freshmen*, *Honcho*, *In Touch*, *Blackmale* and in several volumes of *Friction*. He has also written fiction for children and teens.

**DOMINIC SANTI** (dominicsanti@yahoo.com) is a former technical editor turned rogue whose stories have appeared in many dozens of publications, including *Hot Daddies*, *Country Boys*, *Uniforms Unzipped*, *Caught Looking*, *Kink* and several volumes of *Best Gay Erotica*. Future plans include more dirty short stories and an even dirtier historical novel.

**J. M. SNYDER** (jms-books.com) writes gay erotic/romantic fiction and has worked with many different publishers over the years. Snyder's short stories have appeared in anthologies by Alyson Books and Cleis Press. In 2010, Snyder founded JMS Books LLC, a queer small press, which publishes GLBT fiction, nonfiction and poetry.

**DAVEM VERNE** has never met a magazine rack he didn't like. His fascination for muscle fitness mags inspired "Sporn." His stories have lent themselves to fanciful journeys around the world, secret adventures in college dorms and wild obsessions with neighborhood men, and have appeared in *Fratsex*, *Boy Crazy* and *Erotica Exotica*.

**C. C. WILLIAMS** (ccwilliamsonline.net), after moving several times about the country and through Europe, is now settled in the Southwestern United States with his partner, JT. When not critiquing cooking or dance show contestants, he is at work on several writing projects.

**LOGAN ZACHARY** (loganzacharydicklit.com) is an author of mysteries, short stories and more than fifty erotica stories. He lives in Minneapolis with his partner, Paul, and his dog, Ripley, who runs the house.

# ABOUT THE EDITOR

RICHARD LABONTÉ (tattyhill@gmail.com), when he's not skimming dozens of anthology submissions a month, or reviewing one hundred or so books a year for Q Syndicate, or turning turgid bureaucratic prose into comprehensible English for the Inter-American Development Bank or the Reeves of Renfrew County, Ontario, or coordinating the judging of the Lambda Literary Awards, or crafting the best croutons ever at his weekend work in a Bowen Island recovery center kitchen, likes to startle deer as he walks terrier/schnauzer Zak, accompanied by husband Asa, through the island's temperate rainforest. In season, he fills pails with salmonberries, blackberries and huckleberries. Yum. Since 1997, he has edited more than forty erotic anthologies, though "pornographer" was not an original career goal.

# More Gay Erotic Stories from Richard Labonté

**Buy 4 books, Get 1 *FREE****

**Muscle Men**
***Rock Hard Gay Erotica***
Edited by Richard Labonté
*Muscle Men* is a celebration of the body beautiful, where men who look like Greek gods are worshipped for their outsized attributes. Editor Richard Labonté takes us into the erotic world of body builders and the men who desire them.
ISBN 978-1-57344-392-0 $14.95

---

**Bears**
***Gay Erotic Stories***
Edited by Richard Labonté
These uninhibited symbols of blue-collar butchness put all their larger-than-life attributes—hairy flesh, big bodies, and that other party-size accoutrement—to work in these close encounters of the furry kind.
ISBN 978-1-57344-321-0 $14.95

**Country Boys**
***Wild Gay Erotica***
Edited by Richard Labonté
Whether yielding to the rugged charms of that hunky ranger or skipping the farmer's daughter in favor of his accommodating son, the men of *Country Boys* unabashedly explore sizzling sex far from the city lights.
ISBN 978-1-57344-268-8 $14.95

**Daddies**
***Gay Erotic Stories***
Edited by Richard Labonté
Silver foxes. Men of a certain age. Guys with baritone voices who speak with the confidence that only maturity imparts. The characters in *Daddies* take you deep into the world of father figures and their admirers.
ISBN 978-1-57344-346-3 $14.95

**Boy Crazy**
***Coming Out Erotica***
Edited by Richard Labonté
From the never-been-kissed to the most popular twink in town, *Boy Crazy* is studded with explicit stories of red-hot hunks having steamy sex.
ISBN 978-1-57344-351-7 $14.95

*** Free book of equal or lesser value. Shipping and applicable sales tax extra.**
**Cleis Press • (800) 780-2279 • orders@cleispress.com**
**www.cleispress.com**

# Rousing, Arousing Adventures with Hot Hunks

**Buy 4 books, Get 1 *FREE****

**The Riddle of the Sands**
By Geoffrey Knight

Will Professor Fathom's team of gay adventure-hunters uncover the legendary Riddle of the Sands in time to save one of their own? Is the Riddle a myth, a mirage, or the greatest engineering feat in the history of ancient Egypt?
"A thrill-a-page romp, a rousing, arousing adventure for queer boys-at-heart men."
—Richard Labonté, Book Marks
ISBN 978-1-57344-366-1 $14.95

---

**Divas Las Vegas**
By Rob Rosen

Filled with action and suspense, hunky blackjack dealers, divine drag queens, strange sex, and sex in strange places, plus a Federal agent or two, *Divas Las Vegas* puts the sin in Sin City.
ISBN 978-1-57344-369-2 $14.95

**The Back Passage**
By James Lear

Blackmail, police corruption, a dizzying network of spy holes and secret passages, and a nonstop queer orgy backstairs and everyplace else mark this hilariously hardcore mystery by a major new talent.
ISBN 978-1-57344-423-5 $13.95

**The Secret Tunnel**
By James Lear

"Lear's prose is vibrant and colourful...This isn't porn accompanied by a wah-wah guitar, this is porn to the strains of Beethoven's *Ode to Joy*, each vividly realised ejaculation accompanied by a fanfare and the crashing of cymbals."—*Time Out London*
ISBN 978-1-57344-329-6 $15.95

**A Sticky End**
***A Mitch Mitchell Mystery***
By James Lear

To absolve his best friend and sometimes lover from murder charges, Mitch races around London finding clues while bedding the many men eager to lend a hand—or more.
ISBN 978-1-57344-395-1 $14.95

*** Free book of equal or lesser value. Shipping and applicable sales tax extra.**
**Cleis Press • (800) 780-2279 • orders@cleispress.com**
**www.cleispress.com**

# The Best in Gay Romance

**Buy 4 books, Get 1 *FREE****

**Best Gay Romance**
Edited by Richard Labonté

In this series of smart and seductive stories of love between men, Richard Labonté keeps raising the bar for gay romantic fiction.

**Best Gay Romance 2012**
ISBN 978-1-57344-758-4 $14.95

---

**The Handsome Prince**
*Gay Erotic Romance*
Edited by Neil Plakcy

In this one and only gay erotic fairy tale anthology, your prince will come—and come again!
ISBN 978-1-57344-659-4 $14.95

**Afternoon Pleasures**
*Erotica for Gay Couples*
Edited by Shana Allison

Filled with romance, passion, and lots of lust, *Afternoon Pleasures* is irresistibly erotic yet celebrates the coming together of souls as well as bodies.
ISBN 978-1-57344-658-7 $14.95

**Fool for Love**
*New Gay Fiction*
Edited by Timothy Lambert and R. D. Cochrane

For anyone who believes that love has left the building, here is an exhilarating collection of new gay fiction designed to reignite your belief in the power of romance.
ISBN 978-1-57344-339-5 $14.95

**Boy Crazy**
*Coming Out Erotica*
Edited by Richard Labonté

Editor Richard Labonté's unique collection of coming-out tales celebrates first-time lust, first-time falling into bed, and first discovery of love.
ISBN 978-1-57344-351-7 $14.95

*** Free book of equal or lesser value. Shipping and applicable sales tax extra.**
**Cleis Press • (800) 780-2279 • orders@cleispress.com**
**www.cleispress.com**

Ordering is easy! Call us toll free or fax us to place your MC/VISA order.
You can also mail the order form below with payment to:
Cleis Press, 2246 Sixth St., Berkeley, CA 94710.

## ORDER FORM

| QTY | TITLE | PRICE |
| --- | --- | --- |
| | | |
| | | |
| | | |
| | | |
| | | |
| | | |
| | | |
| | | |
| | SUBTOTAL | |
| | SHIPPING | |
| | SALES TAX | |
| | TOTAL | |

Add $3.95 postage/handling for the first book ordered and $1.00 for each additional book. Outside North America, please contact us for shipping rates. California residents add 8.75% sales tax. Payment in U.S. dollars only.

*** Free book of equal or lesser value. Shipping and applicable sales tax extra.**

**Cleis Press • Phone: (800) 780-2279 • Fax: (510) 845-8001**
**orders@cleispress.com • www.cleispress.com**
**You'll find more great books on our website**

**Follow us on Twitter @cleispress • Friend/fan us on Facebook**